PRAISE FOR
HIGHLAND FIRE

"Magical from the very start."

—InD'Tale Reviews

"Enchanting landscapes, breathtaking betrayal, and heartwarming passion herald Tanya Anne Crosby's triumphant return to ancient Scotland."

—Glynnis Campbell,
USA Today Bestselling Author

"Tanya Anne Crosby is a master of her genre ..."

—Laurin Wittig
Bestselling Author

"Love, honor, suspense, passion... all the good things we love in a Highlander Romance."

—Suzan Tisdale,
USA Today Bestselling author

"Crosby's characters keep readers engaged..."

—Publishers Weekly

"Crosby sets out to show us a good time and accomplishes that with humor, a fast paced story and just the right amount of romance."

—The Oakland Press

"Romance filled with charm, passion and intrigue..."

—Affaire de Coeur

"Ms. Crosby mixes just the right amount of humor... Fantastic, tantalizing!"

—Rendezvous

"Tanya Anne Crosby pens a tale that touches your soul and lives forever in your heart."

—Sherrilyn Kenyon
#1 NYT Bestselling Author

HIGHLAND
FIRE

TANYA ANNE
CROSBY

OLIVER-HEBER
BOOKS

For my husband, Scott, the original dún Scoti.

PUBLISHER'S NOTE: This is a work of fiction. Names, characters, places, and incidents either are the product of the author's imagination or are used fictitiously. Any resemblance to actual persons, living or dead, business establishments, events, or locales is entirely coincidental.

Copyright © Tanya Anne Crosby

All rights reserved.

ISBN-10: 1-942820-38-0
ISBN-13: 978-1-942820-38-3

0 987654321

"Let us go forth, the tellers of tales, and seize whatever prey the heart long for, and have no fear.
Everything exists, everything is true, and the earth is only a little dust under our feet."

—*William Butler Yeats, The Celtic Twilight*

THE CAIMBEUL CURSE

Fire of the candle, heat of the flame,
   Strike a blight on the Caimbeul name.
Gift of beauty I now bestow, and lo,
Accursed his bairn will grow.
Violet eyes and skin so fair,
The last his name will ever bear.
Tempt the Weeper, it be done,
Love's first kiss will bear a son.
On the fortnight of its birth,
Forfeit honor, life and worth.
No' by Caimbeul hand, nor by his will,
No sons, nor daughters blood he'll spill.
By all on high and law of three,
This is my will; so may it be.

ONE

King David's Secret Council
Somewhere in Scotia, 1125

"She's a witch, I say!"

The king blew an impatient sigh. "Simply because minstrels sing it does not make it so. She is skilled in the simples, so what?"

"Nay, Your Grace, I myself have witnessed miraculous recoveries by her hand. Last fall, she passed a maid's bairn through a wreath made from woodbine and the boy's fever vanished."

The King's answering expression was full of mockery. "A wreath, ye say?" A guffaw erupted from the depths of his belly. "Art certain it wasn't a halo instead? Perchance the girl's a saint?"

Quiet laughter sliced through the tension in the hall.

"Saint Lileas," one advisor quipped, leaping at the opportunity to earn the king's favor.

From the far end of the table came a crude jest. "Not with tatties like those, I'll warrant. If she came tae my sickbed, all I'd be wailin' for are those sweet nipples 'twixt my lips!"

The chamber erupted with nervous cackles.

But despite the levity of the moment, the discussion at hand was a sober one. Held in the most private of quarters, with doors closed and guards posted outside, King David of

Scotia had gathered his most trusted advisors, along with a discreet group of influential chieftains. Each mulled over the dilemma he had presented—how to quell the most rebellious of Highland tribes—and how to do so without bringing the clans to further bloodshed. Boorish and weary, the council had been ensconced now for long hours. The chamber reeked of sweat, greed and fear. After so many hours of keeping counsel, the billowing black smoke that crept up from the pitch torches had embedded new layers of soot into the ceiling. Flies had begun to swarm the picked-clean carcass of a hog that sat in the center of the table. No one had allowed the serving wenches to enter to clear the leftovers for fear of being overheard. The ewers were long empty now, and so were the goblets, save for a swallow of backwashed spit from their mouths.

As for the mood prior to the meeting, the empty seats at table were a reminder that not every chieftain held the same influence in David's court. There were a few whose absence was conspicuous—in particular the MacKinnon laird, who was perhaps the greatest thorn in David's side. In fact, were it not for the MacKinnon's interference, they might already have had a valuable pawn on their board.

But it was not the MacKinnon they discussed at length today. At the moment, the subject of the discussion was likely the second greatest threat to David's throne—a Highland rebel, who, while he held no obvious design to plant his arse upon the Stone at Scone, could do much to rouse the clans against David mac Mhaoil Chaluim. These were uneasy times and David had spent far too much of his youth in England. There were many who did not welcome his rule.

The King cleared his throat. "Being cursed is not the same as cursing others—nor do I believe in witches. But for the sake of argument, how would the lass be of use to me?"

"Ach, but dinna ye see, Your Grace? *Everyone* who loves her dies!"

David rolled his eyes. Grunting in discomfort, he shifted in a chair that was made for lesser men. "As far as I know only one man has ever kicked up his toes."

"Aye, though precisely as foretold," the man argued.

David remained unconvinced. "By an auld woman's angry curse? The same auld crone, might I add, who plays nursemaid to the dún Scoti clan. Nay, the plan is ill fated from its conception. The dún Scoti would never allow the girl within a league of the Mounth. Aidan would kill her himself, I am certain."

"Respectfully, Your Grace, I dinna believe that is true," interjected another of his counselors. "There are some who say the dún Scoti would see his clan return to the old ways, when their womenfolk whipped them about by their willies. He indulges his sisters as though they were men. I say he would never harm a hair on the lass' head."

The laird of Teviotdale spoke up now. "He's a milksop like his father."

David raised a brow at Teviotdale. In his considerable opinion, Teviotdale had too little respect for women when he could send his own daughter, unwed, to share a man's bed for the sake of greed. On the other hand, the dún Scoti would die for any one of his sisters. He had recognized that look in the man's eyes. "Would ye say that to the mon's face?"

They both realized, just to prove a point, David would send him north sooner than the serving wenches could clear the table. There wasn't a man among them who would defy the dún Scoti. And now that David had crossed Aidan, he himself would not face the man again. If anyone here thought himself braver than the King of Scotia, David would like to see him face the high chief of Dubhtolargg.

As David expected, Teviotdale gave a nervous shake of his head, and David was appeased.

"Bah!" exclaimed Padruig Caimbeul, who had the most to lose. It was his daughter whose fate they were discussing here today—a fate that might well end in her death at the blade of Aidan dún Scoti. "These are savage mountain folk," he contended. "'Tis like as not they all shared the womb with a blade." He shook his head with conviction. "And yet if there is a chance my Lileas may bring them to heel, it is a sacrifice I am willing to make."

"Aye, but even if she could win him over," argued another. "Who can guarantee the curse is real? The dún Scoti's death is hardly guaranteed."

"Her first husband is dead," Caimbeul argued as though that in itself were evidence enough. He went on to say, "What manner of man dies by his own arrow through his pate save an idiot who is cursed? Nay, of a certain my daughter is marked by a witch, and any mon who loves her will hear Caoineag's weeping within a fortnight of losing his heart."

"So it was proclaimed... so it has already come to pass," offered one of Caimbeul's banner men.

Caoineag the Weeper, was the banshee spirit who haunted the lochs and waterfalls. It was said she could be heard wailing before a death within a clan—faerie tales, all of it, but David was growing desperate.

In the silence that ensued, the guttering torches began to hiss. The smoky room took a toll on David's eyes and lungs. "Caimbeul, she is your only daughter. Are you willing to risk it?"

Caimbeul nodded soberly. "What have I to lose? No mon will have her now."

David pierced him with a dark look. "Be advised... if the dún Scoti doubts her 'tis likely she will die." He was glad he had never met the lass and could not put a face to her name. It would make his decision all the easier.

Caimbeul shrugged, and the room turned more somber yet. The pitch torches in their braces flickered nervously, awaiting David's decision.

"The dún Scoti's death is not guaranteed," persisted his counselor.

"Accidents happen," offered Rogan MacLaren, who had remained silent for most of the conversation. MacLaren's brother had been Lileas' first victim—apparently, far easier than fratricide. "There are other ways to ensure the end we desire," he suggested. "Mayhap Lileas could be persuaded? She has a son..."

Every councilman knew what MacLaren was implying— David did not mistake him. They all knew precisely what

MacLaren was capable of in the name of ambition. He could, in fact, make Lileas kill the mountain Scot—if not to save herself, then perhaps to save her boy.

No one spoke to question MacLaren or to temper the dark thoughts.

"Cursed or nay, I can attest to the fact that no man can resist her," MacLaren continued. "Stuart coveted her even knowing what he might lose."

Caimbeul nodded. "Her suitors were many, despite the knowing... but that was before," he confessed. And then he chortled to himself. "Ha! Now perhaps they do not seem so willing to test the hand of fate!" When no one else laughed, he cleared his throat uncomfortably and slid a wary look toward the King.

David eyed MacLaren meaningfully. "And yet you have resisted her, MacLaren, despite that she lives beneath your roof?"

MacLaren smiled, a subtle turn of his lips that never reached his eyes. "I like my willie well enough," he said, "but I need the head on my shoulders a great deal more." And then he added somewhat somberly, "I do not look upon her, nor do I speak to the lass. She and her son keep mostly to themselves."

"Wise man!" the girl's father declared. "I should have married her to you instead! At least you might have had more wits about you than to lose your heart to a witch!"

David slammed his tankard down upon the table. What manner of man said such things about his own daughter? Even he and his brothers, though they fought bitterly over Scotia's throne, would never have spoken an ill word about their womenfolk. They might have skewered the sons in their beds, but their daughters would never have suffered an instant of scorn. He could not abide a man who did not respect his womenfolk. He scratched his chin, pondering all available solutions. As yet, none with any chance of fruition had presented itself... save this. "What of her son?"

"We keep him, of course... reassurance," MacLaren suggested.

David's question was not overt, but could not be misunderstood. "Despite that he is your nephew?"

MacLaren glanced at Caimbeul. Caimbeul nodded almost imperceptibly. MacLaren returned his gaze to the king. "For the good of Scotland... aye, of course."

"Look at it this way," someone interjected. "If the curse holds true... the lass will go to the dún Scoti with those bonny violet eyes and he'llna be able to resist her. He'll love her, plow her belly, then promptly die. And with the bastard out of the way, the mountain folk will succumb, for without their chieftain they are feeble as auld biddies."

David was certain none of these fools had ever faced one, but he didn't interrupt.

"And if the curse does not hold true... well, then..." The man looked toward MacLaren and lifted a shoulder.

"Tell dún Scoti you wish an alliance between kings! 'Twill feed his ego," advised one of his counselors.

David nodded, warming to the scheme, despite a twinge of guilt. It was entirely possible Aidan would accept the lass, although he did not fool himself into believing he would crave the alliance. However, dún Scoti was far too arrogant to believe himself subject to the wiles of any woman, and particularly a woman his own kinfolk had cursed... and there was one thing that would make the girl far more attractive to Aidan than even sacks full of gold: She bore the blood of the man who had killed Aidan's sire.

David glanced at Padruig Caimbeul. The old man, with his long, dirty gray beard, had once been a fierce warrior. He was still a cold bastard, bargaining away the life of his daughter for his own gain. But that wasn't David's concern. Many lives had been sacrificed for the sake of solidarity. Many more would succumb.

Alas, he had hoped that by awarding Aidan's sister Catrìona to a man of his and Henry of England's choosing that these measures could be avoided. But there seemed no other choice. Aidan's sister had wed a rebel Highlander, and David's plans for alliances were all undone. If there was a chance to unite the clans without bloodshed, this was the way it must be done—through carefully planned marriage contracts and alliances—and he must endeavor to ignore even the most insistent of his guilty pangs. At the instant Aidan might not have his eye upon Scotia's throne, but let him become disgruntled... Nay, the man was too unpredictable. Already, they hailed him as the last *mac na h-Alba'*—*the last true son of Scotia.* He sighed deeply, cursing Iain MacKinnon for a meddling fool.

Aye... but giving Lileas MacLaren to Aidan could work... he might, in fact, accept the girl, if only as a manner to control her father.

Vengeance was a powerful motive.

So was a mother's love.

He looked toward Rogan MacLaren. The man was hard enough to do what needed to be done when came the time. In truth, he thought MacLaren would relish the duty. David doubted he would even have to issue the command. All would transpire as it should, and David need never again consider his part in this ignoble deed, for everything would be concluded without his knowledge.

Caimbeul sat, looking smug, as certain as he was that he held the only viable answer at hand. The gleam in his eye was a hint of the gold payment he envisioned.

"Very well," David relented, seeing no other way. "Offer Lileas MacLaren to Aidan dún Scoti as a bride."

TWO

Two goshawks soared high above the castle, skirting past each other like jousters at a match. Lili thought perhaps they had followed the hunters who had returned this morning. The laird of Keppenach had not been present to join them on the hunt, but she knew he had also returned from wherever he had gone for the simple fact that the laughter about the keep had ceased abruptly and the mood turned grim to match its laird's.

Never mind, for Lili took her pleasures wherever she could find them. Today she had thoroughly enjoyed tending the herbs in her garden—alone, save for the company of her son.

"Look, Ma! Look what I found!"

Lili peered back at the child who came scurrying after her from the garden path, hands cupped together and outstretched. At five, Kellen was the image of his Da. Unfortunately, he was also the image of his Da's brother. He reached her side, lifting up his prize to show her what he had discovered buried beneath the earth. "D' ye know what it is?" he asked a little breathlessly. "Do ye, Ma?"

Lili stooped to better see the etching on the flat, smooth stone. The design was in the shape of a rounded shield, knotted in quarters to symbolize the four corners of the earth. There were many such artifacts to be found in these parts, for Keppenach sat beneath the *Am Monadh Ruadh*—The Red Hills—where the Painted Ones had lived long before them.

"It is a talisman of protection," she said. "'Twill keep ye safe where're ye go."

His little brows furrowed. "A talsman?"

"A charm," Lili explained, noting the confusion in her son's expression. His sweet brown eyes were deep and dark, burdened in a way no child's should ever be. "Like the cross your Da wore aboot his neck."

His face fell into a little frown that looked so much like his father's it made her heart ache. "But my Da died," he said plaintively. "So it didna work."

Lili felt a fierce pang over his words. Not the least for which, one day her son would grow up to learn that everyone else blamed her for her husband's untimely death. Or rather, they blamed the curse that had been bestowed upon her as a child—that same odious curse she had once dared to hope was naught more than blather. Only now she had a dead husband to belie her doubts.

Her son made to throw away the stone. "Nay!" she said at once. "Keep it, Kellen."

He stopped before tossing it, his eyes filling with alarm at having upset his mother. He was such a good boy, so full of affection—too full of worry.

"In this life we may use all the good will the world lends us. Never take for granted even the smallest of favors, my son."

His little face screwed. "But it's just a rock, Mama."

Lili tilted a patient look at her son. "All things are what you make them, son." He peered up at her under furrowed brows, unconvinced. "Remember that naught ever comes to us by accident, naught is preordained." She didn't want her son growing up believing that his destiny lay in the hands of lesser men, or in the words of a foolish prophecy. "Our fates lie in our own hands." She eyed the ancient carving. "Like that stone."

He drew his hand back, examining the stone once more, inspecting it closer, his dark eyes full of skepticism.

"Keep it for another day," she bade him. "You may find you need it."

His little shoulders conceded defeat. "Verra well," he relented, and then he smiled a little crookedly. "I'll save it in my treasure box so no one will find it!"

Lili smiled. His treasure box, a small wooden receptacle that had once belonged to his father, was where he hid all things he valued most. She patted him upon the head. "Good lad," she said. "You are wise... even wiser than your Da."

His dark eyes twinkled and a tiny, sad smile emerged upon his lips. She loved him fiercely in that moment, with a love that was pure and true. One day, she would see him free of his uncle's influence.

"Lili!" a familiar voice rang out.

Speak of the devil.

Recognizing the laird's voice, her son stiffened visibly. Lili touched him upon the head, tempering her reaction for his sake. She pushed him gently away. "Go," she urged him. "Await me in the garden." He stood firmly rooted to the spot, but Lili could not bear for him to witness even one more unkind word from his uncle's cruel mouth. "Go now!" she demanded.

"Yes, mama," he said, but shuffled his feet, hesitant to leave her.

She could hear Rogan's boot steps nearing, his footfall heavy with purpose. "Kellen," she pleaded quietly.

Reluctantly, Kellen turned away, crushing his newly found talisman within his tiny fist, and it seemed to Lili that as he walked away he bowed his head and prayed over it. He looked back at her only once, with the greatest turmoil in his gaze, and her heartache deepened. This was no place for a child to live—not in the shadow of so much bitterness.

When Lili was satisfied her son would not return, she turned at last to face her tormentor—the man who bore the same blood as her husband, the same blood as her son. "Rogan," she said in greeting. But that was all the pleasantry she could muster.

He held his arms outstretched, asking for an embrace that she had never once deigned to give. The thought of touching him, even for the space of a hug, turned her stomach foul.

When she did not fling herself into his arms, his gaze unshuttered, revealing the full measure of rancor behind the dark mirrors of his eyes. "I need to speak with you," he said, his tone clipped. "Shall we walk in the garden?"

Lili shook her head. "Nay, not the garden! I only just came from there." She glanced over her shoulder quickly to be certain her son did not linger. "Mayhap the courtyard?" she suggested a little less emphatically.

"You spend far too much time tending weeds," he chastised, as he peered over her shoulder at her son's retreating back. His black eyes gleamed with something Lili could not name—an emotion she had never spied in anyone's eyes save his.

His soul was black.

"Whatever suits you," he relented, and then he turned and started toward the courtyard, expecting Lili to follow—which she did, of course, even knowing his mood was far too cheery. Instinctively, she understood it boded ill. Not once did he peer back at her or slow his pace, though he must have heard her scrambling to keep up. "It has been four years now since my brother's death," he said.

"Indeed," she replied.

Four years. Two months. Twenty days—every instant full of harrow.

At once her shoulders tightened, fearing the familiar discourse. Six times in four years Rogan had asked her to wed him—and that did not include all the drunken demands she share his bed without virtue of matrimony. Unlike his brother, the man bore not the least tenderness in his manner. He was as crude and cold as the Highlands in winter. At least now he had a mistress to keep him warm at night, but he clearly valued the girl not at all. Poor Aveline. Her father was a bit of a fool if he thought Rogan would come to have any affection for the lass. He would use her up and toss her away, like everything else he owned. The only reason he wanted Lili so desperately was simply because he could not have her.

Rogan stopped abruptly and turned to appraise her in that familiar way that made her skin twitch. He studied her from her slippered feet to her breasts, and only belatedly met her gaze... as though it were an afterthought. Placing his hands behind his back, he rocked backward on his heels, puffing his chest—a stance that betrayed the arrogance within. "As well ye know, I canna continue to support both you and your son without recompense."

Lili swallowed, and averted her gaze.

Here now it began... yet again.

From the ramparts, a few curious onlookers peered down at them, watching, though she knew they would turn askance to save themselves the guilt of doing nothing if he raised his hand. No one defied Rogan MacLaren. He ruled his demesne without question and for most it was simply easier to ignore what they did not want to hear or see. Unfortunately, Lili did not share that same predisposition. What she wouldn't give to be away from here, but it seemed her father had washed his hands of her—and her son—knowing that everything attached to Keppenach now belonged to Stuart's vile brother, including her dowry, meager as it had been.

"Alas, Lili, what am I to do? I have offered endless opportunities to gi' ye a proper title, and ye have refused. 'Tis time for me to get myself a wife and a child of my own."

Aveline?

Surprised, Lili's gaze returned to Rogan's face. But his look was smug, and it gave her a shudder. Rogan was handsome—she would give him that much. But his eyes, deep set and dark, were like pits of burned-out coals. If they had ever been alight with emotion, the light was long expired now. Lili wondered what had happened to make him so terribly cold.

"It leaves me in quite a quandary, ye see, since I canna have ye here once she arrives."

Ach, it was not Aveline.

Alas, but Lili's next thought was to pity the poor woman, whoever she might be. Aveline should consider herself fortunate, after all.

He smirked. "It seems no one of substance will have ye—and who could blame a mon?"

Lili's heart began to beat a little faster. Her mind

stammered over possibilities. Would he cast her away now? Where precisely did that leave her and her son? Mayhap she could go to a nunnery? But what of Kellen?

"Take heart, there *is* a solution," he suggested. "One that will allow ye to make amends with your father and return honor to his name."

His eyes gleamed maliciously and Lili blinked, uncertain what to say, for in truth she had done nothing to bring dishonor upon her father's name. She had been a good wife to Stuart, despite the brevity of their marriage. If, in fact, the curse was real, the mountain folk had cursed her for her father's sins—not her own.

He could hardly have read her mind, and yet it seemed he had. "Ye do wish to honor your father, do ye not?"

Nothing about his smile was reassuring.

Anxiously, Lili glanced over her shoulder, searching for her son, hoping Kellen was nowhere near, for if she refused whatever offer Rogan was about to make, his temper would surely loose the rafters. She breathed a sigh of relief that her son was nowhere to be seen and lifted her chin a little defiantly as she faced Rogan once more. "Tell me, Rogan, what would you propose?"

Rogan took his time answering, as though savoring her discomfort, and then he said at last, "I know of only one man who will have ye as yet..."

Lili squared her shoulders, refusing to be baited. Anything would be better than this, she determined. *Anything.* "And who might that be?"

"Aidan dún Scoti."

The response erupted from her lips without thought. "Nay!" She took a self-defensive step backward, her heart constricting painfully.

Rogan simply stood there, watching the emotions play across her face, enjoying her distress, judging by the smirk that turned his lips.

Aidan dún Scoti was a savage! Tales of him and his uncouth mountain folk were fodder for children's nightmares. His tribesmen were hardly evolved from the

Pechts and Northmen who had once travailed the untamable north. Only men who were as wild and unforgiving as those rugged hills themselves could survive so long so deep in the Mounth. And they would exile her there without mercy!

Lìli's jaw worked angrily. "I said nay! I willna allow my son to be punished this way, Rogan. He doesna deserve this treatment." She softened her voice for Kellen's sake, hoping to appeal to Rogan's better nature. "He is your nephew! You canna exile him to such a savage place."

Rogan feigned offense, his expression practiced, like that of an actor's. None of his emotions ever reached his eyes. "Why, my dear, I would never allow my nephew to suffer the indignities of the barbarous north."

Lìli straightened her back, clenching her fist at her sides, surprised by his response. "What, then, prithee?"

"Ye alone will go."

"What do ye mean, me alone?"

High above them, a hawk shrieked. The sound reverberated within Lìli's skull.

"Just that, o' course. Ye'll go and wed the brute, do your duty to help unite the clans, and leave your son in my loving care."

There was nothing that was kind or loving about Rogan MacLaren. He was, in truth, one of the cruelest men Lìli had ever known. "I will appeal this to King David!" she threatened.

He laughed in her face. "Come now... who d' ye think ordered me to offer ye to dún Scoti in the first place, daft woman?"

"Ach, nay!" she exclaimed, and in self-preservation, backed away, ready to flee.

Rogan reached out and seized her firmly by the arm. "Come," he demanded, his fingers digging painfully into her flesh. "Let me apprise you of the details of your mission for the king."

* * *

DUBHTOLARGG, THE HIGHLANDS OF SCOTIA

The journey north had been long and arduous. Aidan was ready for respite. Tired and ready for his bed, he nevertheless wrapped himself in his breacan.

His sister Lael's tone was fraught with sarcasm. "*King David's* runner awaits ye in the hall."

"Dinna leave the bastard alone!" Aidan demanded, and cursed beneath his breath as his door closed once more.

After riding two days over rough terrain, and after dealing with his sister Catrìona's trials, a messenger from David mac Mhaoil Chaluim was the last thing he expected.

King David, humph!

It was entirely laughable that the man would hail himself as the rightful heir to the throne of Scotia, when the *Sassenach*-loving scoundrel had spent the whole of his youth suckling the teats of English maids. A true Scotsman faced his enemies squarely. They did not hie away when faced with a meager skirmish. And then, after all was said and done, he had lied to the MacKinnon when asked if Catrìona was the runaway he sought. He had stood and bold-faced lied to save himself the trouble of raising his sword.

Aye, they were enemies now, coward that he was.

Were it not for the MacKinnon's presence in the grove where he'd tracked his sister Cat four days hence, he might have ordered all of his twenty warriors to fall upon the arrogant imbecile and hack him down to size. That was the bloody last time he would allow the blackguard under his roof. Had he not learned a thing from his father's trials? Friends were those he knew and trusted, not those who simply employed the name. But Aidan's greatest weakness was a bone-deep desire for peace. Even here in the Mounth, he felt political tensions rising, and he feared there might soon come an end to the years of peace since his father's death.

Well, at least the fool was wise enough not to show up here in the flesh, because Aidan had trusted him once—never again. What he had gotten for his faith was a stab in the back. Peace was not possible amongst these warmongers. Why the hell they could not simply live and let live he could not comprehend. His clan had purposely kept itself apart from Scotia's politics, but that was apparently not enough.

The bastard had come under the guise of friendship and had slipped into his sister's bedchamber in the dead of the night, then had dragged the poor lass south without Aidan's knowledge or permission—intending, he'd said, to give her in wedlock to some bloody border lord. The Reiver lords—all of them—might as well be English, for they were naught but feckless Scots, who gave deference to none. They raided Scots and English alike, stealing everything, including their wives. He wanted to kill David simply for the thought.

It would have been far smarter for him to run a dagger through his shoulder blades whilst he'd slept, because now as long as Aidan had breath in his lungs, he would never trust that *Sassenach* lackey again.

He had only just divested himself of his claymore, but he retrieved it now and re-sheathed it into his belt. Barefoot and bare backed, he might not feel their *guest* was worth bothering to dress for, but when he showed up with the claymore and little else on his back, his message should be clear.

He found the man—or rather boy—quivering in his hall. The lad swallowed a massive ball in his throat when he spotted Aidan entering the room. He was alone. No doubt David feared Aidan would run his messenger through and had sent the puniest of the lot so Aidan would pity the poor dolt.

It worked.

His sister had left Lachlann, his captain to guard the hall. He gave Lachlann a nod, telling the man without words to leave them. The boy would pose no threat, and his guard's presence was not helping the lad's composure. However, Aidan's sense of charity only went so far. He didn't seat himself at the table, but stood instead, peering down at his *guest*. "This had better be good to have roused me from my bed," he warned the boy.

The messenger craned his neck upward, wide-eyed, shuddering. His gaze slid to Aidan's arms, to the blue paint he had yet to wash from his flesh—intricate markings that hailed back to their ancestors. Furious with the abduction of his sister, he had painted himself for war in the woad of his ancestors. He smiled thinly when the messenger met his gaze again.

"K-King D-David s-sends m-m-me," he stammered.

Aidan nodded patiently, wondering ruefully if he looked down at the boy's lap, whether his breacan would be soiled. The boy's entire body was wracked by nervous spasms. "And?"

The messenger licked his lips and Aidan took pity on him. He shouted for his sister, his voice slicing through the silence like a dagger. Lael shot through the door as though she had expected to be needed, looking at first worried, but seeing that Aidan was unharmed, she smiled with relief. Aidan lifted a brow, letting her know that while he appreciated her concern, he was mildly offended by it. "The lad is thirsty," he said. "Would ye be so kind as to fetch him a wee dram?"

His sister's lovely lips turned only slightly at the corners. She tossed a braid of black hair behind her back, and sauntered into the room. "Are ye certain he deserves our good *uisge-beatha*?" she asked haughtily.

Aidan ignored her barbed question. "Are ye hungry?" he inquired of the lad. The messenger nodded jerkily although Aidan doubted he truly understood a single word that had come out of his mouth. He turned to his sister again. "Bring him a wedge of bread as well." 'Twas likely the youth had expended all his energy climbing the bluffs, and Aidan intended to dispatch him the instant he listened to his news, not trusting an emissary of David's to remain under his roof—or in his vale—for a single night.

Lael gave him a twist of her lips, her bright green eyes, so like his own, flashing defiantly, but she did as he bade her, bringing the foodstuffs back from the pantry within minutes of his asking. This time, instead of leaving, she stood and watched, unwilling to leave again now that he had invited her in. Aidan was wise enough to know when and where to pick his battles—especially with the females of his household.

Contrary wenches, all of them, but he loved their impassioned spirits.

The messenger seemed even more ill at ease now, eyeing the jagged blade of the enormous dagger Lael had tucked into her boot. His sister was a master with her blades—a collector, as well. She usually carried the most discreet of her knives hidden from view. Her theatrics amused him, for no doubt she had donned the biggest blade she owned to make a point. She had also smeared blue paint into bold lines across her face, creating as fearsome a visage as she was able with those soft, bonny features. She crossed her arms, watching from a distance, and finally, Aidan sat. He took a seat facing the messenger, hoping it would abate the shivers the lad tried so hard to conceal. "Now," he said. "What is it that David finds so urgent to say to me that he sends a boy into the Mounth in the black of night?"

"Y-Your Grace—"

Aidan stopped him with a hand. "I see no king sitting before you and recognize no king beyond this hall, so dinna address either of us that way again."

The messenger's eyes shifted warily to Lael and then back. "Aye, m-my lord—"

Aidan shook his head again. "I see no lord here either. That title is for *Sassenach* lackeys. Do I look like a *Sassenach* lackey to you?" he asked the boy, his tone gentle, but unyielding. The poor lad jerked his head from side to side. "Aye, then, let us continue."

"W-what would you have me c-call y-ou?"

Aidan was losing his patience now as the hour was growing late. "Aidan," he suggested. "It is my given name and it pleases me to no end to hear it spoken."

His sister snickered at his back.

"Aye, w-well..." The messenger paused for an extraordinary amount of time and still could not seem to muster the simple name upon his lips. Aidan nearly laughed but he was far too weary for mirth. The boy's brow furrowed. "K-King D-David," he began again with some effort, and then as though starting at his own words, his gaze shot up to see if Aidan took offense.

Aidan let it go, simply wanting the lad to leave now.

When Aidan did not react, the messenger continued, thankfully eschewing the use of the title again. "D-David s-sends a bid for p-peace," he said. "He s-says he l-laments having been so heavy handed with your s-sister C-Catrionna."

His back was to her, but Aidan thought he heard Lael growl. The eldest of his sisters was as fiercely protective of their brood as was Aidan. The messenger's eyes grew wide and his gaze flicked toward the woman standing at his back. Aidan watched the boy's pupil's dilate, the muddy color blending with his dark orbs in the dim light of the hall. Through the boy's eyes Lael must seem a fright. And he should be frightened. The lad should count his lucky stars that Cat was safe, because in a fit of temper Lael terrified even Aidan.

An impatient muscle ticked in Aidan's jaw. " Tell me," he asked the messenger. "Do ye condone the abduction of innocent lasses from their beds in the middle of the night?"

The lad shook his head vigorously. "Nay, my l-lo—er Aidan!"

Aidan nodded. "Well, ye see... I have only just returned from saving my sister from the clutches of some feckless lord—a fate mandated by David himself. I abandoned all I was in the midst of attempting to accomplish here and went chasing after her—all the way to Chreagach Mhor—and *then* after all was said and done... I was forced to leave her in the care of strangers because she lost her heart to some bloody Scotsman. Can ye ken how I might not be quite in the mood for treaties?"

"Aye but—"

Aidan interrupted him, and said, just so the lad understood. "Ye are quite fortunate I approve of my sister's choice of husband. If I dinna, I would send ye back to David with your tongue strung upon a necklace."

The messenger gulped, hard. He glanced at Lael and her knives and then gulped again.

"So, then... tell me... what does David propose?"

The messenger's eyes were wide with apprehension. Unconsciously, his hand went to his mouth, as though to safeguard his tongue. He peered back at Lael, and then met Aidan's gaze. "He... er... he wishes to offer ye a b-bride—a-and a seat upon his high counsel."

"A bride?"

"Aye, my lo—er Aidan."

Aidan would just as soon cut off his own bollocks and send them back stuffed in the lad's mouth than to take a seat on David's counsel, much less take a wife of David's choosing. No doubt, he would send the lass north to spy. "And who is it that David would offer me to wed?"

The lad swallowed convulsively, flicking a glance at Lael. "Lileas MacLaren," he said, nearly in a whisper.

Aidan's brows collided. "Lileas MacLaren!"

At his back, Lael shrieked in offense. "The daughter of the man who murdered Da!"

He heard her rush forward, but he placed a hand in the air to halt her. She stopped, though he knew she did not like it.

The messenger recoiled visibly, looking almost as though he would slide beneath the table in self defense.

Aidan grit his teeth, but calmed himself. "So... David would offer me a *cursed* bride?" He knew better than anyone that the lass was cursed for the woman who had cursed her was the same woman who had pulled him and all his siblings from his mother's womb. "You realize that anyone who loves the lass is fated to die?" he explained, as though the entire world did not already know it. Jongleurs sang the girl's misery as a cautionary tale.

A heavy silence met his question... a silence so profound that anyone who knew Aidan might have thought he was contemplating murder. Even Lael remained still behind him, waiting with bated breath to see what he would do.

When the boy's face had grown as pale as sun-bleached wax, Aidan simply threw his head back and laughed. The sound of his laughter boomed like thunder through the rafters.

CHREE

The devil had agreed to the bargain, so Lili was sent north, traversing through woodlands and valleys that sliced through precipitous cliffs.

The Mounth was an unforgiving place—a vast range of corries stretching nearly to the North Sea. Most people traversed them by the ancient road, but there were no roads leading to the place they traveled now.

Dubhtolargg.

She shuddered at the name. The stronghold was named after a king of the Southern Pechts. Nicknamed *dubh*—the *black*—not for his temper, but for his coloring, it was said that, upon his death, his royal blood ran in rivulets down into the mountain streams and flowed red all the way to the mountain loch where *Cailleach Bheur*, the blue-faced mother of winter, slept in her cave. Drawn from her slumber to mourn the fallen king, her tears transformed the glen into a bounteous place surrounded by the roughest terrain known to man. It was to that glen Aidan's people had fled more than two centuries ago, and there remained—in the red hills, stained crimson by the blood of dubh Tolargg.

It was said that David would not rest until he held the mountain tribe's fealty, for to gain their blessing carried nearly as much import as the coronation at Scone—little did it matter that the dún Scoti had not blessed any King since the death of Aed, son of Kenneth MacAilpín. Did David believe she could change that fact?

Lili's thoughts darkened as they made their way through the woodlands—an ancient pinewood forest, peppered with hefty lichen-painted oaks, and knotted wych elms that reminded her of bent old crones with boils and gout in their joints. At their feet crouched juniper, birch, cherry and rowan trees, giving refuge to deer, rabbits and red squirrels. She knew there were also grey wolves and wild boar in these woods, as well as bears, but luckily they did not encounter any along the way. The worst they suffered were a scourge of biting midge—Highland flies—that set them all to slapping at their limbs like self-flagellating priests. Only Aveline, Rogan's mistress, complained. Of course, it wasn't enough that Stuart's brother couldn't spare her his company for these final days of freedom. He had foisted his mistress upon her as a lady's maid—no doubt as his spy to be sure Lili complied with all he decreed.

As they climbed the hills, the forests thinned, and aside from a slight chill in the air, the troupe met with only good fortune on the journey north. Bright blue skies and puffy white clouds prevailed the entire way. Indeed, one might think God himself had sanctioned this plan, but Lili knew better. No matter what path she chose, she would lose. If she didn't carry out this wicked deed, her son would suffer, and if she did exactly as they bade her, her soul would be damned for all eternity.

In the end, whatever choice she made, a part of her would be lost.

Whatever may become of her, she prayed with all her might that God would protect her son, and she took small comfort in the fact that David had promised to look after him now and again. What good was a promise from a man who had sanctioned this plan to begin with? Nay, King David had not spoken the words directly into her ear, but she understood by his demeanor that every word Rogan had uttered had met with his approval.

With a heavy heart, she thought about her son. Abandoning Kellen at Keppenach was the most difficult choice she had ever made. Not even the death of her husband—a good man—had left her feeling so bereft. They had threatened to kill her boy if she did not obey, and the last thing she had spied before leaving the castle was Kellen's sad little face up in the tower window as they had led her out of the garrison.

Did he feel himself betrayed?

Lili felt as though she had betrayed him.

As she was bound to betray her new husband.

But she must harden her heart, for if the choice came down to her son's life or the dún Scoti's—the mountain Scot as he was known to all beyond the Mounth—she would kill the laird of Dubhtolargg in an instant.

By all tales she'd heard of his people, they were a barbaric lot, eschewing clothing and painting themselves as the old ones had. Their clergy were druid priestesses, and their gods the children of the forests—Taranis, Shoney, Fionn, and Sluag. These were the gods of her ancestors as well although much of Scotia—like David—had abandoned the old ways in favor of the Holy Church.

Every so oft, the priest who rode beside her crossed himself, a nervous gesture in which she read his rising fear. For days now she had endured his endless orations, much of which was aimed at saving her soul from the fires of damnation. She was a witch, of course—or so they whispered behind her back—and so they were sending her to the devil.

It might as well be Hell.

Like the faerie glens, Dubhtolargg was not a place good folk ventured and she wished to God that Padruig Caimbeul had not believed himself the one chosen to quash the mountain tribe. Alas, while her father had succeeded in killing their chieftain, under the son's rule the dún Scoti were more feared than ever. And yet Lili was innocent of her father's doings. If they were to punish anyone, why not her father? Lili was not to blame, but she was the one to pay. Aye, were it not for the odious curse the mountain folk had placed upon her as a child, she might have lived a happy life with a husband who died of old age in his bed. Instead, her name was cursed throughout the land, and it didn't matter whether she believed in curses or nay, because everyone else did, and now her son had been ripped from her breast, and would be subjected to his uncle's cruel whims.

Brooding, she cast a glance at Rogan's mistress. Aveline sat upon her mount beside Rogan, adjusting her breasts to their greatest advantage, then peering over at Rogan to be certain he noticed. Ach, what need had Lili for a maid in hell?

In the Reiver Lands—the border lands—where they were half English anyhow, they might have use for silly maids there, but Lili was Scots-born through and through. She didn't need anyone to plait her hair. God's truth, but she had never shied away from work of any kind, nor any task... save this one King David had set before her now.

Birds twittered about them, but the song in Lili's heart was mournful.

Today she would give herself to the man whose kinsmen had cursed her—her enemy, in truth.

Was he kind or cruel?

It didn't matter; she had no choice.

She must keep her faith and do as they commanded, for Rogan had promised unspeakable horrors if she did not. The villain had no heart.

At last, the hillside turned sloping and green and they passed a crumbling stone cairn that sat near a field of wildflowers. From there, the path wandered down a bluffside, into a verdant valley bordered on three sides by corries and on the fourth by a beautiful loch. The valley was defended on all fronts by natural barriers, making it impossible to breach except through duplicity. Not even a well-planned siege could lay these people to waste, Lili thought, for they had everything they needed here to thrive. Truly, it was as though God himself had lifted his hand and blessed these folk. And, in fact, with nary a ripple to mar the silvery surface of the loch below, the water reflected the clear blue sky, so it appeared they were riding down into the heavens themselves. Despite her mood, the sight took Lili's breath away and a sense of something bigger assailed her as she entered the glen... something undeniably ancient and powerful. It was a feeling she had only experienced in glimpses throughout her life and her hair stirred from her shoulders, lifting in the cool breeze that accosted them.

Whatever doubts she had harbored about magic receded in the beauty of this place, for only enchantment could explain this oasis surrounded by barren stone.

Down in the valley, protected from the winds and encircled by berry-laden rowan trees, sat row upon row of stone cottages topped with freshly thatched roofs. The rowan trees, she knew, had likely been planted for protection—a superstition passed down from their ancestors, although she had always thought of it as more lore than truth.

Out on the loch, an enormous structure with a cone-shaped roof sat like a wooden island connected to the land by a pier.

As they wended their way along the shoreline, she spied half-naked fishermen, some of them mooring their boats after a day out on the loch. Darker-skinned than most men she had known, and with hair the color of a raven's wings, they appeared primitive and foreign to her eyes. Standing bareback in the shallows, they watched the small cavalcade pass by, something like mirth alight in their eyes. Torn between anger and fear, Lili bristled at their expressions. By the rood, 'twas good their moods were so light, for hers was black—as black as the sin they had set before her.

"Wicked," the priest muttered beneath his breath, and crossed himself yet again.

His fear was contagious. As they neared the village, a feeling like doves took flight in her belly.

Any moment she would meet her betrothed...

Was he as savage as the tales proclaimed? Did he wear his ancestor's bones for jewelry? Did he bathe? Would she be forced to share his bed straightaway? Would he skewer their priest? For that matter, was there even to be an actual wedding? Or did he simply plan to drag her by the hair into his den?

Her escorts had ceased their banter. Even the priest fell into a daunted hush. The seven of them pressed silently onward. Aveline, who had barely spoken a word all day, now sat taking in their surroundings with wide, fearful eyes. Lili could sense their unease like a tension in the air and her heart began to pound. The palms of her hands felt damp, and she swiped them anxiously upon her wedding gown—a gift from David she would have gladly tossed back in his face if they hadn't been holding her son hostage. It was a gift meant to deceive and she was a bride dressed in the colors of a queen... made to woo a king.

What a farce.

Pulling her arisaid about her shoulders, she tried to still the shivers that suddenly besieged her.

At last, the troupe rounded the wooden island that had blocked much of Lili's view of the village itself, and she saw that the townsfolk had gathered near the beach to receive her. Most appeared the same as anyone she might have known at home, but she swallowed hard as her gaze alit upon the small gathering at the foot of the pier.

A man dressed in barely anything at all—a breacan at least—stood with three women and a young man. Alongside them, stood an old crone with a wooden staff. She knew instinctively by the arrogant stance that this was Aidan dún Scoti.

Her betrothed.

Painted with intricate blue markings wherever his flesh was bared, he watched her approach with canny eyes. She could tell their color even at this distance for they were unnaturally green. The man towered over everyone who stood near him, his shoulders wide and brown—and bare, despite of the lateness of the summer. His claymore, a massive weapon meant to cleave men in two, was sheathed within his belt. His boots were laced and his legs were bare as well, revealing thighs that were as strapping as oaks.

Her heartbeat sped to a painful cadence as her mount halted along with her troupe.

She hadn't even realized they had stopped until her companions slid to the ground to face their welcome party. Even Aveline dismounted while Lili sat frozen in her saddle, swallowing convulsively, unable to rouse herself to move.

Aidan knew without having to be told which was to be his bride.

Despite that she wasn't the only woman to arrive with the little troupe, he could not have mistaken Lileas MacLaren. The other woman appeared pale in comparison.

Seated primly atop her white speckled mare, she was a vision in violet, with chestnut hair and eyes the color of bluebells. Her creamy skin was pale but flawless and he ceded that the tales he'd heard of her were all too true. Confessing to her beauty, he bent to whisper into Una's ear. "She's as lovely as they claim."

The old woman cackled low, leaning upon her walking stick for support. She gave Aidan a knowing glance. "'Twas easy enough to foresee simply by looking at her minny, but dinna e'er say I canna wield a curse!" She nodded proudly, and looked back at the girl, thrusting out her chin as she added a caution, "Her first husband cocked up his toes precisely as foretold, so dinna go losin' your head o'er the winsome lass."

Una had been with them for as long as Aidan had memory. Her hair had never been anything but white and her skin reminded him of the stones they used to build their cairns. She seemed ancient, with her one good eye. Not even the meaning of her name was quite certain, for some called her the great white witch, and others called her The One. Still others whispered—especially when she abandoned them every year on Beltane—that she was Cailleach Bheur herself, the blue-faced mother of winter who protected them from the fury of the Highland winters, striking up corries wherever she willed them. Where she actually went every summer, Aidan hardly knew. She claimed she wandered the Highlands after the snows ebbed and the winds mellowed, plying her trade amongst the neighboring tribes. But she always returned to them late in the summer, bringing with her a sense of belonging as old as time. She was the Mother of their clan, their healer, their elder, and the longest living Keeper. She was also the only mother Aidan had ever known.

Aidan laughed, reassuring the old woman, "Dinna worry aboot that, Una."

"Aye?" Lael challenged. "See that ye dinna, brother mine, for I have eyes in my face, and can see verra well the way ye are ogling her!"

In unison, all his siblings turned to glower at him, and Aidan scowled back at each in turn. In truth, he didn't believe in the curse, but neither would he go losing' his head over a winsome face. Curses and jests aside, there was enough at stake here that he wouldn't take chances with his kin. She was the enemy's daughter. That was something he was bound never to forget. In fact, that was precisely why she was here today—that, and the simple fact that Una seemed to believe the girl was the answer to all their ills.

The little troupe reined in before him, and Aidan observed his bride a moment. Looking much as though she would swoon in the saddle, she simply sat looking petrified, her gaze focused directly upon him. By the sins of sluag, he had seen standing stones with far more life than she was displaying at the moment. For all her beauty, she could have been a bloody totem!

So she would sacrifice herself to the pagan king, would she?

He smiled grimly and when it seemed she would never dismount, Una craned her neck up to look at him, her wrinkled face set in lines of disapproval. "Put that child out of her misery," she hissed.

As he watched, his bride allowed her cloak to slide down her back, revealing a tight-fitting English gown that was constricting enough to shove her breasts halfway to her chin. He crossed his arms. "She hardly seems a child to me," Aidan complained.

"Aye? And what aboot Catriona?" Una countered. "Is Cat a woman or child?"

Annoyed by the question, Aidan frowned at the old woman, for he knew very well what she was trying to say. His sister Cat was a wedded woman now, though he would forever see her as a babe. Aye, Cat may have a right to choose the course of her life, but if her new husband did not treat her with as much reverence as she deserved, Aidan vowed to fly down the mountain and carve the blood eagle from his breast.

Bloody damned Scots.

"Aw, but Una," Lael protested beneath her breath, coming to Aidan's defense. "We're simply havin' a wee bit o' fun."

Aidan cast a glance at his sister—at the bold blue lines she had once again drawn above her brows—paint that made her look as fearsome as any man. Her black hair, so like his own, was pulled back severely into one thick plait, and then plastered back at her temples and forehead with a thin coat of blue paste to keep the strays from her face.

"The paint is itching," the youngest of his sister's complained. "We've been wearing it far too long!" And she bent to scratch her thigh.

In answer, Lael elbowed Sorcha, unbalancing her. "Ye should wear it more oft to remind ye from whence ye came!"

Sorcha hopped to regain her bearings, frowning up at Lael.

"True," said Una. "But this is cruel, and if ye would wear the paint, wear it to honor the gods. For this, they wadna approve."

"What gods?" his brother taunted, all whilst Aidan's bride sat waiting atop her nervous palfrey. Arms crossed, Keane nettled the old woman simply because he could. Aidan knew his little brother cared little about the state of his soul. At his age he worshipped only what lay betwixt a woman's thighs. Aidan had long since outgrown that youthful bent, and no longer cared to sow his seeds in a garden he didn't wish to tend.

The second eldest of Aidan's sisters remained silent. Cailin missed Cat, he knew, and for that he blamed David of Scotia. Unfortunately for the lovely lass seated so stiffly upon her palfrey, at the moment he also blamed David's emissary. And yet if he took her to be his wife, he was bound to give her everything due her as his bride... everything except his heart.

If he didn't kill her first.

She had yet to dismount, he noticed, and before Una could think to elbow him yet again, he abandoned his siblings to "put his bride out of her misery" and bid her welcome. Enough was enough, he decided. Una was right. It was past time to put an end to their charade, amusing though it might have been.

But as he approached, her eyes widened—as though he were wearing his bollocks on his chin—and seeing the horror etched upon her face, he wished he'd left his claymore in his chamber, along with his paint. Inasmuch as it was rumored they walked around bare-assed in winter slathered in war paint, it was not true. The woad was simply a tribute to their ancestors, meant for one of two things—neither of which was appropriate at the instant.

He made his way down the pier, startled to find he had a skip to his step.

Resisting the urge to peer back at Lael, he slowed his pace, hardly pleased to be showing such exuberance over meeting his outlander bride—especially one who likely had treachery in mind.

Lili had the sudden urge to flee.

The closer the dún Scoti came, the bigger he appeared, until he loomed at her side like a pagan stone rising from the depths of the earth.

His hair, black as sin, fell just below his shoulders. Braided on both sides so as to keep it from his face, it was otherwise straight and clean, revealing chiseled, high cheeks and a frown that seemed carved in stone.

Stilling the beat of her heart, she offered her hand politely so that he might help her dismount, and was startled when he ignored it, reaching out to pluck her unceremoniously from her mount. She swallowed her protest as he set her down upon the ground. The beast had lifted her as effortlessly as though she were but a child!

"*Fàilte a mo dhachaidh,*" he said in the old tongue. *Welcome to my home.*

Lili had learned a bit of the old language from the midwife who had come to tend her during Kellen's birth. "*Tapadh leat,*" she replied. *Thank you.*

One brow arched, but she saw a gleam of appreciation in his eyes. "*A bheil gàidhlig agaibh?*" *You speak the old tongue?*

"*Tha, rud beag,*" she answered. *A little.*

Lili was acutely aware that all eyes were fixed upon her now, but she held Aidan's gaze. His green eyes assessed her shrewdly.

Whatever else he might be, he was not the least bit dull-witted, of that she was certain, for she spied keen intelligence in the cool depths of his eyes.

He smiled suddenly, his teeth flashing a brilliant white, and then he turned to one of his men standing nearby. "Disarm them," he demanded at once.

"But we assure you…" Rogan stepped forward, "We come in peace."

Aidan's smile deepened. "Then ye have no need of weapons here," he said in the Scots tongue, and turned to Lili, dismissing Rogan, "You must be weary?"

"Quite," she confessed.

He raised his hand and flicked his wrist to dismiss the crowd that had gathered. And just like that they all went, like rats racing from the shadow of a torch. Peering over his shoulder, he bade the small group of onlookers standing upon the pier to come forward. They did so at once, if reluctantly it seemed.

Lili joined her trembling hands before her as he introduced them one by one, three sisters and a brother.

The bright blue smears on the eldest sister's face were hideous—painted without the least care for adornment—as though she had prepared herself for battle instead of meeting her brother's bride. Her green eyes—so similar to Aidan's glittered with far less welcome—if that were possible. Her black hair, slathered away from her face with blue paste, gave her a severe appearance that was only emphasized by the gleam of the enormous knife she had tucked into her belt— and another in her boot. Her clothes were simple—a clean, rough-hewn tunic of unstained linen. Leather straps crossed her breasts, as though to keep all her womanly parts in one place while she fought. Both her sisters were dressed the same, except that while they too had paint on their bodies, Cailin and Sorcha wore braids in their hair and no paint upon their faces.

The youngest of the lot, Sorcha, was the only one who did not share their dark countenance. With hair the color of Lili's and eyes that were as blue as a bellflowers, she peered up at Lili with a question in her eyes.

Standing beside the child, the crone was as wrinkled as a withered prune with bright white and wiry hair, as though she had been caught in the fiercest of windstorms. She wore a faded black patch over one eye. *"Ceud mìle fàilte!"* she exclaimed. *A thousand welcomes!*

"Mòran taing." Many thanks.

The elder gave her a nod and an odd smile and Lili turned her attention to the sisters, greeting them each in turn, avoiding Aidan's gaze as she addressed his siblings. One was absent, she realized, for the girl had wed a Highlander somewhere near Chreagach Mhor. Lili had overheard Rogan recounting the story to Aveline with no small amount of disgust.

"Welcome," offered the one called Lael, but she didn't make any effort to embrace Lili. That was well and good, Lili decided, for she didn't need blue stains on one of the few gowns she'd brought north.

"Fáilte," said the one called Cailin. The lass' deep red hair flowed about her face like a radiant flame, and her bright green eyes flashed with something like resentment. She was lovely as a rose, probably just as prickly. Not a one of them seemed very pleased to meet her and the feeling was mutual.

The youngest sister lifted her chin, looking sullen, though her gaze lacked the animosity her sisters shared. The girl bent to crudely scratch her blue-painted thighs and then her arms and then finally she thrust a finger inside her leather boot, scratching there as well, giving her eldest brother a narrow-eyed glare.

"If you should need tae piss," the brother offered, standing with arms crossed and refusing to come forward another inch. "I can show ye where tae go, lest ye find yourself with an arse full of nettles."

Lili blinked at the mention of her private ministrations, but held her aplomb and gave the lad an uncertain smile as the old woman thumped him hard upside the head with the end of her staff. The sound was not unlike the smack of hammer against a stone wall, but the lad merely gave the old woman a sideways glance.

It seemed to Lili that she and Lael were of an age—which only made her wonder how old Aidan was. She made the mistake of sparing an upward glance at the laird of Dubhtolargg. He was frowning down at her, his dark brows furrowing in disapproval. "I expected you to bring a son," he said.

But it was the wrong thing to say as far as Lili was concerned. She felt horrid enough for having abandoned Kellen. "Why, my lord?" she asked pleasantly, but with an edge to her words, "So your brother can teach him where to piss as well?"

He smiled thinly and the old woman cackled, popping the laird's brother once more upon the pate of his head. Lili frowned. By the rood, these were strange folk.

"I ken your tongue is cursed as well," the laird remarked, his green eyes glinting and Lili hitched her chin a little higher, noting that she came no higher than his mid chest. But what she lacked in height, she had been given in spirit and if he thought for one instant he could intimidate her with his presence alone, he was sorely mistaken.

"That should come as no surprise to you, my lord as 'twas your folk who cursed me after all." She said it very sweetly, but with an underlying bitterness that would have escaped only the deaf.

The old woman cackled again, striking the laird's brother yet another time. Lili might have laughed in horror but she felt a sudden painful tug on her arm.

As Aidan watched, one of his bride's companions jerked her backward by the arm, whispering something into her ear and suddenly, she blanched, her face falling as she lifted her shoulders and turned once more to face him.

An unexpected wave of fury reared up within him and he fought the desire to trounce the man where he stood. His hand had only been upon her for an instant; he had already released her, but from that instant forward Aidan didn't like the man.

Intensely.

Even more, he didn't like the way he felt—suddenly protective over the Scots wench. The feeling was wholly unwelcome, considering the circumstances.

The daughter of his enemy was his enemy as well, he reminded himself.

But she could not meet his gaze now. "I-I am sorry, my lord. You have the right of it. I am indeed weary," she confessed. "It seems the days of travel have soured my mood."

Her words did not match the fire he had spied in her eyes an instant before—a fire that intrigued him despite that he knew it meant they would not deal well.

Evidently, there was something the lass feared far more than she feared him, and he had a feeling it had to do with her absent son. He tucked the suspicion away to ponder later.

She held his gaze, the violet pools glistening with unshed tears. They seemed to plead with him somehow, but she said not another word.

Confusion warred with anger.

Mo chreach! He had been prepared to loathe his bartered bride. He had been prepared to dismiss her. But he was not prepared for the unanticipated wave of possessive fury he now felt over the treatment he'd observed. She'd looked both mournful and desperate in the same instant and it was a look that confused him beyond measure.

She is your enemy.

Suddenly he found himself angry, for despite that he knew what they were capable of, these feckless Scots, he clearly had not learned from the past, for here she was—along with her entourage—a danger to his clan simply by their presence.

Damn Una. This was her doing, he reasoned, for she had

advised him to this end. All those years ago, she had been the one to curse Lileas MacLaren, and now the old woman claimed she was to be the salvation of their clan. It made little sense to Aidan, and yet that was all Una would say. Unfortunately, merely the sight of Lileas now reopened wounds he had thought long ago healed. Ach, but it had taken him more than thirteen years to banish the memories of that day from his mind. He peered at the old woman at his side.

Una seemed to read his thoughts and gave him a nod.

But Aidan was suddenly blinded by rage. A tiny muscle ticked at his jaw, betraying his emotions, and he realized that if he remained where he stood an instant longer he would betray far more than was prudent.

"See that my *bride* wants for naught," he demanded of his sisters, and then he spun on his heels and walked away, vowing to steel his heart against the Scots witch.

She was not here for love, he reminded himself—neither did he intend to give it.

Four

aking his cue from his elder sibling, Aidan's brother took one last measure of their troop—and of Lili— and with a lifted brow that was an identical match to his brother's, he turned and followed Aidan. Abandoning her to the women of his clan, her betrothed marched down the long pier toward the strange building on the water. Not once did he peer back at her, but it was clear by his stride that he was hardly pleased.

Uncertain what had upset him so thoroughly, Lili watched the brothers go, and somehow knowing Rogan would blame her wayward tongue for this, she refrained from meeting his gaze. Although were it not for her son, she would die a thousand deaths to speak her mind.

"Dinna mind him," the old woman said at her side, elbowing Lili none too gently. "He's a cantankerous auld sack o' wind!"

Lili blinked at the declaration. And despite that the laird's dismissal stung, the grin on the old lady's withered face brought a reluctant smile to her lips, for it struck her as quite absurd that the elder, who appeared to be no less than one hundred if she were a single day, would call the laird of Dubhtolargg *old*.

In fact, her betrothed was hardly an aged man. He was in fine fettle, even if his manners were boorish and left much to be desired.

For a moment, she watched him walk away...

Thankfully, whatever Stuart's brother was thinking, he kept it to himself, or perhaps he simply didn't care to be overheard. Whichever the case, Lili was grateful he refrained from speaking to her. Merely the sound of his voice grated upon her nerves, and—forsooth—at the moment, her nerves were near to shattering.

Brandishing her cane, the old woman ushered them toward the village center. "Come!" she said and took Lili by the arm.

Without having to be asked, a handful of villagers rushed forward to tend their mounts.

"'Tis certain ye'll wish to rest before we sup."

Lili glanced back at Aidan's retreating form on the long dock. He disappeared into the odd building, followed by his brother, and she chewed her lip, trying to determine what it was she was feeling right now—relief?

Disappointment, perhaps?

She was certainly grateful he wasn't some greasy old man with wiggling jowls, but neither had she envisioned him that way. And yet, that his countenance was fair was no reassurance in itself, for Rogan was a comely man and she had learned that comeliness was no guarantee of kindliness.

But Aidan's gaze was hardly comforting.

If Lili felt relief, she told herself, it was only because it seemed she had been granted a reprieve from his company. But that hardly explained the intense feeling of disappointment that lingered after his rude dismissal.

In fact, no man had ever dismissed her quite so. They gave her piteous looks, or they ogled her breasts, or they tried to wheedle her, but none had ever simply cast her aside.

She found herself wondering why the laird of Dubhtolargg had agreed to this union to begin with since he seemed to be wholly unaffected by the one thing other men seemed drawn to: her face. The only answer she could come up with was revenge. Aye, they would wed her to her enemy, in truth. God save her, she must somehow win this battle, lest she become another casualty of war.

"Tonight, we celebrate," Sorcha announced, intruding on Lili's thoughts.

Lili's gaze snapped to meet Lael's in horror. "The wedding?" she asked. Mercy! Nay! Not only was she dreading the moment she would be forced to share the dún Scoti's bed, they had been traveling now for days and she was desperate for a bath.

Once again, the old crone cackled beside her.

Lael shot her a glance as sharp as the dagger she wore strapped to her leg. "We are no' quite so barbaric as that," she replied acidly. "We would hardly drag ye from your sweaty mount and set you willy-nilly before an altar."

Lili's face heated, though she wasn't given time for chagrin. Lael shoved past her, picking up her pace to lead the way, clearly as disgusted by Lili as her brother seemed to be.

Sorcha and Cailin flanked her at once and the old woman fell back to walk alongside Rogan. Aveline followed silently and Lili heard the old woman begin to chatter away, seemingly without regard for any response from Rogan, though she heard Rogan mutter crossly beneath his breath. May God forgive her, but Lili felt an instant of communion with Aidan's siblings, for she realized that it grated upon Rogan's nerves to be treated little differently from women and servants. His ego was boundless. No doubt he had expected to be accorded a king's honor in David's stead, but Aidan had not addressed him once—not even an acknowledgment, she realized only belatedly.

His gaze had been fixed solely upon Lili the entire time.

Alas, but her good humor was quickly tempered by her own disappointment, for clearly, the dún Scoti had judged her and found her lacking.

The man seemed to care not a whit for civilities, nor had she expected him to, judging by the tales she'd heard of him. 'Twas said the messenger who was sent north to barter her marriage had returned with the reek of urine in his breeches. And who could blame the poor lad when faced with a man who, at the tender age of ten, had killed his first foe—two at once if the tales were true?

Not for the first time, she silently questioned her father. *Why?* Why had Padruig provoked these mountain folk? Why had he not simply let them be? They were harming no one living secluded in these corries, but like a sleeping bear, anyone waking him from his slumber may not live to regret it.

Once again intruding on her thoughts, Sorcha reached out to touch the soft velvet of Lili's bliaut. "I ha' never seen a gown so fine!" she said with awe.

Lili saw no reason not to be completely truthful. "Neither have I," she confessed, and when the lass peered up at her in surprise, Lili winked and smiled.

From that moment forward, Sorcha seemed far more amicable, explaining each structure's use as they passed it. There was little difference in their villages, Lili noted, save that these huts were all very well tended. They passed a butcher and a baker and a smith. Behind the huts lay an orchard laden with fruit and berry trees. In the near distance, she spied a shepherd tending his flock upon the slope of a hill, a pastoral view if ever she had seen one. The fact that their bodies were painted for war and they were armed to the teeth only confused the image.

Aidan's sisters walked beside her, while the old woman, Una, prattled on at her back, and one by one their little troupe dispersed. Rogan was given his own quarters while the King's men were accorded a single dwelling to share. Una remained to see the men settled, leaving Lili and Aveline to continue along with Aidan's sisters.

Apparently, until after the ceremony, no one would be permitted within the hall where the laird's family slept—a fact that Sorcha felt not the least reluctant to share. Lili had no complaint about that, except that the house they led her to was meant to be shared with Aveline.

"How crude," Aveline whispered, as she entered the tiny cottage, with its simple wooden furnishings. She ran her fingers along the surfaces of the furniture, finding her fingers clean after leaving each piece. Still, her face remained pinched with disapproval. Lili had an overwhelming urge to remind her that Rogan had no influence here. She didn't know how that could have been made more clear. The gleam of Lael's knives were more than enough warning to apprise Lili to use her manners.

Aveline had a noble bloodline, but apparently good breeding was no assurance of good manners. And yet, while the accommodations were a far cry from the massive stone towers of Keppenach Keep, the cottage was immaculately kept, with fresh rushes on the floor and new thatch on the roof. Clearly, these folk had worked hard to prepare for their arrival and someone had given up their home as it was doubtful they had constructed the domicile simply for them. There were blankets that had been lovingly knitted by someone folded neatly upon the bed, and adornments that said this home was beloved. Regardless of what else she might feel, Lili appreciated the effort they had made in their behalf, even if her betrothed seemed to want nothing to do with her.

Both Cailin and Lael watched from the doorway while Sorcha showed them within.

Along the journey north, they had brought but a single wooden cart. But it wasn't until they brought in Aveline's oversized trunks that Lili realized how meager her own coffers were in comparison. She'd brought only two small chests while the trunks took up half the space of the diminutive dwelling. Sorcha wandered over to examine one of Aveline's trunks. "Are these yours?" she asked Lili, running her fingers over the intricate carvings in the corner of the largest coffer.

"Mine!" Aveline snapped, and the girl withdrew her fingers at once, tilting Lili another questioning glance.

Her older sisters stood with arms crossed, peering at one another without saying a word, but Lili knew they must have been wondering who the true mistress was—clearly not Lili. She didn't fail to note their disdainful glances toward the trunks and then toward each other.

Discomfited by the sisters' scrutiny, Aveline softened her voice. "I meant only to say your blue paint may ruin the woodwork." The trunk was fashioned from expensive oak and the carvings were delicately painted, but there was no paint on the girl's hand. Lili gave Aveline a quelling glance. Very soon, whether she liked it or not, these would be Lili's people as well, and it would be her responsibility to protect them—from Aveline's sense of self-importance, if from nothing else. However, Lili was certain much of Aveline's haughtiness would be tempered naturally once Rogan was gone. Once again noting the silver knife handle gleaming over the top of Lael's boot, Lili nervously lifted up one of the candles sitting atop a table. She brought it to her nose to inhale the lovely scent of beeswax. "Oh!" she exclaimed in surprise. "What an honor to be given the best of your candles!" she said to Sorcha.

From the doorway, Cailin gave a little twitch of her brows.

The eldest of the three sisters continued to watch Aveline circle the room and Lili forced herself to ignore Rogan's mistress, centering her attention on Sorcha and Cailin. "At Keppenach we were not so fortunate. Our candles were all made of tallow."

Sorcha screwed her face. "Oh, they must have reeked!"

Lili smiled. "Indeed," she confessed, meeting Lael's gaze just for an instant. Lael lifted a brow, but that was all she conceded, and Lili returned her attention to the candle in her hand. Decorated by an outer layer of braids, the handiwork was quite ornate. She studied it with genuine fascination.

Still Lael said nothing and simply continued to watch from the doorway, her stance nearly as imposing as any man's, but Cailin walked over to remove the candle from Lili's hands. She turned it over, peering up with a tentative smile. "This one is mine," she declared. "See? We place our marks upon the bottoms so everyone may know." Clearly, she took pride in her work.

"How lovely," Lili said sincerely and continued to scrutinize the braid work. It was incredibly detailed and quite unlike anything she had ever seen. It reminded her a bit of the etchings on the stone her son had found in her garden. "Will you show me how to make one later?"

Cailin gave her another smile, and then seeming to recall herself, she peered back at her eldest sister. Their exchange was indecipherable, but it appeared to Lili that somehow she had won a tiny victory when Cailin turned, lifted her shoulders and said, "Mayhap."

But that apparently did not please Lael, for she suddenly waved her sisters away from their *guests*. The look she gave Aveline was scathing, but all emotion was shuttered when her gaze returned to Lili. "I trust ye will discover all to your satisfaction," she said, slanting a look at Aveline that could have sliced the heart out of a man.

Aveline took a startled step backward and Lili stifled a tiny smile.

"As my sister has said, we prepared a welcome celebration," Lael offered rather grimly. "When ye are ready to sup, simply follow your noses." And then she gathered her sisters and ushered them out of the cottage, remaining just a moment longer to impart a warning...

She centered her gaze upon Lili. "Ye'll find us quite accommodating, but take care. My sisters may not recall what betrayal looks like, but my brother and I will n'er forget." She passed another glance to Aveline, her gaze lingering a second longer before returning to Lili. "I may have promised Aidan my best behavior in your presence, but not even Aidan will fault me for gutting ye from belly to throat if I find ye have perfidy in mind. Dinna betray my kin," she warned, and with that she smiled sweetly, her face suddenly softening despite the war paint. "Welcome to Dubhtolargg," she said, and turned and walked away.

* * *

This was the longest era of peace their tribesmen had ever known.

From the moment of its conception, Dubhtolargg had been plagued with betrayals and deceptions, and it seemed history was bound to repeat itself.

Apparently, Aidan was little different from his father—so

hungry for peace that he would find himself once again bargaining with traitorous devils.

With an explosion of curses, he burst into the hall, angered to find himself in the position he was in—hopeful for a treaty of peace, but heedful of the consequences of letting down his guard. But that dilemma now presented itself with an entirely new quandary. He was torn, feeling intensely protective over his new bride and equally distrustful.

That pleading look in those violet eyes tugged at his heart, but for all he knew she had been sent to gut him in his bed.

It didn't matter. He didn't intend to give her any opportunity to put him in the ground, and whether or not he believed in the curse, there was only a danger for the husband who lost his heart over the violet-eyed wench, and that was something Aidan was not inclined to do—no matter how imploring a look she gave him.

Love was not a part of this bargain.

The only love he bore any woman was the love he had for his sisters, and his mistress was the land of his birth. That would not change, no matter how well his bride packaged her lovely breasts.

His brother sauntered in behind him and Aidan stilled his tongue, ready to rebuke Keane for having abandoned the others, but he was well aware of the example he had set. If possible, his mood darkened as he made his way toward the cupboard to snatch himself a tankard and a pint of *uisge*. After retrieving both, he sat down at the long table, pouring himself a liberal dose, wondering how Caimbeul's daughter fared with his sisters.

Keane sat down and Aidan eyed his brother over the rim of his tankard. "Once we are wed, you *will* afford *her* the respect due her as your chieftain's wife."

There was no need to clarify of whom he spoke, for they both understood very well.

Keane sat watching as Aidan swallowed a hefty draught. The sweet golden liquid burned as it slid down Aidan's throat. When it was gone, he set the tankard down upon the table. "That includes remaining in her company e'en when I canna abide it." And then to himself, he added, "I wadna relish the thought of that bastard giving your sisters e'en the tiniest slight." Again, there was no need to say of whom he spoke, for he knew his brother had spied the exchange that had angered him and sent him on his heels. "In that case, I would return him to David in snippets."

Keane nodded, merely listening, knowing better than to argue. His brother could be a defiant lad, but never with him. He was well aware that Keane venerated his every move. It was both a boon and a burden, for Aidan could never relax his guard. Some day, Keane might well lead the clan in his stead and, to that end, he had groomed Keane from the time of his boyhood, well aware that his own life could end at any given moment. It seemed there was ever some fool who yearned to rule them despite that they made it a point to stay out of Scotia's politics.

For more than two hundred and fifty years their kin had been positioned here in the Red Mounth—not hiding, per se, but neither did they wish to be troubled. After the murder of King Aed in the year 878—by his most trusted friend and advisor—his kinfolk had retreated here to this refuge in order to safeguard the one true relic that could protect and ensure the reign of future Kings over a peaceful nation—a sacred stone that as yet no one even realized had gone missing. In its stead, they had left a perfect replica that not even the priests at Scone seemed able to differentiate, for David was the twentieth so-called king they had crowned upon that other slag of stone. He poured himself another draught and swallowed, considering the replica and the men who had sat their fat arses upon it.

Even once the throne had been returned to Aed's heirs, Aidan's people had made the decision to keep the true stone hidden, for Aed's son and nephew had returned from exile as Gaels, their manner and customs no longer true to the old ways. It was little wonder Aed's nephew had been the first to hail himself as a king of Scotia, for what else was Scotia but a new name for an old land occupied by a new regime?

Such as it was, Aidan's tribesmen were the last of the

painted ones—those the Roman's had once called Pechts. It was a legacy his people strove to preserve. They did not recognize Scotia, nor any of its kings, and he was angry that he had been forced to allow his sister Cat to wed a feckless Scotsman. Simply by virtue of the fact that they hailed themselves as Scoti, the clans were fated to war upon one another, for the real stone of destiny was vaulted deep within the Red Hills. It could only be awarded to a rightful heir—but who should that be? The Pechts were no more and the Scots were bloody traitors and murdering bastards—all of them!

"Get yourself a tankard," he commanded his brother.

Keane was four and ten now. There was little reason not to treat him as a man.

At his command, Keane leapt up so fast he nearly toppled the bench he was seated upon. Aidan watched him run to the cupboard, snatching the first tankard he could find. He hurried back to the table and sat down again, slamming the cup down with a greedy gleam in his eye.

Aidan lifted up the jug, refilling his own cup before reaching across the table to pour Keane a dram as well. Although he had long ago ceased to treat Keane as a child—and he knew full well the lad pinched from the barrels when it pleased him—this was the first time he had ever drank with his little brother. The moment was far more significant than it might appear. Aidan was proud of him. It was long past time to bless him. If indeed Aidan were to expire in his wedding bed, he must have faith in his brother's ability to rule in his stead.

But that was yet another burr in his side—now that Aidan was to wed, his firstborn son should be his rightful heir—a child with Scots blood. That fact burned his gut far worse than a shot of fresh *uisge*.

He poured another gullet full, wincing at the sweet burn in the back of his throat, and then set his tankard down upon the table.

Of all his siblings, Lael was by far the most adept to lead. There was not a fool alive who would gainsay her if he knew what was good for his health. At least it was something to consider…

"Will ye keep your promise to wed the Scoti wench?" Keane asked, coddling his cup before him. "Ye dinna have to," he suggested with one brow raised.

"A mon's word is his honor," Aidan told him. "The price of breaking it—e'en once—is the trust of his clan. Aye, Keane, I will wed the lass, but that doesna mean I'll no' kill her if she proves to be a deceitful bitch."

Keane grinned, lifting his tankard to his lips. Aidan knew he was trying to be nonchalant, but the boy's hands trembled as he peered up anxiously to see if Aidan watched.

"Oh, and," he said, "lest ye forget… *I* am the *only* one who may call my bride a wench. Dinna let me hear such disrespect pass your lips again."

Keane nodded, at last taking a swig of his *uisge*, succumbing immediately to a fit of coughs and sputters. But he drank again even before his hacking had subsided, and Aidan smiled, for Keane was a lad after his own heart.

Keane's face split into a silly grin and he took another hefty chug. When he came up again from his cups he had a new glitter to his eyes.

Aidan rewarded him with a nod and a smile. Their *uisge* was not for the faint of heart. 'Twas said their recipe for the water of life came straight from the faeries who had first led his people to this glen. Like everything in this little slice of heaven on earth, the recipe was a legacy to their ancestors, kept for generations and changed not a whit.

Like the *crannóg* they slept in.

Made completely of wood, the building had been designed to hold an entire village in the event of war, but Dubhtolargg was far larger than it had been when their ancestors had first arrived here. Despite that many Highland villages were now protected by new stone fortresses that buttressed the sky, they had no need of such bastions here. Those monstrous creations of men were monuments to fear. Here they were protected by the land itself—and some would say by the ancient faerie glen where men must pass before coming down into the vale. This was not a country for the enfeebled, and very soon he would discover precisely what Lileas MacLaren was made of. If his bride would seek a warm bed, she would need gather near, for the walls here were no doubt far thinner than those she was accustomed to at Keppenach.

Now it was Aidan's turn to cough, for the thought of Lileas lying naked in his bed sent a surge of lust through his veins that stirred his cock, startling him so that he swallowed his *uisge* down the wrong pipe. *Mo chreach!* He couldn't recall the last time a lass had such sway over his willie. The women of his clan were hardly shy. They held as much dominion as any man, and loved where they would, but Aidan had never been able to stomach the thought of fathering lads with a woman he didn't care to live with.

Enemy or nay, Lileas was a lovely thing, with curves in all the right places and breasts that were far riper than a body so lean should have a right to bear. He reasoned that it must be because she had already borne a child, but her belly belied that fact. She was a beautiful contradiction, his bride—everything about her. And though he had contemplated returning her to her father if she didn't please him, he knew beyond a shadow of doubt that he would not.

In fact, there was no reason to delay the hand fasting, he decided in that very instant. If Lael managed not to kill her this afternoon, he would wed Lileas MacLaren on the morrow.

A tiny smile curled his lip, for the simple fact that none of his sisters had returned with news of Lileas' demise was a verra good sign. In celebration, he poured himself and Keane another cup full of *uisge*. "Drink!" he commanded. "Tonight we celebrate."

If Lileas made it through the afternoon with his sisters, at the very least they would celebrate not having to go to war with her bloody Da.

Five

The instant Aidan's sisters were gone, Lili sent Aveline to retrieve water for the basin in their room. She waited for about an hour, and when Aveline had yet to return, she went in search of water herself and found a well not far from the cottage. But even after hauling the bucket back, Aveline was nowhere to be found.

All the better, Lili decided, for she wasn't accustomed to having anyone wait on her anyway and she preferred not to have an audience while she bathed.

Aveline was likely with Rogan anyway, Lili thought.

Poor girl... she had come to Keppenach as Rogan's ward and though he had wasted little time in bedding her, he clearly did not intend to wed her. He had cast her off so easily. He never showered her with gifts, nor did he publicly acknowledge her as his mistress. Whatever Aveline owned she had brought along with her from her father's home—and quite a lot there was!

With some effort, Lili moved Aveline's enormous trunks out of the way to get to her measly two chests. Lili had brought very little in regards to clothing, but she had stuffed all the herbs she could fit in her coffers. Realizing that once she was gone they would allow her garden go to weeds, she had harvested everything she could. Half the other trunk was full of herbs as well, for the herbs were far more valuable than any dress she owned, including this ridiculous gown David had gifted her with. For her son, she'd left but a few herbs, primarily rosemary to help him ward away the terrible dreams he suffered by night. But she had also left a few medicinals with a nursemaid she trusted. Her son was a healthy lad, though she worried about him anyway. He was her only son and she missed him more than words could say.

They had given her one year to see her new husband dead—one year to contemplate the atrocities they would commit upon her son if she did not obey.

Lael's words came back to taunt her: *My sisters may not recall what betrayal looks like, but my brother and I will n'er forget.*

What did she know? Was betrayal written so clearly upon Lili's face even though she did not even know how she would accomplish the task? Could she murder a man in cold blood? More than anything, for once in her life, she hoped the curse was true, for then she could lay Aidan's death squarely upon his own hands, for it was his kin who had cursed her, after all.

Save for one wee complication... to die from the curse, Aidan would have to love her, and the affection of the laird of Dubhtolargg was something she doubted she would ever earn. Considering the dark look Aidan had given her before he'd abandoned her to his sisters, she would be quite fortunate if he didn't strangle her in their bed on their wedding night.

But of course, she preferred not to think of *that* right now.

She was no innocent maid. She understood what would come and what would be expected of her, and the thought of the bedding made her cheeks flame. An image of Aidan, standing nearly bare upon the dock accosted her, and she shoved it away, unable to bear the thought, for it made her belly flutter and her heart dance against her ribs.

Reining in her wayward thoughts, she rifled through her chest.

Amidst her belongings, there was one small pouch she truly hoped never to open. The tiny brown nondescript sack contained a very deadly concentration of nightshade and hemlock—so potent that one must endeavor not to even touch it with bare hands. Also inside that sack was the ring Rogan had given her—a poison ring so she might lace Aidan's food or drink without his notice.

It crossed her mind to wonder why Rogan would have such a trinket to begin with. If Stuart had not perished in the manner he had, surrounded by witnesses, she might begin to wonder if his brother had intended the device for him. Certainly Rogan was capable of it. Shuddering at the thought, she shoved the pouch with the ring down deeper into her chest, concealing it. Another small pouch, similar in color, was full of rose petals, and she snatched that one out and closed the chest.

Rose petals had many uses, but she most loved to throw the petals in her bath water. These, however, were no longer supple, so she would use them to freshen her wedding gown. She took from her coffers a far plainer bliaut, a deep sapphire blue gown fashioned from soft wool, with light-blue embroidery along the hem and sleeves. She had sewn the dress herself and was quite proud of the result, even if it was worn now with age. As Rogan had intended, she had made her appearance in the lavish gown David had gifted her with, and now she would leave it for her wedding night and wear something far more appropriate to the weather. This far north the night would bring a chill.

Stuart had once told her that the color of her blue gown complimented her eyes—but that was *not* why she chose it.

Besides, she told herself it didn't matter what Aidan dún Scoti thought of her.

In the pouch, there was also a phial of rosewater, which she used to scent her bath water. Not daring to tarry much longer, she made quick work of her bath, donning the gown hurriedly and then retrieving her beloved arisaid from her coffer.

Until she was duly wed she saw no reason not to continue wearing the MacLaren plaid. Stuart might be dead now, but although these were her last days as a MacLaren, some day her son would do these colors proud. For now, wearing the arisaid made her feel bonded to Kellen. The simple fact that she would soon be forced to abandon it left her with a hollow feeling deep in her soul. But she sighed, deciding that once she put it aside, she would save it for the woman her son would wed and prayed she would live long enough to see that day come.

Once her private ministrations were done, she smoothed her gown down around her ankles and then brushed and plaited her hair so that it fell in one thick braid down her back. A few wispy strands could not be contained, but she couldn't bother herself to try. She was too weary and glum and the laird of Dubhtolargg had already shown her what he thought of her—apparently not very much.

What had she expected anyway?

Far from being a love match, this wasn't even a political match. What it was precisely, she had yet to determine, for she knew enough about Aidan dún Scoti to know he had no interest in alliances with anyone. In truth, there was only one thing he could want with her, though Lìli could well see that they had gone out of their way to provide her with all that she would need here. Apparently, at least for the moment, he didn't intend to make her suffer for her father's sins. Still, she couldn't help but feel a sense of impending doom because vengeance could be his only motive. What would be his method of punishment?

Surely he had something planned...

Pondering that with a wary heart, she sat upon the bed she was meant to share with Rogan's mistress and found it plump and clean. Aveline would think it insufferably crude, but the feather bed was a pleasant surprise.

Outside, the sound of the reed rose upon the air and Lìli waited, expecting someone to knock upon her door at any moment. *When you are ready to sup, simply follow your noses*, she recalled Lael saying. Apparently, she had meant that quite literally. When no one came to retrieve her, Lìli suspected no one would and she finally ventured out toward the sound of the reed.

On the beach near the loch, Aidan's kinsmen had built a bonfire. Beyond it, she could see the torches lit along the pier to the wooden fortress perched out upon the water. However, the pier was empty and there was no sight of Aidan. The sky was alight with a deep golden light that reflected upon the glassy water, and despite that a chill had risen in the air, there was nary a breeze and the fire burned true and high.

Little by little, the townsfolk abandoned their daily tasks and gathered around the fire, but their numbers grew slowly, for it seemed no one was in the mood for a celebration. In fact, the looks upon their faces as they gazed at her reminded her of the way the villagers at Keppenach regarded Rogan whenever their haughty master wasn't looking. In contrast, they had loved Stuart, and Lili might have grown to love him as well if she'd had half a chance. As it was, she was grateful to him, for he had shown her the greatest kindness she had ever known. However, he had died within the first year of their marriage, and she hadn't truly had time to know or love him as he had deserved.

Watching the townsfolk gather, Lili stood alone at the edge of the bonfire, ignoring the wary looks the people cast in her direction. As the sun continued to fade, more and more clansmen were drawn to the warmth of the fire. Finally, Aveline reappeared. She stood at Rogan's side on the other side of the bonfire, whispering into his ear. Her face was flushed and despite the fact that the conversation was no doubt in part about Lili, neither of them peered in Lili's direction. Lili felt invisible and alone, an outsider without asylum, but she refused to go join Rogan and his dour-faced mistress. While these were not her people as yet, neither were Rogan and Aveline. They were as much her adversary as was Lael.

At least Lael did not mince words.

Listening to the evocative sound of the reed, Lili drew her arisaid higher over her shoulders, mesmerized by the dancing flames. Watching the crackling timber, she remained rooted to the spot, thinking of her son—the look upon his face as she'd left him alone—and she swallowed a knot of grief that arose in the back of her throat.

Suddenly she felt more than heard the presence at her side

and turned to find Aidan dún Scoti standing beside her. She had not even heard him approach.

He was no longer bare-chested, nor was he painted, and he had traded his claymore for a simple dirk that he had sheathed within his belt. Wearing an unstained tunic along with his breacan, there was nothing savage about the man's appearance now save the look in his eyes. They were cold and hard, and for the longest instant, he held her gaze transfixed, then he eyed her arisaid with narrowed eyes.

Lili pulled the cloak around her shoulders defensively and met his gaze without flinching. "'Tis cold, my lord. I have no other."

Was she baiting him?
Aidan wondered.

Clearly she did not come to him with open arms, but neither did she strike him as being a contrary wench, despite her earlier mettle. And yet she stood before him, wrapped in MacLaren colors for everyone to behold.

Was it a message for him perhaps—that she might wed him but her heart would always belong to another? Or was she simply cold, as she'd claimed?

He reminded himself that until they were wed she had a right to wear whatever she chose, but it rankled nonetheless. For all his outward calm, he felt like stripping off her accursed MacLaren cloak and covering her with his own. But to do such a thing had far greater consequence than simply assuaging his wounded pride. The women of his clan would as soon box a man's ears than to put up with his jealousy, and yet he felt a twinge of it now. Still he held his tongue, battling through strange emotions that assailed him. In all his years he had never felt possessive over any woman. Foreign as the feeling was, he recognized it nevertheless and didn't like it one bit.

He couldn't see much beneath the arisaid, but she had changed into a simpler gown. He spied a glimpse of the dark-blue wool beneath the plaid. His sisters, Cailin and Sorcha, had changed, as well, although Lael had refused. The eldest of his sisters was as stubborn a wench as any who had ever breathed—even more headstrong than their mother had been, but Aidan could barely recall much else about the woman who had borne him. That fact alone rankled, and his new bride—the woman who would share his bed—was the daughter of the man he held responsible for her death.

"Widowhood suits ye," he remarked. "Though dinna become accustomed to it, for I dinna intend to be so accommodating as your first husband." He crossed his arms, his countenance dark as he again fixed his gaze upon her odious MacLaren cloak.

Averting her gaze, Lileas peered across the bonfire, where her companions stood huddled together. She seemed to be weighing her words, her jaw working slightly as she stared at her companions. "I am no more responsible for my husband's death than you are for your father's," she suggested.

"Is that so?"

Her violet eyes snapped up to meet his. "Aye, my lord, it is."

"My name is Aidan," he corrected her. "Here we do not adhere to haughty English customs as the rest of Scotia seems inclined to do."

"Mayhap," she allowed. "But ye are now my keeper and thus my lord, are ye not?"

Mo chreach! The wench was no more subservient than his bloody sisters! And yet though he felt a stab of anger over her words, he did not truly wish her to be anything less, he realized. He took a deep breath, summoning patience before speaking. "I am neither your keeper nor your husband as yet, *mo chroí—my heart.* And, in fact, I am reconsidering the wisdom of inviting the woman whose hands bear the blood of my father into my bed."

"Would that you had decided sooner!" she dared to scold him. "But *I* did not kill your father, Aidan *dún Scoti.* Your people cursed an innocent child."

Hearing the name her kinfolk called him, the Scot from the hills, Aidan grimaced. By the sins of sluag, he was no bloody Scotsman! "Aye," he argued, "though your father did—in cold blood I might add. If, in fact, your life has been accursed, *mo chroí*, you may blame Padruig Caimbeul, not my kin."

Illuminated by the rising flames, her violet eyes seemed to deepen to a shade this side of black. "I never said I blamed your kin."

"And yet you do?"

The question was a challenge. They both knew very well that there was enmity between them—enmity that stemmed from circumstances far beyond this moment—beyond any words that had ever been spoken between them.

Her eyes glistened by the light of the fire, but she dared to lift her chin. "As you blame me?"

That too, was a challenge.

The bonfire grew brighter, crackling in the twilight.

Aidan was well aware that now that he had arrived, those of his kinfolk who had avoided the celebration before were drifting into the circle. They were watching him and his bride. Even the children looked to their chieftain for direction, for if these guests rose up against them, he would be the one to lead his warriors to their defense.

But this was no warrior standing before him.

She was a woman... a woman unlike any he had ever known.

She looked like an English loving Scot, sounded like a Scot, but her eyes gave him a feeling of kinship that he should not in good conscience share with a woman whose father had committed such atrocities upon his clan.

And yet... he had agreed for her to become his wife. At some point, he *must* find a way to put aside their differences and embrace her... for the good of all.

Unless he truly planned to kill her for her father's sins... and what true justice was there in that? Revenge, although he had certainly entertained those notions, were not the reason he had agreed to this union. It was not his duty to conquer. It was his duty to protect the stone, and the best way to accomplish that was to stay out of petty wars.

He gazed across the fire at her companions, wondering if

their treatment of Lìleas were somehow a trick, a scheme to pluck at his heartstrings... for despite his resolve not to be affected by the lass, he sensed her torment just the same. It weighed the air around them like a black cloud... invisible but there... like Una's visions—things he could not see with his eyes, but he could certainly feel them.

"Why did you agree to wed me?" he asked suddenly, needing to know.

She peered up at him, her violet eyes reflecting the bonfire. Tiny flames danced in her gaze. "I could ask the same of you?" she countered. And once again, her chin lifted defiantly.

She was a quick little temptress with a depth of knowing in her eyes that unsettled him. But verra well, he would play her game if he must. "And to your mind... what would be the acceptable reply?"

"For peace," she professed without hesitation.

Aidan nodded, suddenly at a loss for words, for while he wished to say the same, he had not brought her here for that reason. Vengeance was never truly his motive, he reassured himself once more, but somewhere inside a fire cooled at her answer. And yet her presence here at Dubhtolargg was only assurance that her father would not bear arms against them, so long as he valued his daughter. If he did not value her, then they held no advantage at all. She was simply a viper in their midst, spying for her Da and for David mac Mhaoil Chaluim.

Could he afford to trust her?

If she spoke the truth... could he wipe the bitterness from his heart and take her at her word? After all, she was right; she was not her father.

Aidan felt the scrutiny of his clansmen acutely. As his brother had done, they would treat his bride as he treated her, following his lead. Until he knew more, he could not condemn her to his people's discrimination, but neither could he signal them to be off their guard. In spite of the fact that Una's prophetic words had moved many to accept her with a wary eye, not all were so convinced the daughter of their enemy could, in truth, be the salvation of their clan. But that was exactly as it should be. He studied her in silence, aware that all eyes were upon them.

Despite her lovely features, her face was drawn with fatigue. At the moment, she was staring across the fire. Aidan followed her gaze.

It had completely escaped his notice earlier that the man who had seized her by the arm was also wearing MacLaren colors. Her husband's brother—information he had gleaned from Una. Those two—the laird of Keppenach and Aveline—were colluding... but the question remained: Was his lovely bride a part of their scheme?

Time alone would tell.

"It seems to me that ye would draw more strength in numbers," Aidan remarked, curious as to why she stood alone when her brother by law and his company were present.

Lileas straightened, wrapping her plaid more tightly about her shoulders, and eyed him meaningfully. "I draw my greatest strength from solitude."

Damn. But she would fit right in with his saucy sisters, he thought. Never in all his life had he been dismissed so thoroughly. Though, in truth, he wasn't entirely certain that's what she had done, it certainly felt like it. Had she been any other woman at any other given time, he would have obliged her at once. However, duty kept him rooted to the spot.

The tension in the air crackled like the pinewood at the center of the flames. Across the fire, the pair in question turned to look at them, and discomfited by Aidan's scrutiny, once again averted their gazes as though his attention made them uncomfortable.

"Who is the woman?" Aidan asked.

As nothing else had, the question seemed to deflate her. She sighed and peered down at her feet. "My lady's maid. She is to tend me."

Aidan lifted a brow. "Seems to me she has her duties confused."

A tiny burst of surprised laughter escaped her lips, and she turned to look at him then.

In that instant, there was no guile in her expression at all. Despite the tension in their discourse, she smiled softly and lifted her chin. "I am quite certain her duties are clear to her, my lord."

"Aidan," he insisted. "Though if ye canna bring yourself to speak my name, at least use the Scots word. I can stomach it far better."

"Laird," she replied, and in that moment, she appeared for all the world a martyred bride.

Because she is, he reminded himself.

And still, unlike most men even, she held his gaze, her violet eyes haunted and beautiful. Not for the first time, they spoke to him in a way that made him feel wholly uncomfortable. Though, damn it, if he considered her plight, it would pull at his heartstrings and he could simply not allow that to happen.

Arms crossed, his gaze was drawn again across the fire toward her companions. The reed played on, children laughed, and every knowing eye remained fixed upon them.

Mayhap his heart was not so steeled against her as he'd thought and he felt a new peril rising, one that had little to do with the distant ring of battle swords.

It was not too late to send her home, he told himself.

It was the Highland custom to enact a trial marriage. A woman, or a man, could renounce a spouse at any time, but for the first year it was understood the marriage was provisional... to be certain, especially in the case of a chieftain, that his wife could bear him a son. But he was not obligated to hand fast with this maiden. He could send her home before they spoke the words, and right now, that was his inclination... except...

His gaze scanned the gathering, searching for Una.

As elusive as the old woman could be at times, she was always around when he needed her. However, tonight she was nowhere to be found, and his skin prickled with annoyance.

Once again he considered the lass at his side, torn.

She was beautiful standing there, her face awash with golden light, her dark hair bound in a healthy braid down her back. Her lashes were long and her lips looked soft and lush. He longed to see what she wore beneath the arisaid. The simple fact that she had changed out of that ridiculous gown she had arrived in pleased him immensely, for now she appeared the same as any of the women of his clan.

She glanced up at him, her violet eyes speaking to him still, words his mind did not comprehend, but his heart seemed to understand nevertheless... and he felt disquieted. Despite everything he knew, he yearned to make her feel welcome, wanted to let his kinsmen know he accepted her—at least for the moment—but he found himself at a loss for words. And though his fingers itched to unclasp his own plaid from his shoulders and offer it to the lass instead of the one she wore, he held them fast at his side.

She was his enemy's daughter.

Soon she would be his wife.

Which of the two should he acknowledge when he looked into her eyes?

Six

"Aidan!"

The voice belonged to Aidan's youngest sister. Ill at ease with *guests* in their midst, Aidan's hand flew to the hilt of his dagger, ready to leap to Sorcha's defense. Alone, she ran toward him, sweat pasting her chestnut-colored hair to her face. Clutching her skirt in her hands to keep from tripping in her haste, her face was a mask of distress as she came to a breathless halt beside them, her eyes glassy with unshed tears.

Aidan drew the dirk from his belt, but Sorcha pushed it back. "Nay, Aidan!" she cried. "I went to see Dunc," she explained before he could jump to conclusions. "To see if he was well enough to attend the celebration. He'll no' waken! His minny weeps at his side for fear of the sweating sickness. Now I canna find Una—what shall I do?"

Aidan was about to set out toward the weaver's hut, but Lileas touched his sister upon the shoulder. "What ails the child?"

His sister's cheeks were flushed with exertion and her face contorted with worry and fear, though she did not recoil from Lileas' touch—a fact that would have raised Aidan's brow were he not contemplating young Duncan's plight. Of all his sisters, Sorcha had been the most furious over Catriona's abduction, blaming David for stealing her elder sister from her bed. While Lael and Cailin were much closer in age to Cat, Sorcha had looked to Cat as a mother as well. Lael might be the eldest, but she was hardly maternal in nature.

"I dunno," Sorcha exclaimed, shaking her head. "Like the rest, the sickness came quickly. His fever began only this morn."

"Will you take me to him?" Lileas asked, and Sorcha nodded without hesitation. Lileas turned suddenly, meeting Aidan's gaze directly. "May I?" Her hand automatically touched his bare arm and he felt her touch like a pulse of lightning.

Aidan hid the shiver that coursed through him and fought the urge to move his arm out of her reach, as though her fingers burned his flesh. But his body reacted with a vengeance, hardening his shaft like a poppet on a string.

He stared at her a moment too long, unsettled, and then peered down at the slim fingers resting upon his arm. She too must have peered down because their gazes lifted at once and the sincerity in her violet eyes took him by surprise.

For a moment, his brain was too muddled to think clearly. She was asking him to allow her to go help Duncan.

She was a noteworthy healer, he reminded himself. He didn't trust her, but neither could he deny Duncan her healing prowess. When finally he was able to shake off his stupor, he nodded, bemused, and watched her hie away with Sorcha.

Once she removed her fingers from his flesh, Aidan felt the separation acutely—like a man whose arm had been lopped off. The sensation startled him.

"This way!" Sorcha demanded, and his lovely bride went chasing after his youngest sibling without sparing another word or glance for Aidan... as though she were completely unaware of the way her touch had affected him.

Confused, Aidan held back only another instant, then followed, half expecting a Caimbeul spawn to continue where her father left off—only picking them off one by one, beginning with the children first.

But she wouldn't dare.

Surely she wouldn't dare.

He picked up his pace, assuring himself that, woman or nay, if the damned enchantress dared to harm a single hair upon the boy's head he would toss her, along with that *siùrsach—whore* lady's maid—and her brother by marriage into the bonfire. Aye, and then they would turn the celebration into a funeral and burn them all upon a pyre.

Lili struggled to keep up.

All she could think of in that instant was that a child lay ill and it could very well have been her son. She hoped to God someone would return the favor were Kellen in need and it filled her with grief to know that she would not be at his side if he called out for her in the middle of the night.

Somehow, she must find her way back to him.

As she hurried away from the bonfire, she tried to keep up without twisting her ankle. It was difficult to find her step without faltering along the rocky terrain. Hurrying behind Sorcha, she was blind to the glances Aidan's kinsmen gave them as they hurried into the lowering night. In her concern for the child, she was oblivious, as well, to the fact that her betrothed was marching like a henchman at her heels.

"What can you tell me of the illness?" she asked Sorcha.

"No' verra much. It begins with fever and shivers, and then I'm told, terrible sweats."

That description could be most anything, Lili fretted.

"So Duncan isna the first?" she asked, tripping over a small rock along her path.

Far more surefooted and rushing up the hillside like a woodland sprite, Sorcha answered without looking back, "Nay."

"How many before?"

"Three."

"How many recovered?"

"None." The girl peered back at Lili with a sense of foreboding in her clear blue eyes, though she didn't stop, and neither did Lili, despite that it occurred to her suddenly to worry over contagion.

"Is anyone else ill in this particular house, Sorcha?"

"Nay," the girl replied, and finally she stopped before a small cottage way up on the hillside and threw open the door.

Inside, amidst a circle of flickering candles, a young woman with black hair sat upon her knees at the bedside of a young child, weeping softly. Lili took in the boy's appearance first. His hair was soaked and plastered to his face. He reminded her of Kellen, with his dark hair and long lashes that fell thickly upon high cheeks. His skin was ashy, but not gaunt, proof that his illness was not long and lingering. In spite of the pallor of his skin, he appeared to Lili like a well-fed, healthy child. Sorcha claimed he'd fallen ill only this morn. What sort of illness came so quickly and spared no lives?

The mother's eyes lit first upon Sorcha, but now she peered at Lili and her eyes widened with alarm. "Nay!" she cried, rising up to face them. "*You* stay away from my child!"

"Glenna, she only wishes to help," Sorcha pleaded in Lili's behalf. She stood between them to keep the woman at bay. "Remember, Una said she was a skilled healer?"

The woman was lovely, but Lili did not wish to anger her for she was quite tall and thickly built. "Nay!" the mother persisted, and then attempted to sidestep Sorcha to get at Lili. "She will kill us all given the chance—just like her Da!"

Lili started at the accusation. Until this instant, she had not precisely placed herself in these people's shoes. All her life she had felt persecuted by these folk, despite having never known them. Their curse had followed her like a devil's hound. But for once, she considered what her father might have done to earn such hatred—a hatred so impassioned that they would curse a man's firstborn child. Until this instant, she had considered herself a casualty of men's politics, and whatever her father had done only typical for men playing at war. But like Rogan, her father could be cruel. She realized that better than anyone. However... war brought out the worst in both sides, did it not? She was as much a victim as any other.

The young mother glared at her, and Lili resisted the urge to shrink back out of the cottage door, somehow sensing it would gain her little respect among these folk.

In her hysteria, the woman shoved Sorcha aside. "I said nay!"

Lili swallowed. She would not fight this woman, but neither did she intend to leave if she could help the poor boy. Her gaze fell to the child lying abed, examining him from afar while the mother railed at her, saying what Lili had no clue for her attention was now on the son.

A rush of cold air blew in as the door opened once again and a deep voice boomed from the doorway. "Enough!" The woman hushed at once. "Allow her to tend the child," Aidan demanded.

"Nay, Aidan!"

His tone brooked no argument. "If she can help, Glenna, allow her to do so."

To some degree, Lili was accustomed to that ambivalent look, for so often her patients were torn, needing help, yet fearing her nonetheless. Very often, if she could speak with them alone, they soon came to realize that she was simply a woman, nothing more. Trading kindness for animosity had always served her well. No matter what their differences, they were both ultimately the same—mothers who worried for their children.

Reluctantly, Glenna stepped aside.

Grateful for Aidan's interference, Lili moved past the worried mother and bent at once, putting her hand to the boy's forehead. His fever raged, burning his flesh. Forsooth, but she could have baked an egg upon his cheek so hot was his skin to the touch! She peered up at the mother, looking beyond the hatred to the terrified woman behind the dove gray eyes. "Did his belly trouble him at all?"

The woman wrung her hands, peering at Aidan for reassurance. She turned to look at Lili and for a long moment simply gazed at her. She must have read the truth in Lili's gaze—that she simply wished to help—because she shook her head at long last.

"Could he have eaten something sour?" Lili persisted.

The woman shook her head again, and then came forward to stand beside Lili, her motherly concern outweighing her enmity. "Nay," she said. "He was fine. He simply said he felt cold. Then the fever followed. There was no vomiting, nor did he move his bowels, but he has been shivering just so for hours."

Lili nodded, lifting the boy's shirt, inspecting his belly.

"No rashes," the mother offered quickly, understanding instinctively what it was that Lili was searching for. Lili glanced at his hands, and then his feet, and then felt the area beneath his arms and about his neck. There were no telltale bulbous, but his skin was damp and the bedclothes were soaked with this sweat.

"No bites either?" she asked the mother.

Glenna shook her head no, her eyes full of anguish, and then she knelt beside Lili, grasping her son's hands into her own. "He's my only son. His Da is gone. He's all I have. Please," she begged.

The child slept the sleep of the dead, as though he were already gone. But his breathing, though quick and shallow, was steady, Lili noted. "How long has he been this way?"

The mother sniffed back a sob. "Hours now. I have not left his side." She peered up at Lili. "I wanted to go for help, but dared not leave him alone." She peered back at her son. "Thank God for Sorcha!"

Counting the woman's cooperation as a small victory, Lili asked, "Has he eaten or had anything to drink since he became ill?" While many believed it was best to sweat out impurities and not to introduce the possibility of more, Lili knew through experience that the sick craved water, and she believed God would not allow a body to crave something it should not have.

"Nay," the mother replied.

No doubt, that was a good part of his exhaustion, Lili was certain. "Have you any *vin aigre*?" she asked. Lili used the bitter concoction for many things, but it seemed to help rid the body of infections at times like this. Indeed, if she held any sort of magic at all it was the knowledge of the *vin aigre* potion, for it cured all manner of ills.

The woman nodded, looking confused. "A fresh batch,

but 'tis yet unfiltered. I was going to begin preserves for the winter store."

"Even better," Lili assured her. "The mother of *vin aigre* is the best part. Bring it to me," she bade the woman. "Along with water."

"Water?" the mother asked, looking even more confused.

Once again Glenna turned her gaze to Aidan, looking for his direction. He had yet to come fully inside, but now he let the door close behind him, shutting out the night air as he met Lili's gaze, assessing her. There was nothing she could do if he chose not to trust her, and he had no reason to do so, but she hoped he would. Her eyes pleaded with him.

With the door closed, the candles no longer flickered uncertainly. Their flames burned tall and strong, illuminating the room somewhat better. Lili straightened her spine, waiting for Aidan to decide, but it seemed she waited an eternity while he made up his mind.

"Do as she says," he commanded finally.

That was all Lili needed to hear. She was aware of his lingering gaze, but she had nothing to hide—at least not at the moment. She would never harm an innocent child, no matter what threat loomed before her—in truth, not even to save her own son, for what manner of monster would that make her?

Killing Aidan dún Scoti was not the same.

At least that's how she confessed herself.

She glanced at the pot hanging in the hearth. "Is that empty?"

The boy's mother was still gathering the items Lili had requested. She placed a bucket of water on the table. "Aye," she said, seeing the direction of Lili's gaze. "'Tis clean as well since he has not eaten since yestermorn. I had no stomach for food myself. Retrieving this bucket of water was the last thing he did for me before he became ill, and then he had no thought for food or drink."

Lili rose from the child's bedside, taking the small bucket of water from the table where the woman had placed it. Reaching inside, she inspected the sides, looking for slime—

any indication the water had been sitting too long. She found none, but just in case she took the bucket to the small pot hanging over the hearth fire and poured the water inside the cauldron, saving a little to bathe the child. It sizzled as it settled into the bottom of the iron pot. Beneath the cauldron, the fire was already burning hot and she lowered the pot into the flames.

"What are you doing?" the woman asked now, her voice fraught with worry. Lili took a little bit of the *vin aigre* from the cask on the table. Making sure she scooped up as much of the unfiltered cider as she could, she poured a goodly amount into the pot, and then looked at Sorcha and said, "Do you recall the smallest of the coffers brought into my cottage?"

"Aye," Sorcha said.

Thinking only of the child lying abed, she sent Sorcha after a small dark brown pouch that contained various medicines.

"What is she doing?" Glenna asked Aidan once more. "She is making a brew to poison my son!"

Lileas turned to look at the woman, meeting her gaze directly, her eyes full of compassion. "You have my word, Glenna, I'llna put anything in your son's mouth I am no' willing to drink myself. Dinna worry, I have used *vin aigre* many times in just this way."

Aidan watched her closely.

She was behaving like a worried mother herself.

He couldn't fathom what this new sickness was. The illness had only begun since his return from Chreagach Mhor—first one fell ill, then another, and another followed. The malaise took their young and old so swiftly that there was scarce time to build their pyres before the fever took them. Next, it would seize the healthy among them, withering their numbers as not even their enemies had managed to with their bloodthirsty blades.

Glenna's eyes continued to plead with him, beseeching him to intervene—begging him not to take the side of his Scot's bride...

In Aidan's mind's eye, he saw Padruig Caimbeul looming

over his father's lifeless form, his long gray beard splattered with blood. They had come to Dubhtolargg under the guise of friendship, supping at their tables and partaking of their *uisge* and then all together had risen up in the middle of the festivities and slaughtered half their clansmen while their noses were still deep in their cups. It was the gravest of transgressions amongst Highlanders, and yet the Caimbeuls had done so with impunity, as though they felt justified in re-enacting the betrayal that had originally brought Dubhtolargg its name.

In fact, they had not even known about the hidden stone. They had come simply to appease their monstrous pride—to say they had driven the chieftain of Dubhtolargg to his knees. They had raped his mother, as well, and then left her with a babe in her belly. That child was Sorcha, and it was then, on Sorcha's birthing and his mother's deathbed that Una had cursed Padruig's firstborn child. Not even Sorcha knew the truth of her patrimony. His clansmen had kept it from her on pain of death.

Staring at Lileas' back, he watched her tend Duncan, wondering whether she intended to give that poor child *vin aigre* to drink. Simply the thought of the bitter taste of the rancid wine made his gut churn. Yet his "bride" certainly appeared to know what she was doing. Is this what Una had meant when she claimed Lileas was to be the salvation of their clan?

Resigned though she was to his will, Glenna wrung her hands with worry, her attention returning to Lileas.

Aidan felt torn, uncertain what to do, or what to say. He had no intention of weakening his position toward Lileas. Healer or nay, she was still Padruig's daughter.

But she continued though she was weary; he could tell by the lines of fatigue in her face. No doubt they had traveled days to reach Dubhtolargg, and knowing how little time had passed since he had sent the messenger back to David with his agreement, there was not much chance they had rested much along the way. Still she had not complained after learning there was a *celebration* intended to mark their arrival, despite that he had half expected her to behave like an English miss and hie to bed for a week before showing her face again.

As he watched, she worked without complaint. With the bucket and a rag, she returned to Duncan's bedside and pulled the blankets down, then stripped the boy to his bare arse. Rising again, she set the cloth into the cask and let pure *vin aigre* flow over it. Then she returned to the bed, wiping down the boy's skin again, dipping the rag into the bucket and wiping him again. He didn't understand any of it, but it made a certain sense. The *vin aigre* would surely kill anything it touched. When Lileas was finished with the potion, she stripped the top covers off the bed, and without asking stole the blankets from his mother's bed, giving the boy dry bedding.

"Aidan, please," Glenna begged once more. "The night air will kill my son for certain!"

Aidan vacillated. Where the hell was Una when he needed her?

He could not risk second-guessing the old woman, for he knew she held the best interests of their clan. While he might not trust this child of Padruig Caimbeul, he trusted Una without fail. He blew a sigh, and shook his head, holding up his hand to command Glenna to calm herself. "Let her tend the boy," he commanded. He did not mean to sound so hard and unrelenting, but he could not think just now.

Glenna obeyed, but her lips trembled and she lowered her head and wept and Aidan cursed profusely beneath his breath.

Lili was grateful for Aidan's show of trust, but her sense of relief was short-lived, for it was only once she had the child completely undressed and was laving his body, cooling it with the water and sponge, that it occurred to her to worry about which pouch his sister would retrieve from her coffers. She was not accustomed to perfidy and did not know how to think like a conspirator! Unlike Aveline, she did not even know how to be a woman, apparently, for neither with the dress that David had given her, nor by her own wiles, could she seem to make the laird of Dubhtolargg look at her with anything less than disfavor. And yet it should not matter how he looked at her, for she was no more pleased with this arrangement than he was.

But she would be even less pleased—as would he—if his sister returned with the wrong pouch!

She tried to remember exactly where she had placed the small bag she had sent Sorcha after and hoped it was at the top of her coffers. She had many such pouches, all of them similar in appearance. Only one could see her bound to a pyre and burned alive, for it contained the means to kill not only Aidan, but all his kin as well.

If that were not enough, there was no way for her to explain away the ring. It was an instrument of murder, pure and simple. Made of bronze in the shape of a five-pronged crown, the ring was designed so that the bearer could quickly dump poison into a cup without ever having to remove it from his finger. She had never seen its like. Inlaid with lovely etchings along the sides, it appeared to be ancient and delicate, but it was deadly and clever.

She waited with baited breath for his sister to return, laving the child's body, while trying as best she could to keep her mind off death by fire. Her father had once claimed she would burn upon a stake, like the witch she was. Lili swallowed hard, terrified that his prophecy would come true.

His mother had said the boy was unmarked by any rashes, or any lesions that may indicate infection, and he was. Whatever it was that plagued him was invisible to the eye. He didn't seem to be in any pain, though she had a small amount of willow bark if he awoke in need.

Dear God, would Sorcha choose the right pouch?

Lili had shoved the other down deep into her coffers. In her curiosity, would the girl decide to explore? Would she think to question the hard lump if her fingers encountered it amidst Lili's softer garments?

Feeling Aidan's presence at her back like a threat in the room, she held her breath, staring at the boy's pale face, watching him breathe.

What in God's name would happen to Kellen should they

discover her treachery?

David would have no use for him, and Rogan would never embrace him truly. If anything, he probably considered her son a threat to his holdings—holdings that he now held only because Stuart was dead, but her son was the rightful heir to his father's demesne.

Lili held her breath so long it hurt—until the door burst open and Sorcha came dashing inside, clutching the bag in her hand. She expelled a breath she hadn't even realized she held. By the rood, the girl had chosen the correct bag! Taking it from her quickly, Lili clutched it in her hand for an instant, thanking God—any god, every god—for the reprieve. She swore to be more careful from here forth.

Fortuitously, this particular bag was filled with various herbs, including rosemary and juniper, which would, when burned, help to purify the air itself. Until the boy awoke, he would not be drinking her concoction of *vin aigre*, so this must do for now. The sack contained more, but until she knew these people a little better, she would not dare practice earthier skills.

As the other occupants of the cottage watched, she crushed the juniper and rosemary together and then set it into a shard of pottery to burn. Then, finding another small piece of pottery that would weather flames, she filled that as well, then lit them both. She didn't dare meet Glenna's gaze as the thin ribbons of smoke climbed into the air, and instead she went back to the boy's bedside, well aware that the door opened, once again letting in a rush of cold air, and then slammed shut. When she turned to see who had come or gone, she met two horrified gazes—neither of them Aidan's. The look on both Sorcha's and Glenna's faces were near mirror images.

SEVEN

Aidan was no longer certain he was doing the right thing allowing Lileas to tend Glenna's son, so he went in search of the only person he knew who could help him decide what to do: Una.

He knew her well enough to know where she must have gone. She was the only one who dared spend time in that grotto she called the cradle of *Geamhradh*—*Winter.*

His thoughts in turmoil, he made his way over the hillside where the shepherds tended their flocks. None of his clansmen would think to question why there were more men watching over these hapless sheep and goats than was necessary, nor that their shepherds wore claymores strapped to their belts that could slice a man in two with scarcely any effort.

They didn't question why, because they knew.

He passed his captain, seated atop a boulder. Lachlann's massive sword rested at his feet, the blade reflecting the rising moon, for it was growing dark now. With a smaller gleaming knife, he whittled away at something in his hands, but Aidan couldn't tell what it was—no doubt one of his wooden carvings. The other "shepherds" were settled at strategic points upon the mount, all of them visible to one another, but not to outlanders who might not know the lay of their land, or the caverns and boulders that pocked it.

"Ha' ye seen Una?" Aidan asked.

"Yup," the burly warrior replied and pointed up the hillside.

"That's what I ken," Aidan said, and grumbled beneath this breath. Damned old woman! He was saddled with a new bride because of her and she couldn't even linger long enough to be certain all went as it should.

He climbed the bluff, all the while cursing to himself, for despite the fact that there were easy enough scrambles along the way up, the path was steep, and not for the first time, he wondered how Una's frail body could make it up the hillside without putting her out of breath, even in winter with treacherous, icy rocks. Once the snows fell, even the guards kept their vigils from lower upon the hill, yet Una came and went.

Along the hillside there were a number of smaller caves, but not all of them were so extensive. Only one had suited the purposes of their ancestors, though it seemed as though it had been created precisely for their cause. Aidan made his way toward that one, passing the smaller yawning holes in the rock face that often gave their children sanctuary during summer storms.

They kept their store for the winter in the entrance to the main cave—all foods that did not necessitate cooler air to keep fresh. But the tunnel didn't end there. The following cave, naturally formed, full of mist and colder yet, was where they stored more perishable items. And it might seem to anyone who didn't know better that this cave was where the underground caverns should end, with the mist rising from unseen crevices, but if one looked carefully, or knew exactly where to find it, there was a small hole in the ground and a ladder that descended deeper into a grotto. That was where he would find Una, and then, deeper yet, was where they kept the destiny stone.

Aidan descended the ladder into the belly of the mountain, and certainly enough, he found Una standing at her worktable staring into her *keek stane*—a crystal stone she claimed could reveal past and future. As always, the room was shrouded in mist, and cold enough to freeze his bollocks under his breacan.

Una was so entranced that her staff lay forgotten at her side, despite that it rarely left her hand, even whilst she slept. Her *keek stane* lay cradled in a wooden box, a luminous green crystal that was concave on one side and convex on the other. To Aidan, it appeared like no more than a hunk of crystal, for it never revealed any more than its translucent nature while in his presence. But Una seemed to see things no one else could see in her scrying stone and betimes Aidan could *feel* it in the air, like a prickling under his skin.

Una's eyes had yet to leave her stone, but she waved him into the room. "Come in, come in," she bade him.

"I've come—"

"I know why ye've come, ye lout. Come in and sit down," she commanded him as no one else ever dared. "Let me finish, and then I shall speak wi' ye anon."

Aidan knew better than to argue with this female in particular. As cantankerous as Lael could be, his eldest sister was nothing compared to Una in a fit of pique. The old woman's temper made even seasoned warriors quake in their boots—especially while standing within reaching distance of her staff.

Trusting her, and resigned to do as she bade him, Aidan sat beside her at the little worktable, in the only chair available. Usually, the single chair in the room sat near the braced torch, where she often squinted by its light to read her manuscripts. The fact that the seat was now at the table only strengthened the impression that she must have known he was coming.

But of course she would know that. She had led him into this travesty and she knew him well enough to know he would expect her counsel until it was done.

"I need to know... will the boy die?"

As a test of sorts, he didn't tell her who, and wondered if she had remained in the village long enough to learn of Duncan's illness. Then again, if she knew Glenna's son was ill, why wouldn't she come to the boy's aide? It was Una they all turned to whenever anyone grew ill, for despite her eccentric ways and her moodiness, she held a wealth of healing knowledge.

Una's hand froze over the *keek stane*, where it seemed she had positioned it to either keep out the light so she could better see within or, more likely, to hide the stone so Aidan could not see what was simply not there. She gave him a disapproving glance, as though she'd read his thoughts and said, "Ach, if he does 'twill save you the trouble of hand fasting and then mayhap your life in the end."

Aidan frowned. "What the bluidy hell is that supposed to mean, auld woman? Ye dinna say my life would be at risk!"

Their relationship was not a simple one. As the woman who had pulled him, feet first, from his mother's womb, he would love and respect her until the day he died, but it was never certain what mood you would catch her in, and she did not respect him back when he blenched over her bad temper. After many dozens of raps upon the head, both when he raised his voice and when he did not, he simply treated her the way she treated him. And thankfully, she never rapped him before his clansmen. Any castigations she deemed worthy of inflicting were always privately done and Aidan realized she dealt every blow with love, so he abided it.

She gave him a weary glance, rolling her eyes. "Ach, Aidan. Your life is *always* at risk. You're the chieftain of this clan, di ye forget? Or di' ye lose your wits already o'er the winsome lass?" she asked irascibly.

"Of course not, but you sold the woman to me as the savior of our clan—now ye tell me she could be the death of me yet. Make up your bluidy mind, auld woman!"

She lifted one white brow. "No one has said both things canna still be true."

The words slipped from his tongue, but he regretted them almost at once. "I am beginning to doubt this was the right thing to do."

In fact, it may have been the worst thing he could have said, for Una glowered at him, and the mist surrounding them seemed to rise and coalesce, so that he did not quite see her bend to retrieve her staff, but when it cleared, he saw the staff was in her hand. The opalescent jewel in the claw seemed to wink at him.

Simply because he was a student of the old ways did not mean he did not know the stories passed down by the Holy Church. Moses had used his staff to part the Red Sea, Pharaoh's magicians had transformed their wands into writhing snakes, and then turned the waters blood red by its touch. Una's staff betimes seemed to raise a mist that swallowed the Highlands whole. Just when he felt his faith slipping away, she somehow scared the devil out of him with her tricks and that one-eyed glare that made her look every bit the blue-faced Mother of Winter.

Una watched him across the table. Her *keek stane* forgotten for the instant, she cast her one-eyed gaze toward Aidan, all traces of her earlier good humor diminished. Her unnaturally green eye seemed to glow in the dim light, pale and luminous like the crystal *keek stane*. She held her staff upright, her knuckles turning white to match the weathered ash wood in her hand, and she hissed, "Ailpín blood flows through your veins, the first whose blood stems from me and mine!"

They were of a lineage that flowed true and straight—kin to the Ailpín king who had once wed a Pecht princess. But Aidan's frown deepened, and so did his doubts. "What answer is that to my question, Una? David also bears the blood of Kenneth mac Ailpín, and yet you do not believe him fit to rule."

"David's blood is not so pure as yours," she countered, narrowing her one good eye and lowering her voice.

Her cryptic answers were not appeasing him. In fact, they were confusing him all the more and it vexed him. "Bollocks! David's blood flows red the same as mine!"

"David mac Maíl Choluim is far from his origins," she answered calmly. "He is like a tree whose roots are exposed and will no longer sustain him."

In his temper, Aidan slammed a hand down upon the table, though unlike most who may have flinched at his temper, Una did not. He waved a hand, dismissing her answers—all of them—growing angrier by the instant, for while they sat here mincing words, a child lay dying, and Aidan might well have hurried him to his grave. "None of this has one thing to do with my question," he told her. "I *must* know! Did I do the right thing allowing Lileas to tend Glenna's son?"

Una relaxed her hold upon her staff, letting it lean once more upon the table, and said, as though it were idle gossip she were recounting rather than talk of treachery. "Your Scots bride may betray you at least once before she finds her true path, but I do not know what form that betrayal will take."

"Ach! Are ye telling me Dunc may, in truth, die?"

She sat straighter, the mist rising once more. "I *did not* mince words, Aidan *dún Scoti!*" Chill air swirled about the room, like icy fingers beneath his breacan and she smiled thinly, knowing how deeply the barb would sting. It was one thing for Lileas to use the epithet, another yet for Una to wield it.

Mo chreach! If it meant he must trust in things he could not see and words he could not comprehend to be a Pecht, mayhap he was in truth more a Scot. He could not seem to see any truth or find peace in Una's words. He rose from the table, considering how much damage may have already been wrought in his absence. If he left now, mayhap he could prevent further damage to the boy?

He didn't know what to say, for he felt foolish now for having sought Una at all—and for not trusting the one thing that had served him well enough throughout his entire life: his gut. But he could not bring himself to leave without a kind word, for Una had been their keeper from the instant he'd given his first wail into the world. "Thank you," he said, his tone tight with worry as he made to leave.

"Aidan," she called to him, after he'd put his foot on the ladder.

Filled with turmoil over his thoughts, Aidan turned to meet Una's bright gaze across the misty room.

She said, "The mon who never questions his path is oft blinded by the sight of his own feet."

Aidan hesitated, closing an eye to consider her advice. But

it made his head hurt. As perplexing as it might seem, there was nearly always reason to her madness. This moment, however, he did not recognize wisdom in her words.

"Look to the stars to sustain your faith," she added.

Although he hadn't a bloody clue what the hell she was talking about, Aidan nodded, and left her at her worktable. Without another word she returned to her *keek stane* and Aidan climbed the ladder out of her tomblike hovel. As always, he felt the chill ease a bit as he ascended. On his way out of the tunnels, he lifted up a wheel of cheese, thinking that if aught would sustain him it would be auld Morag's cheese.

Morag was long gone, but her cheese filled their caverns still, for they hoarded it greedily, knowing it would be a long age ere her daughter learned to make it as well as her minny. Protected by beeswax and immersed deep in the caverns, most of Morag's remaining wheels were near to seven years old now, and a handful were almost as old as Aidan.

Bouncing the small wheel in his hand, he thought of Una's words: *Look to the stars,* she'd said. What the hell could she mean by such a queer thing?

He made his way out into the night air, where a thin layer of fog swirled at his feet, fine as a winter morning breath. The mist followed him out of the cave with a whoosh and settled like a sheet over the landscape, as though the entire blanket of Highland fog that crept out over the Mounth was born in the depths of Una's grotto.

He thought about their ancestors who had first come here... the stories that had been passed down through the ages. As the tales went, his clansmen had picked their way over these desolate mountains, and as they moved further into the Mounth, the corries had risen up behind them to bar their return. In the night sky, it was said they were guided by faeries who led them to a vale that was verdant and fertile despite being surrounded by hillocks of stone. To this day, it was said they stood guard on the ridge above the vale. Their bones were laid to rest in the old cairn at the top of the ridge and that same cairn also stood guard over the faerie glen beyond it, a field that bloomed even through the bitterest snow.

Buried in that story was a shred of truth, but Aidan had come to realize that the rest, like the beeswax surrounding the cheese in his hand, was chaff to be discarded. The blooms they spoke of in that glen above the ridge were merely harbingers of spring—the hardy *cròcas*, with its yellow center and lavender petals nearly the color of his bride's eyes.

The night was black now even though the sky was clear—as clear as that *keek stane* that never seemed to yield any true visions as far as Aidan had ever known. He sighed, for they were simply an old woman's ramblings. What was real, was the wheel of cheese in his hand right now. Aye, and what was real was the fact that wee Dunc was suffering near to death at this very instant and he'd left a stranger to tend him—the daughter of their enemy at that—no matter that she was soon to be his wife.

If the boy died, how would he forgive himself?

How could Glenna ever forgive him? He will have failed her as her chieftain, for he was sworn to protect her and all others unto his dying breath.

Thank God Sorcha had remained with them to keep the peace. As soon as he walked through the door he would send Lileas out of Glenna's home. Aye, that's what must be done. Those violet eyes had weakened his resolve. But no more. He was chieftain here and he must do what was best for his kin—that and never less.

He glanced down at the wheel of cheese in his hand.

Bloody hell, how could he enjoy this treat while Glenna mourned?

Mayhap he would give the cheese to Glenna but what the devil would Glenna do with a wheel of cheese and a dead son? By damn, instead of becoming easier, it seemed his path grew more difficult every day.

Suddenly, he realized he was staring in the direction of his boots—not that he could see anything through the blanket of fog that had enveloped his ankles. He knew this mountain path as well as he knew the back of his hand and he was surefooted enough—had never stumbled through these hills like an awkward lad chasing after a wiggling arse.

The mon who never questions his path is oft blinded by the sight of his own feet.

By fog, more like, he thought, and chuckled, shaking his head.

Look to the stars, she'd said as well.

Peering up at the cloudless night sky, his gaze was drawn to the south, where the corries rose to their steepest point. It was said that the Mounth had been formed by Cailleach Bheur herself, and that wherever she went, she had dropped stones from her apron and in their places had risen the Highland hills. In her hand they said she kept a hammer... to beat down the hills when they rose too high, shaping them as she saw fit to protect those who dwelled within her realm. Faerie tales, of a certain, but there were some things he sensed were part truth. And still other things he could not take at face value, for they required that he cast away all logic.

His mother used to tell him those stories.

The sky in the north seemed clearest tonight. Stars twinkled fiercely and he thought about his mother's eyes—what he could recall of them—that twinkle she'd had whenever she'd gazed upon her children. That sparkle had all but vanished after their father's death, and during her final ten months upon the earth, whilst she carried an outlander's bairn, the twinkle in her eyes had extinguished entirely. The day he'd buried her, she had gazed at him with the dead eyes of a stranger. And still he'd had trouble letting her go.

Ach, if they buried everybody that ever lived within the vale, every inch of land would be marked by a grave, but alas, they did not, save one: his mother.

Although his baby sister shared the same Da as Lileas, Aidan had never once looked at Sorcha with the same disdain he felt for his bride. Could he ever see Lileas through kinder eyes when she had been raised by the butcher who'd killed his father?

As he walked down the hill, pondering that question, he suddenly spied a falling star, and then before he realized, he saw another, and yet another. One after the other they shot across the night sky like burning missiles and he was watching so intently that he stumbled, obviously not quite so sure footed as he'd believed. With a yelp of surprise, he tripped over a stone and tumbled down the hillside, rolling to a halt over a particularly rocky spot. Sharp pebbles poked him in the arse and back. *"Mac Bhàdhair fhuileach thu!"* he exclaimed. *Son of a cow's bloody afterbirth!*

The night went deathly quiet.

After a moment, from across the hillside, he heard Lachlann's deep voice call out to him. "Aidan?" There was a question in his name.

Embarrassed, Aidan rose to his feet, peering about to see who might have witnessed his fall down the hillside. Likely everyone had heard his cursing, but he didn't have to admit anything to anyone. The fog was too thick for anyone to have seen. Aye, so he could simply walk away without a word. The mist was thicker now, obscuring the view, but he didn't wish to worry anyone lest they come running with blades swinging, so he called out, "Carry on. All's well!"

But it wasn't; he was so unnerved by the rare display in the sky and his tumble down the hill that he forgot to look for and retrieve the wheel of auld Morag's cheese. Shaken, he made his way straight for Glenna's cottage, thinking only of Una's words.

Look to the stars sustain your faith.

E1GHT

If the fall hadn't rattled his brain, the sight that greeted Aidan when he entered Glenna's cottage made him feel as though he had certainly gone daft. He couldn't have been gone more than an hour, so the last thing he expected to encounter was Lileas and Glenna holding hands together across the bed where young Duncan lay sleeping. His sister Sorcha was no longer present.

The scent of burnt pine—or something like it—permeated the air. One of the candles at the child's bedside had extinguished, leaving the room a little dimmer, but he was quite certain his eyes were not playing tricks upon him.

Lileas peered up when he came in the door, looking wearier than she had when he last saw her.

"Where is my sister?" he asked, shutting the door quietly behind him.

"She went searching for ye."

A shot of trepidation flew down Aidan's nape and his gaze at once fell to the child in the bed. "Is he—"

"Nay... he but sleeps."

Relief sidled down his spine. "Good," he said, and collapsed into an empty chair near the table, stunned. "For what reason does my sister seek me?"

Lileas shrugged, her gaze averting to the crown of Glenna's dark head. The woman had clearly fallen asleep against her will, for she lay in the most damnable position, reaching across the bed to grasp Lileas' hand.

Willingly?

Lileas sighed, noting the direction of his gaze. "I ken what it's like to worry o'er a sick bairn," she offered. The tone of her voice revealed as much as her declaration and Aidan experienced a moment's regret for the accusation in his question earlier in the day. It was clear now that leaving her son was not her choice, for she was a mother at heart.

"Duncan isna a wee bairn any longer," he argued gently. "The boy is eight or thereabouts, but I ken what ye are saying." He kept his voice low, but there was wonder in it, for he still could not quite fathom how his bride had won fierce Glenna over in the short time since he'd left them. There was no other explanation for the fact that she had let down her guard enough to fall asleep, exhausted or nay, and had willingly given Padruig's daughter her hand in friendship.

Or had she?

Once again his eyes sought their joined hands upon the bed, doubting the sight even as he stared at the fingers that lay clutched together so intimately.

Damn, but he'd half expected Glenna to have plucked out Lileas' hair given half the chance—and he might have even half hoped for it, because he didn't want to want this woman.

Glenna's Da had been one of those slaughtered during Padruig's betrayal. And later, her husband had been one of the good men lost when Alasdair mac Mhaoil Chaluim reigned as King of the North and his brother David ruled the lands south of the River Forth. Alasdair had hounded him to join in quelling his younger brother's rebellion, for David's army had outnumbered his by far. When Aidan had refused to embroil himself in Scotia's politics, Alasdair had responded with raids upon their glen—never confessing his part, of course. Instead, he had blamed his brother David, though of that crime, at least, Aidan knew David was innocent, for David had had his hands full trying to control his territories far to the south. The youngest of Malcolm Ceann Mohr's sons was not well favored by the Scots, and particularly not by

Highlanders he was trying so hard to rule, for he had spent nearly his whole life under the influence of English kings. Thus Glenna had good reason to loathe outsiders, and Aidan had returned, fully intending to adhere to her wishes and remove his Scot's bride from her home. Alas, but if the woman should lose her son, that show of respect seemed the least Aidan could do.

Apparently, there was no need.

Somehow Lileas had managed to find a bridge between them—through the boy, no doubt. Both of them were mothers, he reasoned, and only a mother could truly know another mother's pain or fear of loss.

Lileas was no longer paying attention to him, he realized. Her attention was centered upon the child, and Aidan sat quietly, watching her tend the lad, deeply affected by his conflicting thoughts. Una said she would betray him at least once before she found her true path... To watch her, he did not think she was capable of killing a child.

So what the hell did Una mean?

The room remained silent but for the sound of Glenna's soft snores. After awhile, Lileas released Glenna's hand and rose. Removing her arisaid, she walked around the bed to place it upon Glenna's shoulders, covering the sleeping mother as best she could. Aidan was heartily glad for the fact that it was not Caimbeul colors she wore, but that she had done so without sparing Aidan a word, or even a glance to see if he had noticed, moved him so that he could not think clearly in her presence. A simple act of kindness on her behalf should not make him let down his guard. Nay! He *must* not allow it. The risk to his clan was far too great. Without a word, he stood and let himself out of the cottage, letting her tend the child in peace—at least for the moment.

He needed air.

Nay, he needed a moment where he was not staring at his bride's too-bonny face and those silken curls that had come free from her dark plait, making him yearn to smooth them back out of her weary face. As she clearly had with Glenna, in just a few short hours she had already begun to bewitch him.

His father used to say that only fools were certain of themselves. Wise men were full of doubts. If that were true, Aidan was, at this instant, the wisest man of all.

In the distance, he spied the glow from the bonfire. Music and laughter carried through the night—a good sign that no one's head was as yet on a pike.

On the other hand, their Scots *guests'* heads on pikes might actually provide for quite some entertainment for his men, but he knew them well enough to know they would never defy him, not even for the sake of revenge. Nay, their *guests* would have to do something vile to earn that fate, and even then his men would have come running to retrieve him first. It was more likely that, simply knowing his warriors would guard their backs, his clansmen had had enough *uisge* by now to overlook the hated Scoti in their midst.

More raucous laughter reached his ears and he relaxed a bit, thinking about the shooting stars he had spied earlier, wondering if that could be what Una had been referring to. His mother had been named after them... but she was long gone now and had nothing left to tell him. Certainly, he had seen many falling stars before tonight, but never three at once. And yet, even if the signs were divine, what the hell could they possibly mean?

Nothing, he decided. They were simply stars... stars that had fallen from grace.

Like his faith.

He stood for a time, enjoying the sound of the reed and the cool night air. Fall was near and there was a bite in the air. Soon, the blossoms in the fields would fade, and the grass would turn to gold. No matter that it heralded the coming of winter, this was his favorite time of the year, for these were the nights when a man could be grateful for a good woman in his bed...

He shuddered involuntarily at the thought of Lìleas—not in revulsion, he was surprised to confess. A sense of anticipation began to stir in his belly and it set his nerves on edge...

Did she entertain thoughts of the bedding as well?

Surely, she did, for she was a woman grown, with a child already and one dead husband—aye, she would know exactly what was to transpire between them once the words were said.

Would she revile him, or would she embrace him and enjoy the coupling? That look in her eyes... what it was he didn't know, but it wasn't revulsion.

Those violet eyes held the power to unman him.

Sucking in the fresh night air, he smelled traces of the bonfire, and then belatedly—much too belatedly, as far as he was concerned—he thought about his sister Sorcha and resigned himself to go and search for her to be sure all was well.

As for those other two lackeys of David... although he had no doubt they had already spied the men he had assigned to guard them, he wanted to make damned sure they felt his presence as well. If the least sign of treachery arose, he would slit their throats faster than they could open their mouths to scream—and that included the *siùrsach* maid.

A traitor was a traitor.

In the silence of the room, Lili bowed her head and prayed, taking comfort in the fact that the boy's breath now seemed far less labored. She had done everything she could for the lad and now all they could do was wait. She prayed for herself as well:

Holy Earth, Mother of us all
Help me be me strong in spirit and gentle of heart
Let me act with wisdom, conquer fear and doubt...

In the dim light, she turned to study the boy's mother. Glenna was young—mayhap no older than Lili. Sleep had softened her features so that she almost looked like a child herself. Dark-haired and with a darker complexion than Lili's, she seemed not all that different from Lili, not really.

Her gaze searched the room. In one corner sat a weaver's loom, and beside it a pile of bundled sheepskin that had yet to be cleaned. On the woman's shelves Lili spied different colored tinctures—mayhap stains for her wool? A half woven strip of tartan hung over the back of the chair seated near the loom and another lay folded upon the floor. Lili recognized it as the same weave as the one that covered the bed in the cottage she had been given to sleep in. They were the colors of Aidan's tribe—blood red and forest green.

The candles here all looked familiar as well. She lifted one beside her that had already burned out, searching the bottom for a familiar mark. She found the symbol Cailin had shown her on the bottom of this candle as well, and considered that these people lived as though they were one, sharing skills and trading their wares.

At Keppenach, although Lili had never really encountered any ill will, the villagers all clamored for more, eager for their share. At harvest time, Stuart had listened to many a grievance, settling debts for men who hardly seemed willing to compromise. More than like, if one villager had not enough gold to buy an item, he went without until he could. Or he stole it...

It was too soon to know for certain but Lili had a sense of something different here—as though these people were truly a clan united.

She shivered, and her eyes were drawn again to Glenna's sleeping form, to her own arisaid draped about the woman's shoulders.

The night had grown cold.

Lili was freezing.

Rising from her knees, she went to the hearth where the fire was beginning to wane. She took the pot from its hook and set it upon the floor. Then she put new wood upon the fire and stoked it, reviving the flames. There was hardly any need to keep the *vin aigre* potion warm, so she left it where it was to cool, hoping the boy would awaken soon. She had a great desire to see the color of his eyes. Were they gray like his mothers, or were they dark and deep like her son's? Or green like Aidan and his siblings? In all her life she had never seen more green-eyed men and women in one place.

In the meantime, while she waited, she was certain Glenna would be hungry when she awoke, so she set about preparing a meal from Glenna's pantry, intending to have it ready when the pair awoke. There was no way Glenna would be able to care for her child if she didn't first nurture herself.

God's truth, so much had happened since they had arrived that Lili felt as though she had been here a sennight already. She had never been wearier than she was at the instant, but there was something innately sound about what she was doing. She didn't stop to question why she felt so much at home for the simple fact that it filled her with guilt.

Aidan had left her alone with Glenna. Did that mean he trusted her? Had she somehow passed some test?

If so, she was both grateful and mortified at once because if there was one thing Aidan should never do... it was to trust her.

Nine

With a groan of satisfaction, Rogan plucked a small rock out of his arse and tossed it away, then brushed another from beneath his shoulder blade. By God, these people lived like savages, forcing a man to seek his pleasure behind boulders in stone-littered fields. At least the low-lying fog gave them some measure of privacy. He returned his hand to Aveline's there upon his chest, squeezing gently. "If she canna do it, you must do it for her," he commanded her.

By the saints, he stood to gain far too much to allow Lìleas to fail, for once it was all done, he would also inherit Caimbeul lands through his marriage to Lìli. He and Padruig had settled the matter outside of the King's council. The old man would not live forever and he had no living sons and only one daughter. His good fortunes had all withered with his daughter's curse. In exchange, Rogan had agreed to give him a hefty payment of gold. Now between Rogan's suborn and King David's payment, Padruig Caimbeul could no doubt buy himself the loyalties of many, but what did Rogan care if he waged war against David himself when Rogan stood to inherit anything the greedy old lecher appropriated from hence forth?

On the other hand, Aveline's father stood to lose much if Padruig were to suffer itchy fingers for her father's territory lay directly south of Caimbeul land. Teviotdale was weak and old and her only brother was a milksop who buggered pretty men.

But there was no reason for Aveline to know any of it. For now, it suited him well enough for the stupid lass to believe there was a chance he might some day wed her. That her father had risked his daughter's virtue by sending her to live at Keppenach without a promise of marriage was none of Rogan's concern—such was the idiocy of a border lord. It only surprised him that he had not filled Aveline's belly with a brat yet, for he had plowed her unremittingly since her arrival at Keppenach.

What if he could not father sons? The idea of leaving all he owned to Stuart's half-mute son did not settle well with him. Aye, the child could speak, but no matter how kindly he treated the boy, with the intent of winning over his mother, the little bastard simply stared at him with those nut-brown eyes that gave Rogan a wretched and unwelcome feeling in the pit of his gut.

"Do not worry, Rogan. I will not fail you," Aveline promised. She splayed her fingers across his bare chest. She had the speech of a well-born heiress, he thought. Too bad her nose was too long and her eyes were the color of baby's poop.

They had discovered a quiet place to lay together, and now that he was well sated, he allowed her the privilege of resting her head upon his chest. That too suited him, for there was a rising chill in the air that he was beginning to feel now that the heat of his ardor had cooled. Aveline was not Lìleas, but she knew how to please a man, that much he would give her.

If it turned out that Aveline was barren, mayhap he would keep her around even once he and Lìleas were wed... just in case his brother's wife proved to be as cold in bed as her demeanor.

Damned Lìleas, for she was an ice queen, who rebuffed him at every turn!

At least it comforted him to know that Stuart could not have gleaned much more from his frigid bride, for he had never witnessed much affection pass between them, despite that Stuart's heart had grown soft over the lass. How the hell his brother had ever put his child in her belly was a mystery to Rogan, for he could not imagine Lileas willingly spreading her legs for any man. But he would plow her good and often once she was finally his—curses be damned. Bah, he didn't believe in witches or magic! And if anyone were to ask his dead brother, Stuart would agree. Stupid bastards hadn't even bothered to look to see whose fletching was on the arrow they had yanked out of his brother's eye. All things that went up, must of course, come down, and Stuart had not been the only one to send an arrow into the air that day.

Tonight the stars were bright, and he sighed, imagining the gold he would earn through David's favor.

"You know I would do anything for you," Aveline swore as she stopped to pull gently at a single hair upon his chest. That annoyed him, but he said nothing. He needed her to continue to serve him for the moment, and so he would say nothing to cool her ardor, particularly now that he would be forced to leave her once the wedding took place. That was the agreement. Only one of them could remain with lovely Lili, and it must be Aveline.

Aveline blew a sigh across the hairs of his chest. "I love you, Rogan," she said breathlessly.

The words soured Rogan's stomach, but he forced himself to repeat them, and considered the fact that he really didn't need Lileas' love. Padruig had the right of it. He didn't intend to fall prey to her wiles the way his brother had. Loving her wasn't necessary to his purpose. All he had to do to raise his cock was simply look at her face, for he had never once in his life seen a woman so bonny as Lili. Aye, it was her face he saw when he loved Aveline. Her body he spilled his seed into. Her tremors he imagined beneath him. But love had aught to do with it.

Now her father's lands were another matter entirely— those he could love. In fact, the thought of ruling both Stuart's and Padruig's lands filled him with an avid lust that not even Lileas' body could arouse.

Aveline continued to pluck at the hairs upon his chest and he covered her small hand with his in order to still her movements, and peered up at the stars. As he lay there, he spied a shooting star—and then a second, and a third and his cock stirred with excitement. It was a sign from God that his aims were true. "Did you see that?" he asked.

"Nay," she replied, lifting her head. "What was it?"

Rogan smiled to himself. It was meant for him alone, he decided, and opted not to share. "Naught," he lied and pushed her onto her back, rolling atop her and peering down at her with glee. "When all 'tis done, ye'll want for naught," he swore. "I will reward ye handsomely, Aveline."

"*You* are my reward!" she declared, and the look in her eyes as she peered up at him was full of devotion.

Rogan's grin widened, for that's the way he needed her to remain.

The thought of all he would possess once the deed was done hardened him more fully, and he slid down to free his cock from between their bodies, positioning himself at the entrance of her skinny body, taking great satisfaction in the way her head lolled backward and her small breasts rose to beseech him. She moaned softly and he thought in that instant how easy it would be to snap her neck if he so pleased... and mayhap that's what he would do when it was all over... *if* he decided a concubine wasn't necessary.

He moved his hands along her arms, until he reached her wrists, pinning them to the pebbled ground. All the while she moaned and squirmed beneath him like a cat in heat, responding so wantonly to his touch that she did not seem to care that she was razing her back flesh with tiny stones. Once he had her hands secured, he thrust himself inside her, reveling in the cry she gave, even more pleased that she did not look at him, for with her head turned and her dark hair splayed across her face under the moonlight, he could pretend she was Saint Lileas instead. "*S e luid a th'annad,*" he snarled, his pleasure heightened by the fact that she did not understand the old tongue, for she was nothing but a lowlander bitch and slut.

* * *

"Have ye gone and lost your *bride* already?" Lael asked, her brow arching with censure when she spied Aidan alone.

Aidan said nothing in response, but he came and stood beside her, crossing his arms and peering about in search of their *guests*. It seemed that save for a handful, every last clansman was present tonight, enjoying the *uisge* and weather. With scarce few days remaining before winter was upon them, they were undaunted by the threat of Scotsmen or potential illnesses. The Scoti were few enough to warrant being ignored, and the illness, no doubt, they were determined to pay little heed. It was far easier to deny it than to acknowledge there was a scourge in their midst. But poor Dunc would make four dead now, and Aidan worried over that fact.

It wasn't his sister's style to leave off. Like a dog with a bone, she would amuse herself until there was nothing left to chew over. "I thought I'd ne'er see the day when my brother chased a *Scoti* aboot like a hound in heat!"

He gave her a quelling look, but let her have her moment of pique. He understood precisely why she felt the way she did. He felt that way himself, and was disgusted by the entire situation. It pained him more than a little to defend Lileas, but he felt compelled to do so after what he had witnessed. "I left her tending Duncan," he said, but that was as much as he had any desire to reveal.

"'Tis what Sorcha said, but she also said you left Lileas and Glenna to kill each other in your absence. Wouldn't it be far simpler to send your Scoti bride home if ye dinna want her?"

Aidan didn't know what he wanted. "I left her with Sorcha, and went to seek Una's counsel. In fact, it was Sorcha who left those two alone, not I." He gave Lael a pointed look, and then uncomfortable with her scrutiny, looked away.

Lael was studying him, her canny green eyes unrelenting. Of all his siblings, she knew him best of all. There was hardly a thing he could conceal from her knowing gaze. "She thought ye might be worried and wanted to ease your mind. Apparently, Lileas and Glenna found a way to embrace one another."

Aidan peered at her to find that her expression was as sincere as the tone of her voice, and he was grateful for the respite. What he needed right now was his sister's true counsel, not a hellion who was bound to see him squirm in his boots. "I noticed." And again he marveled over it. "What of the others?"

Lael's tone once again turned taut. "The brother and the *siùrsach* are coupling in the field like a pair of horny rabbits. Fergus watches them from afar."

Aidan laughed at the thought of the ancient warrior, with his shriveled willie watching those two coupling. Fergus, the dirty old goat, would never take his eyes off them for a second, and his sister knew it. But what he might be doing up there while watching Aidan didn't care to contemplate. "And what of the priest and the others?"

"Over there." She hitched her chin in the direction she intended him to look. "The priest hasna left his post by the fire. He sits there worrying at his beads and staring into the flames—intoning prayers for our souls, no doubt. The other three have all remained by his side the entire night."

"They look a bit as though they feel themselves cornered by wolves."

Lael leaned into him, grinning suddenly. "Ach, but they are, are they no'?"

Inasmuch as outsiders called him dún Scoti, his spirit animal was the wolf, and it was that name his father had affectionately given him and his siblings as children. He was, as his father had said, the strongest of his wolf pups. But memories of his sire were difficult for him to process without anger and so he preferred never to dwell upon them, especially not now when he was trying so hard to find a way to embrace this Scoti bride he had accepted in the name of peace. "Where is Sorcha now?"

Lael's grin faded. "Who knows? Like as not she's with Una as she was seeking you. Or mayhap she has returned to Glenna's?"

So should Aidan be, he realized, as he spied Cailin and

Keane creating some mischief together near the *uisge* kegs. He could tell by the looks upon their faces and by their stealthy movements that they were up to little good. He gestured in their direction. "Make certain whatever plan those two are hatching doesna bring our men to blows with our guests."

Even as he said the words, Keane returned to where their sister Cailin lay hidden, carrying a burning stick. Through experience they knew the *uisge* was quite flammable. If anyone doubted it, they had only to ask Fergus who no longer could grow hair on one side of his face, because he'd made the mistake of taking a candle to his cups to look for a hair swimming in his drink. He never found the hair, and lost full half his beard.

"Damn him!" Lael exclaimed, and she was already racing in their direction as his little brother lit a fuse of cloth behind one of the barrels. Thankfully, they kept the kegs on the beach near the water. He considered the boy he had shared drinks with earlier this afternoon, and frowned. Had he truly thought Keane a man already? This moment brought that fallacy into stark clarity. His brother was yet but a truculent boy. And Cailin, while she looked every bit like a woman grown, she was nearly as much an imp as her brother. Aidan remained long enough to be certain Lael reached them in time. Both Keane and Cailin saw her coming and hied away in fear, and fortunately for the evening's continuity, the fuse had been a long one and his sister reached it in time and tamped it out, then went hurrying after the runaways while their guests stood with their backs to the kegs, completely oblivious to his brother and sister's antics.

Aidan winced over how close they had come to wasting good barrels of *uisge*. And yet if he were honest with himself he would admit that he might have liked to see all four Scotsmen bolt out of that rigid stance they now held, as though they had claymores propped up their arses. All the while his kinsmen reveled around them, they looked like a crop of stone statues. But no matter that it had been intended as a jest, it might have led to far worse than four men diving for cover, and he shook his head over his brother's stupidity, for he knew well how Keane's mind worked.

Tomorrow, he would have another talk with the lad and impress upon him that this was not a game they were playing. The peace of their clan was now at stake. And with that reminder for himself, he started back toward Glenna's hut.

Ten

Scrambling down the ladder, Sorcha called out for Una. It always seemed so much colder down in Una's grotto than anywhere else along the hill lands. Sorcha was quite certain winter itself was birthed here in this spot—at least her brother jested it was so.

"At last!" Una exclaimed. "Di' ye bring my *uisge*, lass?"

"'Tis here," Sorcha declared, raising her hand to show it, but she nearly fell before the last two rungs.

"Careful now," Una admonished her, and then once Sorcha had her two feet planted upon the ground the old woman bade her to come in and sit down beside the brazier while she worked at her table with mortar and pestle.

Sorcha carried the pint of *uisge* over to Una's table and set it down, then stood to watch, examining the brownish powder in the stone mortar. "What are ye doing?"

"Preparing sorcerer's violet!" Una revealed, with her usual flare for the dramatic. "Picked from the Faerie Glen on the thirteenth day of the moon!"

The old woman's excitement was contagious. "Ach! Ye went to the Faerie Glen?"

Una nodded. "I did! On the thirteenth day of the moon," she reiterated, with a conspiratorial wink.

Only Una usually ever visited that place up on the ridge, but she had brought Sorcha along once this past spring, warning her that only those who were pure of heart should ever dare enter. Cailin and Keane said it was just a silly field full of flowers, but Una believed it was special and Sorcha tended to agree with whatever Una said. Despite that Una sometimes didn't make much sense, Sorcha thought she was the wisest person she had ever known. "What will ye do wi' the sorcerer's violet?"

Una's one good eye twinkled mischievously. "Crush it fine, then serve it to Aidan and to Lileas on a houseleek riddled with worms!"

Sorcha made a disgusted face. "Ewww. I dinna believe they will eat it."

"They will if they wish to ha' wedded bliss," the old woman said with conviction.

Sorcha imagined the houseleek with wiggling worms, topped with the fine brown powder and decided she would rather have marital discord than stomach such a horrid fare. "Aye, though I dinna believe ye'll convince Aidan to eat that," she announced. "He doesna even like his Scoti bride!"

"He likes her well enough," Una argued, "And yet, my dear child, that is precisely why I must ensure he eats it."

Betimes the old woman confused her, but Sorcha enjoyed watching her work.

Grinning happily, Una continued to pound the mixture in her mortar, rendering it into a powder so fine that it looked like brown smoke billowing beneath the pestle in her hand. She took a pinch of something else, and tossed it into the mixture. "Your minny used to watch me work just so," she disclosed.

Sorcha sank down to her knees, resting her chin upon the worktable. "Before she had wee ones?"

"Aye..." Una lifted a white brow. "Long before she wed that brute Da o' yours... and then she lost all interest in an auld woman and her craft."

Sorcha knew she wasn't complaining, for Una often told stories about the old chieftain and her minny together... how they had loved each other so dearly, and every time she spoke of either there were wistful tears in her eyes. Una had loved her minny and her Da both, and she wept bitterly whenever she spoke of their deaths. Sorcha had even found her crying one time near Caoineag's Pool. She'd followed the sound, thinking that *finally* she would spy the Weeper wailing in the falls, but she'd found no one there but Una.

Sorcha wished she had known her minny at least. Her Da had been murdered the year before her birth and her mother fled this world bringing Sorcha into it. Sometimes that made her feel very guilty.

While Una was distracted with chatter, Sorcha stood and leaned over the table to hold her nose over the concoction Una was crushing. "It smells like myrtle," she said.

Una gave her a nod. "Ye have a verra good nose," she complimented Sorcha. "It pleases me greatly ye have an interest and aptitude for these things, for despite what all may believe, I willna live forever, child. Mayhap some day ye will take my place?"

Sorcha sank back down to her knees. "I would, but I have no magic," she protested. "How can I take your place if I have no magic, Una?"

"Ah, but ye do," the old woman argued. "Ye simply dinna heed your truest nature, child."

Sorcha's confusion must have shown on her face, for Una went on to explain, "Ye ken Lileas is good and kind, do ye not?"

Sorcha nodded.

"How do ye ken?"

Sorcha lifted a shoulder.

Una smiled patiently. "Aye, but ye do. You have the knowing, child, and I will teach you the rest... if ye are willing?"

Sorcha grinned. "Will ye also teach me to raise the corries?" she teased. Everyone knew what folks whispered about Una, most especially Una, but Una never admitted or denied a single whisper.

Una merely winked at her. "If ye are truly ready to learn, there is a wealth o' knowledge to be gleaned. Lileas knows this as well... I sense she is drawn to the auld ways."

"How do ye know that?"

Una hitched her chin. "Mayhap because I am auld," she suggested. "We auld folk have our ways. Or mayhap 'tis because I have the knowing as well. But if you must find a reason for every last thing under the sun, there are answers that will always elude you."

Sorcha considered that bit of advice briefly, her thoughts immediately turning to her brother's lovely new bride. "Do ye think Aidan will keep her?"

Una snorted so hard at the question she blew a cloud of myrtle dust into Sorcha's face. "Ach, child, d' ye think the lass a dog? Nay, the question isna will Aidan keep her, Sorcha." She waited a moment, mayhap to see if Sorcha would provide the answer before she could, but Sorcha didn't really know what she was supposed to say. Finally, Una said, "The question is will Lìleas stay?"

Sorcha considered that, too, and then thought about the curse. Despite that she liked Lìleas well enough already, she didn't wish to lose her brother to any silly curse. Now that Cat had gone away, Aidan was the only one of her siblings she could truly talk to. Keane and Cailin liked to tease her far too much, and Lael was far too busy sharpening her many blades. "Aye, but, Una, if Aidan grows to love Lìleas, won't he die too?"

Una's head began to bobble, as it always did when she was considering a question. "Ach, well ... as to that... I fear the words of the curse are verra, verra strong, forged in the fires of anger... but there is something far more powerful than hate, my child, and with a far greater magic than any this auld woman could conjure."

"Love?" Sorcha provided, somehow knowing the answer.

Una considered her more closely yet, studying her, her head beginning to bobble again though somewhat less perceptibly, as though she were far deeper in thought. "Aye," she said finally, "but it must be true love. Anything less will ne'er do."

Sorcha thought about the old woman's counsel for awhile, and then considered asking how they would know if love was true, but deep in her heart she believed she already knew the answer to that one too, even if she could never explain it. Besides, Una was certain to answer with more confusing riddles. "Una... ye said Lileas is to be our savior... is that because of the sickness?" she wondered aloud.

She'd overheard Glenna's fearful prayer that, "the terrible sweating sickness please not revisit their clan." Once before, many years before Sorcha was born, had they suffered a similar plague that had swept like a blaze through their glen, killing full half their numbers... but it happened long even before Aidan's birth, and long before anyone living had memory. Only Una seemed to recall.

Again the old woman seemed to lose herself in thought. She sighed deeply. "In truth," she said after a long time, "I did not foresee that... but there is a far more dangerous plague in our midst... one for which Lileas may in truth be the only cure. However, this plague I speak of is not one of the flesh, Sorcha. It is one of the heart and mind."

"I see," Sorcha said, and her head began to bobble too. Somehow, as she pondered the dilemma, she thought of Duncan, and sensed all would be well. It wasn't a vision or a prophecy, just a feeling down deep in her gut, a sense of overwhelming peace when she saw his face in her mind.

The old woman grinned down at her suddenly with that knowing look she often had, and smiled and said, despite that Sorcha never spoke her thoughts aloud, "Indeed, he will be fine. Now, child, pour me two fingers, and go and grab my book from my chair and bring it to the table."

"Yay!" Sorcha exclaimed, and she ran to seize the book in question. Made of sheepskin and bound with leather, it was never to be touched without Una's permission, for it was old and delicate as a spider's web. However, it didn't mean much without Una's stories to go along with it. Carefully opening the book, it fell upon the page it always seem to open to while in her hands, to the symbol of the wolf. "The companion to the forest God," she said, remembering as she tapped the ancient symbol with a finger. Una had told her once that all the symbols in the book had been painted in blood. Her brothers and sisters—all of them—were born under the spirit of the wolf. Aidan often wore the howling wolf's head painted boldly upon his chest.

The old woman nodded sagely. "Courageous and full of honor, but betimes blinded by his loyalties."

Sorcha's brow furrowed, distracted. "Una... Why are all my brothers and sisters wolves, but I am a raven?"

Una's lips thinned and she plied her pestle with renewed strength. "Alas, child, but that is a tale for another day."

Contenting herself with that answer, because she knew Una well enough by now to know that any secrets the old woman harbored would be yielded only when she deemed it was time, Sorcha curled up next to the brazier with the book and listened to Una tell stories, until she fell asleep on the wolf-skin rug, wrapped in her woolen cloak.

* * *

This time, it was Glenna who was awake when Aidan returned to the cottage.

Duncan's mother was sitting by Duncan's bed, supping on a steaming bowl of stew.

Along with the lingering acrid scent of *vin aigre*, the cottage smelled of stewed cabbage and he realized belatedly that he hadn't a thing to eat or drink all day except for a few drams of *uisge*. His stomach grumbled in protest.

Taking her turn at sleep, Lileas rested at Duncan's side, a wet rag still clutched within her fist. Dark circles were forming beneath her eyes, visible even in slumber.

"Are ye hungry, Chief?" Glenna asked.

Aidan nodded, but he threw up a hand, urging her to remain where she was seated by her son's side. "I can get it myself," he assured.

But Glenna ignored him. Putting down her bowl, she came rushing to help. "Nay, Lili has yet to eat as well. I will get you both a bite. Please sit," she demanded of him.

Stunned by the familiarity with which she had addressed the woman sprawled upon her son's bed, Aidan sat. "She doesna look quite in the way to eat," he suggested, scratching curiously at his chin.

Glenna laughed softly and ladled another heaping spoonful into a bowl. "She only just fell asleep—Duncan's fever has subsided!" she said, sounding far cheerier than he'd heard her be in quite some time—in truth, since her husband Ranald died. "He opened his eyes and drank a bit of broth!" She handed Aidan the steaming bowl with a hopeful gleam in her eyes. She peered down at the stew in his hand once he took the bowl. "I must have her recipe. There was little enough in my pantry, but this soup is quite good!"

Aidan's spoon stopped halfway between the bowl and his mouth. He peered up in surprise. "Lili made this?"

Clearly, she hadn't poisoned it, for Glenna lived to tell the tale. And she was spooning another bowl for Lili as well. Glenna nodded sheepishly, peering back at him. "I realize after all... she isna her Da," she confessed, looking apologetic.

Damn, Aidan thought. So she had not only assumed the role of savior in this house, but cook as well. No wonder Glenna had softened toward the lass. Only one day she had been here. One single day and she had already won over Glenna and apparently Sorcha as well. Ach, she must be a witch indeed—or a saint. He wasn't quite ready to decide which as yet. What he did know, however, was that she had earned herself a good night's rest, and then a hearty breakfast come morning, and he fully intended to get her both once he finished his stew. And with that in mind, he hurriedly emptied his bowl, insisting that Glenna leave off with serving another, assuring her that he would see to Lileas' needs.

Setting his bowl down upon the table, he bid Glenna good night, insisting she report Duncan's progress first thing in the morning. And then eyeing the arisaid that was puddled on the floor where Glenna had slept, he removed his own breacan, despite knowing the night air would be cold on his back, and he covered Lileas with his own cloak, then scooped her up into his arms.

Too weary to protest, she mumbled sleepily and tossed her arms about his neck.

"Burn the other," he ordered Glenna without a backward glance. "She won't be needing it any longer." By damn, he wasn't about to stand by and allow his wife to wear another man's plaid!

ELEVEN

The sound of lapping water was like a gentle nudge to Lili's waking thoughts. She opened her eyes, disoriented, for it was not a sound she was accustomed to hearing.

Dust motes danced upon the rays of light that slid in beneath the wooden shutters, and for a moment, she was uncertain how she had come to be in this room though she had the vaguest impression of being carried into the chilly night air in the middle of the night, and clinging to the warmth of the man who carried her.

Her face burned a little at the recollection.

She was alone for the moment, but a glance about revealed that her coffers had been delivered here sometime whilst she'd slept and she was not so naive she didn't realize immediately in whose room she slept.

This was the laird's chamber.

Aidan's belongings were everywhere—woolen blankets with the rich reds and greens of his plaid, a collection of daggers along one wall and a tapestry with the depiction of a howling wolf at its center. Everything about the room reflected the man who inhabited it. There was nothing soft here, no adornment simply for the sake of it. Her coffers sat on the floor next to the bed, but otherwise the room was immaculate, though the walls and floors were made of wood, which gave it a sense of crudeness that couldn't quite be dispelled, even by the large, ornate bed that was the focal point of the room. Like a dais, it sat in the center of the chamber, turned so it was positioned at odds with the walls and she had the impression it was positioned so he could more easily guard the door. She wondered if he slept with his claymore under the bed. Heaped with heavy blankets, and large enough to sleep four people, she wondered, too, with burning cheeks, whether the laird of Dubhtolargg had lain here with her last night. He very well may have, for the bed was enormous and they could have slept at opposite ends without ever touching.

That thought alone made her scramble from beneath the covers, for the last thing she wished to do was have Aidan find her still lying abed and mistake it for an invitation—a bedding after the ceremony was soon enough!

Abandoning the warmth of the covers, she faced the morning chill, and was drawn at once to the window, where the promise of sunlight peeked in through every crack in the wood. She opened the shutters and peered out to discover that, as expected, she was somewhere in the dwelling out upon the water, and the sight that greeted her took her breath away.

It was strange, but lovely to look out over the loch so near her window, with the sun shining down over the glassy surface. In truth, it was not such a terrible sight to wake to... and she would not mind at all ... save for one simple complication...

Aidan dún Scoti.

Her gaze returned to the bed, and she wandered back to the monstrous piece of furniture, inspecting the other side, running her hands over the blankets where he would have lain. The sheets were cold, giving her no clue as to whether he had slept here or nay... only that he would have been long gone.

Her emotions were conflicted, for he was her betrothed, a man feared by David of Scotia... the man whose life she must find a way to end... and yet, he had shown her gentleness last night, bringing her here instead of dumping her into that tiny bed with dirty Aveline. He had allowed her to rest in comfort and warmth … without touching her. Her clothes were still intact, only her shoes had been removed. Those were not the actions of a barbarian.

She tried to convince herself that what she did was for the good of Scotia. David seemed to believe Aidan was a threat to the peace of the clans. Through his tales, she had, in fact, envisioned Aidan as a great painted brute, with greasy hair and bloodstains on his clothes—and his people as war-mongering, bloodthirsty fiends, who walked around gnawing the meat off bones. It was an image David had painted first, and Rogan had seen fit to embellish.

But it was not the truth.

These people were no different from her kin. The stories were all lies. These were simple folk, mayhap, but otherwise much the same as any other clan.

That truth unsettled her, for it meant that what she was about to do was far more self-serving than she would like to believe... and yet... for her son, she would move the *Am Monadh Ruadh* themselves.

Next to the brazier, she spied a small ewer with clean water, along with a bowl, and went to splash her face, hoping that once she was done she might then awaken from this nightmare and find herself in her bed at Keppenach, with her son's sweet little hands caressing her cheeks, bidding her to waken.

Kellen, sweet Kellen, how does he fare?

The water in the ewer was icy. It stung her skin, but she welcomed the sensation, and wondered if there was a private place along the loch where she might bathe. She didn't dare undress here for fear of being discovered. As for her arisaid, it was nowhere to be found and she realized she must have left it at Glenna's, and then began worrying over Glenna's child, wondering how he too fared.

After Aidan had left them alone, she and Glenna had talked at length... mostly about their children, but Lili had wept, despite her resolve not to. Tears would change little, she realized, and in truth, she had deceived the poor woman, for Lili's sins were far greater than the simple act of abandoning her son. This morning, she felt guilt-ridden over all the kind words and thanks Glenna had offered.

Would she thank her later? Once her chieftain was dead?

Doubtless not, for it was clear these people loved their laird—something Lili could never afford to feel. So she hardened her heart, considering her own flesh and blood. She had a task to accomplish here and softening toward these people was not to her benefit.

And yet... she couldn't—wouldn't—have treated Duncan any differently. Children were innocents.

The door suddenly opened, and Lili spun about, smoothing her gown down around her hips, feeling more discomfited than ever before in a man's presence for she was guilty, despite that no one was accusing her of anything as yet.

Aidan held his breath.

He had fully expected to find her lying abed as it was early yet, but she stood with her back to the morning sun peering in through the unshuttered window. Its golden light surrounded her with a shimmering halo, and he was wholly unprepared for the sight of her.

She reminded him in that instant of a kelpie—a spirit half horse, half woman who tempted men with their beauty to ride them and then plunged them into the loch to drown.

He was drowning in those violet eyes, even as he stood on dry land.

Realizing that she must be weary beyond measure, he had allowed her to sleep while he rose to tend to matters at hand. Now it was long past time for her to break her fast, and he had already given the ladies leave to dismantle the tables and clear the hall. Thus he'd brought her a tray replete with nourishment—everything from bread and cheese to boiled eggs and berries. It was the first time in his life—ever—that he had felt compelled to serve anyone in this way. The tray in his hands felt awkward and heavy.

"Ye're awake," he said stupidly.

The sound of his own voice annoyed him.

She nodded, looking like a beautiful, terrified doe, faced with a hunter and his bow. Her gaze immediately dropped to the tray in his hand and to his chagrin, Aidan's cheeks warmed, and he felt a keen desire to drop the tray and walk away. But he didn't. He held his ground as bravely as any warrior facing death.

But she was hardly the image of death... she was beauty incarnate, even with her hair mussed and her dress wrinkled after having slept in it all night long. The soft blue wool traced her curves like a lover's touch.

He liked this gown far better than the courtly costume she had arrived in. He only knew it for what it was, because the very first time David had come to Dubhtolargg, after his brother Alasdair's death, in an attempt to secure Aidan's loyalties, he had brought along his English wife, Maud. They had stayed but a single night, for the countess of Huntingdon had been none too impressed with their meager lifestyle and had pressed her husband to return her to her beloved home south of the border.

Last night, he had lain beside Lileas, the distance between as wide as a river and yet so narrow that it had tormented him. Her silken hair had beckoned to his callused hands, to test the softness of it, unravel it from her braids and lay it about her like a pillow of velvet. And yet he hadn't dared, for touching her may have proven his downfall. He had never in his life wanted to lay with a woman more than he wanted her—most especially after all he had witnessed yesterday—her kindness toward his sister and toward Glenna and the boy.

This morning, her curls had worked themselves free from her braid and fell in disarray about her face, a deep chestnut cloud of waves. Her cheeks were pink and her violet eyes bright and mesmerizing—a like color to the gown she was wearing now—a fact he had completely missed last night in the dim light of Glenna's home.

He realized now he was staring and averted his gaze, walking over the bed to set down the tray he held. "I thought ye may like to break your fast," he said, smoothing the covers away from the tray. He felt like an awkward boy, no different from his brother Keane, and he didn't particularly enjoy the feeling.

"Thank you," she said, but she didn't move from where she stood watching him, like an animal frozen and ready for flight. If he said the wrong thing, she might vanish before his eyes.

Ach, but she was probably accustomed to fancy talk and fancy folk, and he was but a simple man.

Besides, he had never actually wooed a woman before now, and he couldn't be certain that's what he wished to do at any rate, even should she welcome it.

The entire situation was confusing.

"I had your arisaid burned," he said, for lack of knowing what better thing to say. He wanted her to understand that she was his bride now, and that he fully intended to follow through with their bargain. In fact, he planned to wed her as soon as possible—tonight, as long as they weren't burying a child, and it seemed as though, thanks to Lileas, wee Dunc would be fine.

Lili blinked at his words.

He'd burned her arisaid?

Like a frightened little girl, she had remained frozen in place, waiting for him to speak. But once he did, she wasn't at all certain she had heard him correctly.

By the rood, what would possess a grown man to do such a childish thing? If *that* was not uncivilized behavior, Lili didn't know what was! She cherished that woolen cloak, and it was not as though good wool should ever be wasted, no matter what colors they bore.

"Why on earth would you do such a thing?"

He turned to look at her, his hands going behind his back, his green eyes glittering fiercely. "Because... I willna have *my bride* wearing another man's colors. Do ye ken, lass?" He spoke calmly, without the least trace of anger, but the possessive tone of his words sent a quiver down her spine.

Lili bristled. "I am *not* your possession, nor indeed your

wife, my lord—not 'til we have said the words!"

"Aidan," he persisted. "Ha' ye spent so much time with bluidy *Sassenachs* that ye embraced their customs as well as their tongue?"

Lili hitched her chin. "I've spent *no* time with the English. Lest ye forget, 'tis Caimbeul blood runs through my veins! I am a Scot the same as you!"

Too late, she realized it was the worst thing she might have said to him, for he stood suddenly, his jaw working furiously, though he said nothing in response.

"I am *not* a Scot," he said, enunciating slowly.

Regretting her outburst, Lili tried to soften her words somehow, and still remind him that she had a choice in this matter—even if she truly did not. "But *I am*—through and through—and I must remind ye, as such, I am free to wed where I choose!"

He narrowed his gaze and the muscles in his arms twitched beneath his tunic, as though he held his hands restrained behind his back. "Ach, but isn't that why ye're here, Lileas Caimbeul? Because ye *chose* to sacrifice yourself to the odious mountain Scot for the sake of peace?"

His calm demeanor did not fool her. In fact, he looked far more dangerous in that instant than he had since the moment she had met him—despite that he had discarded the war paint and claymore.

Lili experienced an instant of true fear under his scrutiny.

"Nay," he continued, his jaw working still. He took a step nearer, closing the distance between them, his eyes spearing her more deeply than any of the blades upon his wall could manage to do. "In fact, what was it David claimed? Not simply peace betwixt our clans, but between *all* Highlanders—of which I am, despite that I canna stomach the notion of brotherhood with Scotia!" When she said nothing, he continued. "Di' ye realize it was a damned Caimbeul who stood and watched as Giric murdered his king in cold blood?"

Lili shook her head, uncertain of what king he spoke. She knew nothing of the politics of men. But David was alive when last she saw him.

"Aye, they whispered into Aed's ear as friends... all the while their daggers were poised at his back..."

It dawned on Lili suddenly that he was speaking of a betrayal that was more than two centuries old. It was no wonder these men could not get along, for they clung to past injuries as though they were fresh wounds! Why could they not simply leave the past where it belonged?

"So, aye," he proposed, "dinna remind me whose blood runs through your veins, for then I must also recall that treachery is your truest nature."

He glanced down at the tray of food he had brought her and his look was one of disgust, as though he regretted the gesture.

Lili tried to reason with him. "You speak of ancient histories, Aidan! 'Tis long past time to set the insult aside."

"Ancient histories? Insult, you call it?" His hands left his back, and formed twin fists at his side as he took an angry step toward her. Lili had the immediate impression that had she been a man, she would have found herself flat upon the ground. "Mayhap ye dinna recall it was your Da who walked away from a feast of friendship with my kinsmen's blood upon his hands?"

Lil's eyes widened in horror.

"It took us years to wash the bloodstains from our hall," he said bitterly.

Of all the scenarios Lili might have envisioned, that was not one. She had always pictured her father in the midst of battle with Aidan's father, not supping at their table. When a man was invited into another man's hall, it was to be considered sanctuary. Now she understood why Glenna had greeted her the way she had, with such venom.

And yet she could not bring herself to believe it without question. There *must* have been some treachery that had driven her father to it? Even Padruig would not betray such an ancient pact.

"It would serve ye best to recall I am no Scot," he advised her. "Nor will I ever be one, and this is something you must accept to be my wife." His eyes glittered with dark promise.

In that instant, Lili could not believe the injuries committed by both parties could be so easily healed by their union... nor was it bound to, for her marriage to this man would only widen the rifts between the clans.

But if he repudiated her now, mayhap there was hope as yet?

"Aye, but I *am* a Scot," she countered, "and you cannot fashion me into something I am not! Mayhap after all you should return me to my father?"

For the longest moment, he simply stared at her, and Lili held her breath as she awaited his response. If he sent her back... even before the ceremony, mayhap then she would be freed from her burden? Or would David then blame her for sending his plans awry, and what then would happen to her son? She both wanted desperately to know the answer and feared to the depths of her soul that he would send her on her way.

His eyes burned with ire. "Did ye willingly choose this union, Lileas?"

Lili held her tongue, for nay, she had not chosen this. It was commanded of her, but she could not say so. Those hands he held at his sides—hands that only moments ago and borne in the peace offering that now sat upon the bed—could snap her neck only too easily were he to suspect her true reason for wedding him.

Something in her expression must have angered him for his eyes darkened yet more. "Did you choose to be my bride?" he persisted.

"Aye! Of course!" Lili relented.

He unclasped his breacan quickly, with deft fingers and then hurled it at her. "This then is your cloak and none other. If I doubt you for an instant, Lili, I will send you home with a message for your father. That is my promise. So then prepare yourself. Tonight we stand before your priest and mine and say the words you claim you wish to speak, and never again will you remind me of your Caimbeul blood, for tomorrow when you awaken, you will awaken as my wife, the lady of Dubhtolargg!" He turned suddenly and walked out the door, leaving her alone.

Twelve

By all that was sacred, Aidan should have sent her home.

In that furious instant, he might have—especially considering Una's words, that she might be the death of him yet. But something had prevented him—whether it was the look of fear on her face, or something else, he did not truly know, but there was no denying his decision had not been entirely unselfish or even sensible.

He wanted her.

It was pure insanity, given what he knew about her Da, and the risk he took in keeping her in his home, but he wanted Lileas with an intensity that could not be denied. He told himself it was Una's prophecy that compelled him.

But it wasn't true.

He hadn't a bloody clue how this one woman could save their clan, nor even what it was she was supposed to be saving them from, but he craved her with a madness not unlike a drunkard craved *uisge*—and with a lack of constraint that startled him. He was not a man who indulged in excesses, nor did he condone self-indulgence as a way of life. That roistering sense of avarice was the hallmark of the bloody English—and Scots like Caimbeul who loved their *Sassenach* riches more than they loved their honor.

Aidan was no monk, but that was precisely why he kept his dwelling simple, even stuck as they were between tribesmen at war—even with the precious treasure they harbored. There was more to life than simply filling ones coffers, and building walls to keep out pillaging hoards. Nay, but the way of his kinsmen was a communion with the land itself and the true treasure of the Highlands was its country.

Even the stone they guarded paled in comparison.

But he would never keep Lileas against her will, for that would make him little better than those he strove not to be. All she would have had to say was that she did not wish this union, and he would have sent her on her way before nightfall, and with far more security than her father had delivered her with, for no one could ever say that Aidan did not value the gift of life, and a woman deserved no less than any man—even if Caimbeul blood coursed through her veins.

But she feared *something*...

Something had drained the blood from her face more swiftly than a cold steel blade to her throat. Once she had challenged him to send her away, her skin had turned as pale as his tunic as she awaited his response.

For answers, he sought Lachlann, to see if the man had any insight after watching her companions last night. Whatever they were after, he would discover it, by God, and it would please him to no end to take out his frustrations on that weasel of a man who called himself her brother by law.

* * *

How does one prepare for a wedding one does not want?

Lili enjoyed the meal Aidan brought her with all the enthusiasm of a condemned man with his final meal—not that it wasn't delicious. He'd offered her a bit of everything, with boiled eggs that tasted as though they had been freshly picked this morn, bread that was still warm from the oven, and a handful of berries. It was more that her guilt weighed like a fat stone in her belly, and her self-condemnation multiplied with every bite. One thing was certain; his kinsmen knew how to eat, judging by the way they broke their fast. But the fact that he might have gone out of his way for her didn't settle well, so while she gorged herself, the sour feeling in her belly only grew until it became an ache.

Of course, it didn't help that she hadn't eaten a true meal for more than a week now, and then last night she had gone to bed with little enough, save for a taste of the stew she had cooked for Glenna and her son.

She couldn't get Kellen out of her mind this morning. Would they see that he ate well? Would they allow him to play in the sun at least once every day? Would they keep him away from the men at arms? He was a boy, after all, and curious, but she didn't trust Rogan to keep him safe. In fact, aside from the one nursemaid, there was no one she felt she could trust at Keppenach, for they all vied for the new lord's favor, and those who didn't feared to incur his wrath. It was amazing how quickly alliances turned once the tide shifted in another direction. But of course, Stuart had never truly inspired loyalty—not the way Aidan seemed to command it from his people.

At the bonfire, Lili had not missed the looks his kinfolk had cast in her direction—particularly once their laird had arrived. Only once it seemed Aidan would not strangle her where she stood had they relaxed enough to drink and be merry. And yet, none of them had approached her save Aidan.

How would they embrace her once she and Aidan were wed? Would they accept her? Would they trust her? Inasmuch as she hoped so, she also felt terrible for the way she would betray them.

But that was then, and this was now. The task she must see to this morning, if Aidan meant what he said, was to prepare herself for a wedding celebration—but how to begin, when even his sisters, save for the youngest all seemed to despise her?

She could ask Glenna for help, mayhap? Or Cailin? Lael, it seemed, would as soon see Lili skewered by one of her many blades. And Aveline would be no help at all. Even if the woman did not have eyes solely for Rogan, Lili still could not justify having a maid to carry out her every bidding, when it was perfectly clear the women here saw to themselves. Lili had not even indulged herself with a maid at Keppenach, for she had not been accustomed to it. It was not the way of a Highlander.

Pacing the room, she eyed her coffers, wondering whether she should wear the velvet gown David had gifted her, or whether she should choose one of her own more modest dresses. These folk were far more practical, and she felt instinctively that wearing the lavish gown would undermine her purpose here. They would never embrace her if she set herself apart. She was better served by simply being herself. But what to wear?

She didn't care what Aidan thought, she assured herself, though she did need his people to embrace her so that she could accomplish the task that had been set before her without a thousand eyes cast in her direction.

She couldn't help but remember the way he had looked at her when he'd come into the room this morning—as though he'd coveted her. It was a look she'd recognized, for he was not the first man to gaze at her just so, and yet, nothing about his demeanor from the moment she had arrived had given her the first inkling he was pleased with her. To the contrary, it seemed he had looked her over and found her lacking and then he had taken his leave. And yet this morning... that look in his eyes... it gave her a quiver every time she thought of it. Not even Stuart had gazed at her so hungrily—like that open-mouthed wolf emblazoned upon his woolen tapestry.

Setting aside her tray of food, she went to her coffers, and nibbling at her lip, she opened the first one, pushing back the lid and then stood and stared at the velvet gown that lay folded on top. She would not wear that, she decided, but now she wished she were like most women, and had more to her name, for it was that dress, the one on her back, or another at the bottom of her chest that hardly seemed suited for a bride dress. She had nothing more.

Mayhap Glenna would have something she could borrow, although Glenna was far bigger boned than she.

Just when she thought she might have to unfold the purple velvet and iron out the wrinkles, or set out to find Glenna's cottage, both Sorcha and Cailin came knocking at Aidan's door.

"My brother sent us," Cailin offered. But she lingered in the doorway, even once the door was open to admit them. In her hands she held a pale blue gown and a circlet of silver, adorned with intricate braids. She lifted the circlet and said, "This was our mother's." Only then did Lili see the howling wolf head at its center, set in a crystal moon.

"Ye'll be the first to wear it since," Sorcha disclosed, her eyes full of admiration as she spoke of her mother. "She was a Pecht princess!"

Touched by the gesture, Lili waved them inside. She would know of their traditions so she might honor them.

* * *

Aidan found Lachlann exactly where he had last encountered him, seated atop his boulder, only today, instead of whittling away at wood he sat carving from a wheel of cheese with his dirk. Aidan recognized auld Morag's wheel at once. He had completely forgotten about it after yesterday's tumble. He frowned.

"Want a piece?" Lachlann asked, noticing the direction of Aidan's gaze. Aidan shook his head, and mistaking his dark look, Lachlann defended himself. "I found it lying right here on the ground—a faerie gift!" he swore. "You know I wadna take a wheel without asking!"

"I know," Aidan said.

The burly man explained, "I've had me a fierce craving for one of Morag's cheeses for nigh on two weeks, and then suddenly it was here at my feet. Sometimes, prayers are answered!"

He sounded so excited that Aidan didn't wish to disappoint him with the truth. "So it seems." Damn, but he might as well enjoy a wee slice since he had planned to serve it for breakfast this morning, and now it was half gone, vanished into the depths of Lachlann's vast belly. He scratched his jaw, and relented, "Aye, then, gi' me a wee taste."

He sat down for a moment to talk with Lachlann, and Lachlann carved a *wee taste*, handing it over, grinning broadly, clearly pleased to share, though only willing to part with as much as he was compelled to. Aidan had little doubt the entire wheel would be gone before Lachlann e'er rose from his boulder.

He swallowed his *wee* slice and held out his hand again, requesting another, and though he grimaced, Lachlann complied at once.

"What do ye know of MacLaren and the *siùrsach*?" Aidan prompted.

Lachlann shrugged, carving away at his cheese just as fast as he could. He swallowed the pieces nearly whole. "What is there to know? Fergus said the two went at it twice in the field and then he deposited the wench in her bed and stumbled along to his own. As Lael bade him to, he then stood watch outside MacLaren's door for the remainder of the evening but the sour-faced Scot never showed his beak nose again."

Aidan nibbled his piece of cheese, savoring the flavor as it was meant to be enjoyed—slowly—while Lachlann tossed his down as fast as he could.

None of the Scots party had shown their faces to break their fast this morning... but then again, no one had invited them. In fact, he had made it quite clear that their hall was off limits until after the nuptials. His people would not sleep or eat under the same roof with deceiving Scots until they were certain all chance of treachery was diminished.

"What of the others?"

"The priest and the stone statues? They stood by the fire until the priest fell asleep on his arse—quite late—and then all of them went back to the cottage—probably to bugger each other while the priest watched." He laughed at his own jest, then held up a slice of cheese before popping it into his gob. "Want more?"

"Aye, ye greedy bastard! Why dinna ye save a bit for later anyhoo?"

Lachlann patted his belly. "A mon's gotta eat," he

declared.

"Aye, well if ye dinna stop now, ye'll no' be shittin' for a week, I vow."

Lachlann laughed as he carved a more generous piece for Aidan, probably in hopes that Aidan would not ask for another before the entire wheel was done. Greedy whoreson. It rankled only because Aidan had craved that cheese for himself, and he would have shared far more than Lachlann seemed inclined to.

"Dinna fash yourself," Lachlann avowed. "I ha' ne'er met a mon as yet who can out-shit me." He winked.

Aidan answered with a grin, but that was one competition he had never been inclined to join. It was painful enough to spy those burly son's of whores standing upon their boulder on the mount, shouting in victory across the vale as they left their malodorous signatures for God and man alike.

Dirty bastards.

Resigning himself to the loss of his cheese, Aidan stood, ready to go, realizing that despite Lachlann's rabid attention on the wheel of cheese, if Lachlann had perceived any nuance of danger, the man would have forsaken every meal to keep them safe. So, then, let him enjoy his *faerie gift* in peace. "Ha' ye seen any of their lot today?"

"No' a hair on their greasy heads."

"Not even the *siùrsach*?"

Lachlann shook his head.

"Aye, well... be certain someone sets an eye upon them soon, and dinna allow them anywhere near the caverns."

"Dinna worry, Aidan. The entrances are all being guarded, and Fergus is to come and tell me the instant those listless bastards leave their beds."

Aidan peered around to see if he could spot any of his men along the bluff. Because he knew where to look, he spied Turi's black head behind a boulder, but no on else. "Good."

"'Tis like as no' they're hiding in their beds 'til David's lackey comes to save them from the mean mountain folk." He chortled then, clearly enjoying the thought. "I dinna think they trust us a wee bit."

"The feeling is mutual. I canna stomach a mon who willna face his foes."

Lachlann nodded his agreement, and then arched a brow. "Speaking of foes, will ye truly wed the Scoti lass?"

"She's not dead yet," Aidan offered somewhat seriously. "I suppose I will."

Lachlann belted out another peal of laughter, his belly quaking unevenly like a sack of meal.

"Tonight the deed will be done," Aidan revealed, and lest Lachlann suspect his motives, he added, "I'd not draw this out longer than we must. Alert the rest of the men. I'd have everyone on guard and watching for *any* sign of treachery. Come tomorrow morn, I want these Scots—all of them save Lileas and her skinny maid—gone from the vale. I canna rest easy until the rats have gone away."

Lachlann nodded, understanding the burden Aidan carried, for he was a good five years older than Aidan. He too remembered that treacherous supper. "What of wee Dunc?" he asked, changing the subject.

"I'm away to Glenna's now," Aidan disclosed. "To be certain 'tis meet to wed, and we are no' instead obliged to bury our dead. The boy was much recovered before I sought my bed last night."

"Good. Good. I wadna like to lose another so soon and wee Dunc is a verra good lad." Lachlann peered down at the last slice of cheese. He seemed to consider it a moment, hesitating, but then offered it up. "Go on and gi' it to Glenna, then... for Dunc... tell the lad 'tis a gift from the faeries and twill see him strong again. He likes auld Morag's cheese."

A tiny smile curled Aidan's lip as he reached out to accept the burly man's gift for the sick child. He envied Lachlann's faith and as he met his clear blue eyes over the wheel of cheese, he knew for certain that whatever doubts he shouldered, he would bear them alone. "Aye, I'll gi' the lad your best," he promised, and then he offered him a wink and said, "His minny too." And then he reached out with his free hand to pat Lachlann's shoulder in friendship and with pride. More soberly than he had before, he added, "Ye're a good mon, Lachlann. 'Tis proud I am to ha'e ye at my side."

Lachlann gave him a narrow-eyed look, peering up through russet lashes. "Bah! Go on wi' ye now! Ye speak as though ye're off to the gallows, chief. 'Tis a wedding we gather for," he re-assured. "They wadna dare the same ruse twice."

Aidan nodded. But they would, he knew, and if treachery was the aim of these Scoti, then tonight would be the night. "Well, if they do... see that we're prepared for them," he commanded.

"Dinna fret, chief. We will be. If treachery be their scheme, we'll be feedin' them their beating hearts from the tips of our blades tonight." He lifted his dirk, and held the well-honed blade up for an instant to show its gleaming edge, and then he wiped it across his tongue to remove the remainder of the Morag's cheese before re-sheathing it into his belt.

ThRTEEN

Whatever exuberance Cailin lacked, Sorcha made up for emphatically. The youngest of Aidan's sisters was a wee bit of a cyclone, leading everyone about by their noses. She was ten and three going on twenty, and not even her elder sister seemed able to resist her wiles.

Lael, on the other hand, simply would not join them. They encountered the eldest of Aidan's sisters in the hall as Sorcha pulled Lili along by the hand. Cailin shuffled behind them bearing her wedding dress and Lael eyed the dress with clear disapproval and stabbed Lili with a look of disdain.

Attired in garb that made Lili feel as though she were still planning to go to war, there were knives strapped to every limb, but there was no sharper blade than her tongue. "Ye canna miss your scrawny maid," she said. "The woman has been picking her nose beside the pier since Aidan left this morn. We make no apologies for no' allowing her inside, an' ye may tell her so!"

Clearly, she did not trust them and made little pretense over the fact. Thankfully, neither of her younger sisters followed her lead, and seemed happy enough to leave Lael to whatever business she was attending. Her expression dour, she marched through the hall while Lili, along with Sorcha and Cailin ventured outside.

As Lael claimed, Aveline stood beside the dock that led to

the great hall, but her hands were folded before her, and she appeared for all-the world a little lost dove. For the first time since she'd met Rogan's mistress, Lili suffered a pang of guilt for not embracing her more fully. Forsooth, but Aveline did not make it easy, though soon enough they would be alone amidst these people and she knew Aveline must be feeling as distressed as she was, even if the girl would never confess it. As they passed, she took Aveline by the hand, and following Sorcha's lead, they wandered from cottage to cottage, drawing out the womenfolk, until they had a train as long as any Lili had ever seen.

Reluctantly at first, mothers and daughters joined them, bringing along ribbons and a sundry other items to help Lili dress. Nervous or nay, it was difficult not to enjoy herself while Sorcha ran about like a little imp, spurring laughter wherever she went. Lili found herself forgetting—at least for the moment—that this wedding was entirely a farce. She jested with the mothers and complimented the daughters, and all the while, the men gathered, watching from a distance, as though taking their cues from their womenfolk. To Lili's way of seeing it, it seemed that once the women began to relax and laugh, the men somehow found it permissible to enjoy themselves as well.

From where they stood at the edge of the village, she could see the men's numbers growing in the field below the hillside and it appeared to Lila as though they were tossing trees about. She had to ask. "What are they doing?"

"Tossing cabers," Cailin revealed. "Every year, we freshen the wood for the *crannóg*. The logs canna be cut too short, and only the strongest may help carry the wood from the forest, so of course, the dolts must turn it into a sport, as they do with aught else."

"Aye," one woman interjected, "dinna follow any up o'er the mount!" She pointed to a rise up on the hill, where Lili spied a particularly large boulder. "You would regret it at once." She plugged her nose and waved away an imaginary foul scent.

Sorcha leaned close. "There are some who compete to see

who can lay the biggest log," She nodded portentously. "If ye know what I mean."

Horrified, Lili nevertheless giggled. Surely Aidan, as chieftain of this clan, would never enjoy such a crude sport! Inasmuch as they seemed so much more courteous than Rogan would have had her believe, this was not an example of civilized behavior, and she could not imagine Stuart or her son competing in such an endeavor. Not even Rogan would have enjoyed such a vulgar sport. Thankfully, she wasn't given much opportunity to contemplate it overlong, for they started up the hillside to Glenna's house to see how Duncan fared and to inquire as to whether Glenna thought she might join them. Lili hoped so, for the greater part because she hoped that Duncan fared well enough for Glenna to leave him for a few moments of respite.

There was no way Lili could have predicted the outcome of Duncan's fever, for she hadn't had time to do much aside from keep him comfortable. All that she could surmise was that he was young and strong and his body had wanted to recover, but, in truth, his improvement was as much a mystery to Lili as the illness itself.

"Has Duncan eaten yet?" she asked Sorcha.

Sorcha nodded. "He drank more of the *vin aigre* potion, too, but he dinna like it."

Lili was pleased to hear it. "It may seem contrary, but 'twill settle his belly."

Sorcha giggled. "Aye, but Dunc has never had a problem filling his belly. He's a little piggy," she disclosed.

Unlike Kellen. Her son was not given to eating well. Had he been in Duncan's shoes, she loathed to consider the outcome. It made her heartsick to even think of it. Whatever else she did, she must find a way back to her son as quickly as possible, though if she thought of that right now, she would be fit for nothing more than weeping, so she banished the thoughts from her head as best as she was able.

It was a lovely day, despite a bit of a chill. The trees were only beginning to turn, and the grass was still green. The rowan trees were full with leaves, and a few lone flowers sprang here and there along the fields. It was easy enough to forget that all was not goodness and light. Even Cailin's mood lifted as they went, and she carried the wedding dress now with a new skip in her step, joking along with Sorcha.

Glenna must have heard their approach, for she came outside, smiling, her gaze centered upon Lili. "Duncan is sleeping," she disclosed. "But only after devouring the remainder of your stew. You must tell me how you made it!"

Lili's cheeks heated. "It does seem anything made by someone else always tastes better than our own," she offered politely, and knew it must be true, because she did not have a bent for cooking. The most she had ever done in the kitchen was to provide herbs for the cooks, and she had merely used a few to flavor a simple soup, naught more. "May I see him?" she asked.

Lili wanted to be certain there was nothing more she could do. The wedding preparations could wait if Duncan should need her. And yet, even the thought of what was to come— after the hand fasting—couldn't make her hope for less than a full recovery for the child. Still, she at least hoped to linger awhile. Despite that Sorcha's excitement was catching, and it heartened her to have so many womenfolk joining their party, her heart was not in this celebration. Her stomach roiled at the thought of seeing Aidan again and her nerves prickled and grew more taut as time passed. Soon, they would find themselves alone, and how could she give her body to a man and not her heart?

Glenna nodded, but she seemed to hesitate a moment. Finally, she pushed open her door to invite her in. "Certainly. Ye are welcome here always."

Her cheeks were flushed and her hair was windblown, but she was lovelier for the smile that lit her bonny face. The sight of it took Aidan by surprise, for it was the first such smile he had ever seen upon Lili's lips.

He couldn't help but wonder whether he could inspire such a miraculous thing, for he would see her smile often... if their marriage be true.

Doubt was a cloak about his shoulders.

He had remained tense all day, and felt a need to work it out with the cabers, except that there was far too much to be done to ensure his people would remain safe tonight.

Could this woman truly be a catalyst for peace?

He wanted to believe it.

Through the open door, belatedly he spied half the village lassies waiting outside Glenna's door, and he blinked in surprise. Either Sorcha was as much a sorceress as Una, or his bride was an enchantress as well, for it seemed to him that she had won over two score or more. Ach, the way she was going, she would soon have the entire village under her spell. He decided the work must be Sorcha's, for his youngest sister could be impetuous and full of joy. Hers was a force not to be denied—which was curious for unbeknownst to both, they shared the same blood.

"L-laird," she stammered, seeming to start at the sight of him.

Aidan smiled grimly, for she still could not seem to say his name.

Lili's heart stopped.

In that moment, it seemed all others fell away and she was aware of no one but him. His presence was palpable in the little cottage. The way he was looking at her practically stole her breath away.

On purpose, she had left his plaid in his room, preferring shivers to his cloak. For these final hours, she had not wished to be reminded that she was to be his, but his gaze possessed her nonetheless.

His shoulder-length hair seemed darker in the light of Glenna's cottage, and the breadth of his shoulders seemed to stretch the length of the room—which was perfectly ridiculous, for he was a man, not a giant.

"I dinna realize ye would be here," she said awkwardly. "I merely wished to see Duncan."

"These are my kinsmen," he reminded her. "Every last woman and child are my concern."

Outside, the tittering and chatter ceased abruptly at the deep tenor of his voice—as though suddenly guilt swept over the lot of them for having enjoyed themselves in her presence.

"Of course."

His eyes skewered her, and she had the immediate impression that he regretted their arrangement. Uncomfortable with his scrutiny, she averted her gaze to the bed, where Duncan sat atop the covers nibbling on a slice of white cheese.

Glenna rushed to his side. "Do ye remember, Lili?" she asked.

The boy nodded and said politely, "Thank you."

Lili gave the child a tentative smile. "You're so verra welcome, Duncan. I have a son about your age," she told him.

The boy nodded. His brown eyes were indeed the color of her son's. "My minny said so. Will ye bring him here to live as well?"

The simple question strangled Lili's voice. For an instant, she could not respond. As she understood it, Kellen would never see this place, for once Aidan was dead, she would be free to leave—if his people didn't kill her for her betrayal. She nodded nonetheless, avoiding Aidan's gaze. "Ye would like him?" she said. "He reminds me a bit o' ye."

The boy smiled and took another bite of his cheese. He held up the tiny sliver that was left, showing it to her. "D' ye see what the faeries left me?"

Sorcha marched over to the bed. "Ach! 'Tis but a sliver of auld Morag's cheese!" the girl pointed out. "If a faerie left that, she stole it from—"

"Sorcha!" Aidan interrupted, his voice like thunder in the little room.

The room fell silent, and all eyes save Lili's averted to Aidan.

He stepped forward, standing so close behind Lili that she could feel his body's heat through her dress. "If it pleases Dunc to think so, who are we to disagree?"

Sorcha gave her brother a questioning glance and whatever silent message he gave her kept her lips sealed though her brow furrowed.

"We've come tae see if Glenna would like to help prepare the bride," Cailin offered. She stepped forward, pulling her youngest sister back away from Duncan's bedside. She bent to whisper something into Sorcha's ear, something Lili could not hear, which caused Sorcha to give Lili a wary glance—the first such look from Sorcha since Lili's arrival. Sorcha nodded imperceptibly, and Lili had the oddest sense they were keeping something from her then. But then again … there was likely much these people would not say until they knew her far better.

Wholly aware of the man at her back, Lili met Glenna's gaze. "Would ye come?"

"If ye would enjoy it," Aidan suggested, "I'll stay with Dunc for awhile."

"Ach, nay! I dinna need a nursemaid!" Duncan protested. "I am already eight!"

Duncan did seem well enough, and Lili so wanted Glenna to come along. Sorcha was young, Cailin still a bit tentative, Aveline was a mute, and Glenna was the first female friend Lili had ever had. However, it surprised her that Aidan would offer to sit with the boy himself.

"Well," Glenna said hesitantly. She looked toward Aidan. He nodded encouragement, and she relented, "Verra well." She smiled then, and dashed to one corner of the cottage, retrieving a blanket and racing past Aidan. Lili followed her out, but not before turning and sparing Aidan a final glance, but it was a mistake, for the look in his eyes made her heart skip its natural beat.

"Come now," Sorcha demanded, seizing Lili once more by the hand.

To Lili's dismay, her feet seemed not to want to move, and she nearly tumbled onto her face as Sorcha pulled her out the door.

Aidan watched them go.

In that instant while their gazes held, Aidan spied far more than he would have liked to see. He saw a lonely woman, who despite everything, craved to be accepted by his people. She might fear him, in truth, but the look in her eyes as she'd invited Glenna to come along reminded him of a little girl who had no friends.

Ach, but he was drawn to her in a way he had never been drawn to any woman before, and wanted to take her under his arm and love and protect her. But these were things he could not afford to feel.

Not yet.

Mayhap never.

He watched them go, torn between what his heart and head were saying.

FOURTEEN

D id they truly believe he could not see the lout standing guard?

Rogan was not stupid. He realized Lili was weak. If he could accomplish his work for David without her, there would be no need to leave her here amongst these barbarians. He had not missed the way Aidan dún Scoti looked at her. Like all the rest, he coveted her in his bed and it rankled— more because she seemed to welcome his attention.

It gnawed at his gut to think of her lying prostrate beneath the hulking savage, purring for his cock—not that Rogan thought she had the first inkling how to please a man. She was a cold bitch. Every time he tried to embrace her, she recoiled from him, and the look on her face made his stomach roil. The bitch believed she was better than he was—she, a woman cursed, considered herself worthy of a better man! What effrontery!

But Rogan had her son... that was at least some reassurance Lili would complete the task they had set before her. As a worst case scenario, he would leave her here to do her work as planned, though he must make certain Aveline knew her duty and continued to remind Lili about the dangers to her son should she fail.

And yet, if he could save her the trouble... King David would no doubt thank him all the more, for despite that

David was far too righteous to confess his desire to see them all dead, he would hardly mourn their loss. Had he not sanctioned this plan to begin with? Aye, and David understood precisely where that path led, no matter that he did not voice it. The King was desperate. He wanted Aidan's tribe smitten from the face of the earth, for while they might not call themselves Scots, the Highlanders counted them among the noblest of clans, and nearly every king since Aed had tried to woo them to no avail... and then sought to see them dead when it was clear the dún Scoti would never bend their knees.

Rogan contemplated that fact as he stood and watched the barbaric hoards compete with trunks of trees upside their backs, pitching them like children pissing off a cliff.

He glanced at his own men, standing near the priest—one more delicate than the next. It had been planned that way apurpose, to help set the dún Scoti chieftain at ease, for who could count a single one of these bastards to be a threat? They sickened him. And the priest was the worst of the lot, for he sat there crossing himself continuously and counting his rosary as though prayers alone could save him from the wrath of the dún Scoti.

Nay, but it would take wits not brawn to defeat dún Scoti. In his time of greatest glory, Padruig had come here like a hammer, considering himself such a force that there was no chance the dún Scoti could survive him... and yet they had. Indeed, they had thrived, which only made Rogan reconsider his tack.

His gaze reverted to the boy called Keane.

The lad stood among the competitors on the field, his shoulders puffed with the pride of youth. Until Lili produced a child, the boy was Aidan's heir. Mayhap that was where he should target his efforts? When the elder dún Scoti chieftain had been slain along with half his kinsmen, Aidan had survived to see them prosper.

Aye, if Lili could do her worst here... mayhap he was better served by killing Keane, for with the lad dead, there would be none left save women to lead these mountain folk... and who the hell would follow a stupid woman?

In the distance, he spied the procession of ladies heading toward the shore of the loch and his cock stirred, for he knew Lili would be among them.

She had already begun to work her sorcery here, it seemed, nursing some child back from the brink of death. Ach, if there was any witchery to her at all, it was that knack she had for healing. Aye, but that was yet another fortuitous affair, for it seemed there was some mysterious malady plaguing these people. Mayhap with very little effort, they would see the end of their days … with a bit of help.

His gaze returned to Aidan's arrogant little brother.

If he could not kill Aidan himself... mayhap he could still find a way to undermine the clan...

* * *

As though the Mother of Winter herself had inspired the Highland mists, holding back the approach of wintertide yet one more day, the morning's fog retreated into the belly of the mountain, leaving a carpet of green sprawled before a late summer sun. The sound of laughter murmured through the rowan trees and a gentle breeze shimmied the leaves.

Hope rose like a second sun, brightening the mood, and Lili allowed herself a moment to pretend she was a bride for the first time, free of the sins of her father and her duty to the crown. It was easy to do with these joyful people.

The women led her to a secret place along the loch where the bluffs rose high alongside it, and there, cascading into a small pool, she discovered a spectacular waterfall. It was like nothing she had ever seen before, and she stood, mouth agape, marveling at the sight, while every last woman in their gathering undressed and tossed aside her gown. One by one they dove, naked, into the crystalline pool, screeching over the cold, though hardly fazed enough to keep them dry.

Lili laughed, horrified, for she had never once in her entire life been naked under the sun—and never in the presence of so much nudity. All shapes and sizes, these women were completely devoid of modesty, it seemed.

Aveline looked at her aghast, stepping back from the edge of the pool as though she feared they might drag her in the crystal clear waters. The look on her face made Lili giggle all the more. "I will if you will," she challenged Aveline.

Poor Aveline shook her head vehemently, and Lili could hardly believe she had suggested it anyway. She waffled, suddenly self-conscious about her pale complexion, for these women all had sun-kissed skin. These people clearly enjoyed their lives and did not worry overmuch about keeping their skin unstained by the sun.

From the pool, Glenna shouted up at them. "Ach! Ye havena a thing we all dinna have, ladies! Come and get yourselves clean!"

"Aidan will thank ye later!" someone shouted and laughed, the sound bawdy.

The women giggled, and Cailin splashed water at the bank toward Lili.

"What if someone should come?" Aveline fretted.

The womenfolk squealed with laughter, frolicking in the water. Lili peered up along the rise of the hill to see if any of the men were watching, but they were alone here by the pool. What could it hurt? In truth, they had all the same parts, and why should she be so modest when they were not? She removed her shoes and tentatively set them aside.

Aveline, who must have sensed her thoughts, appeared horrified. "God will abandon you!" she warned. "The devil will find you!"

"Ach, 'tis but water," Lili argued, still not quite convinced she wanted to go in. But everyone was having so much fun. In all her life, she had never been in the vicinity of so much laughter, and she envied these people their ease with one another.

"Come in!" Sorcha demanded.

Lili found herself grinning, though she still couldn't move her feet. She laughed, shaking her head, nibbling her lip, terribly tempted, but years of modesty kept her toes rooted in the grass. The cool damp blades felt sinfully good beneath her feet.

Mindless of the wee chill in the air, Glenna and another woman Lili knew as Birgit both came flying naked out of the pool, their nipples puckered and their lady hairs dripping wet. They began to undress her, giving her no choice in the matter, lest she pitch a fit and refuse.

"Oh, my!" Aveline exclaimed, and her hand flew to her mouth.

Lili shivered.

"'Tis far warmer in the water," Sorcha promised.

In less than two minutes, Lili was bare as the day she was begot, standing under the bright afternoon sun. She had a sudden attack of conscience, but to her dismay, her clothes went back into the loch with Glenna and Birgit, and unless she wished to don her wedding gown, or someone else's clothing, there was no way to avoid this.

Giggling nervously, she took a running leap toward the pool and plunged within, flopping on her belly, and shrieking over the skin-numbing cold. The entire entourage laughed aloud, and so did Lili as she came back up, spitting icy water from her lips. At once, she sank to her neck, and peered up at Aveline, who sat shivering alone upon the bank.

* * *

The raucous sound of laughter floated up over the hillside.

Aidan knew instinctively that the women were up to mischief. The rest of the men knew it as well and they immediately abandoned the cabers in the grass and started down toward the loch.

"Nay!" Aidan threw up a hand, halting them at once. He had no bloody clue why he should give a damn, but he did. Wearing a scowl the size of the ben itself, he barred their paths and waved them all back to the cabers. "Ye'll no' be hounding the lasses—no' today!" he apprised them one and all. The thought of even a one of them seeing his bride unclothed left his belly sour—never mind that many of their own wives were down there as well. Aidan would have none of it, tempers be damned. If they thought they would set eyes upon his woman even before he had a chance to do so himself they were sorely mistaken.

"Awww, Aidan!" whined Keane.

Aidan pierced his brother with a warning glare.

"'Tis certain Meara is with them as well!" his brother complained.

Auld Fergus came forward and smacked Keane in the back of the head with the butt of his palm. "Ye ha'e no idea what to do with my daughter anyhoo, whelp! 'Tis nay your laird tells ye and nay it is!"

Aidan was grateful for the old warrior's backing, for he knew good and well that he could give no plausible reason that would suit the lot of them, for his reaction was simply not rational. They were not a modest folk, and on a sunny, warm day they might all be bathing together in the loch, men and women and children alike. There was no cause for him to be up in arms. "Go on back to the cabers," he commanded them.

With gloomy expressions—all of them—his men all returned to their games, casting Aidan disgruntled glances all the while the women's laughter continued to taunt them from a distance.

For his part, Aidan could not shut out the sound. It beckoned to his curiosity and tempted him beyond reason. It surprised him that his bride seemed to have infiltrated his clan so thoroughly in such a short time. It either boded very well, or not at all.

Throughout the day, he kept an eye on their Scots *guests*. At the moment, they were huddled together, watching the competition with bored expressions. So he used that as his excuse for not allowing the men to celebrate with the womenfolk, ordering them to keep an eye to their backs.

Lachlann was with Duncan now. Thank God Turi and the rest were still in their positions up on the hillside. Until he sent new guards to replace them, he could rest assured that they, at least, would not lose their wits for wont of *uisge* or women.

But Aidan was distracted enough that he did not see Keane slip away. Nor did he notice the Scots' numbers were reduced by one.

FIFTEEN

After the brisk swim, Lili felt refreshed by the waters of the loch, her dark hair clean, wavy and free. In so many ways, the day's festivities reminded her of a Beltane celebration, for the womenfolk blessed her as they dressed her, singing in the old tongue:

Bless thee true and bountiful,
Thee, thy spouse and bairns.
Bless all those within thy keeping.

All that was missing was a maypole, although Lili might as well be one herself, for she was surrounded by flailing arms, hands and song:

Satisfy thy soul and shield thy loved ones,
Protect thee in truth and honor,
Bless thy land and all the vale for thy people.

They sang with abandon, while their daughters hung bits of ribbons on the hem of Lili's gown. For the space of the day, she could almost forget how she had come to be with these folk, for it seemed as though they had forgotten as well.

"'Tis lovely ye are," Glenna offered.

Lili recognized the sincerity in her tone, softened tenfold

since the moment of their meeting. It gave her a pang of regret for what was yet to come.

Her dress, far less lavish than the purple velvet gown David had gifted her with, was soft and worn with age. According to Cailin, the robin's egg-blue dress had been worn by the brides of seven chieftains, and then each time put away to be worn by the next lady of Dubhtolargg. That they had allowed Lìli to wear it, made her throat thick with emotion. Not even her own mother had shown such joy for her first wedding to Stuart, and in fact, her parents had very nearly ushered her out the door. With a sack for her dowry, they'd bid her good riddance. Unlike her father, her mother had not been unkind, but she had never dared gainsay her father, and Padruig Caimbeul had blamed Lìli for the demise of his good fortune from the instant he'd heard about the curse from a wandering minstrel. As far as Lìli was concerned, the simple fact that her father believed it had created a self-fulfilling prophecy, for though she had made it her life's mission to study the old ways, she had found no proof that curses existed. From her studies she had gleaned merely a knowledge of herbs, and by it she had become a skilled healer. Although, admittedly, she did every so oft include some earthy ritual, just in case. What could it possibly hurt? Some things could not quite be explained away. Like the feeling she'd had upon riding into this glen. Or the way she now felt after having bathed in the loch—in a sense reborn. Or even the connection she felt to things unseen whenever she allowed faith into her healing. Or for that matter even the intense *knowing* she felt when she peered into the veil that fell over the eyes of the ill—aye, for she often knew when they were destined to pass from this world to the next. But these were all things she kept to herself. Nay, she was not a witch, but neither did she deny the possibility that magic existed, for what else was faith but a form of magic? And yet to accept that fact, also filled her with a sense of gloom, for how could one accept the possibility of magic, and not accept the fact that she might, in truth, be cursed? It *could* be true that Stuart had died because of her... and it *might* also be true that Aidan would die as well. If so, it would make her task here go all the simpler, but she hoped it wasn't so. And yet... that made no sense at all, for one way or another, she would be responsible for Aidan's death. But somehow, it seemed far worse to consider that her betrayal would come only after he gave her his love.

Dinna worry about that, she reassured herself. Aidan dún Scoti would never give her his heart. She was simply a pawn in a game of politics, no more—a way to control her father and David, though the jest was on Aidan dún Scoti, for no one valued her, and in truth, they had already guaranteed her death should Aidan discover her ruse—that, or her son's should she fail.

But she would not fail.

Up on the hill, they could hear the men playing at their games, though surprisingly, not a one showed their faces by the loch... save for young Keane, who spied on them now from some place up high on the bluff.

Glenna's cousin Meara had spied him first—mayhap because she had been searching for him—and the two were making sheep's eyes across the way. So long as it was just him, the women did not seem to mind and simply ignored the lad, continuing to prepare Lili for the ceremony. Each of them pinned ribbons to her dress, a symbolic gesture to show they embraced her as the chieftain's bride. But with every ribbon, her sense of guilt increased tenfold. And whenever she considered taking joy in their traditions, the sight of Aveline, with her pinched face, only served to remind her that none of this was real.

Aveline's brows were set in thin lines of disapproval while she watched Meara preen naked in the pool. "Do ye not worry they will be tempted?" she ventured to ask.

Meara was the last to leave the water, while practically everyone else was already dressed. Aveline, on the other hand, was the only one who had refused to bathe, and her greasy hair lay heavily around her face, defying even the gentle breeze.

"Ach, but nay!" Glenna said. "Where there is a will there

is a way for young folk. Worrying over it never made a wee bit o' difference. Anyhoo, 'tis Meara's right to choose. If Keane gets a babe of the lass, he will do what is right."

"Those two have been flirting since the day they were born," Cailin added, and rolled her eyes.

"But he is just a child himself," Aveline argued. "'Tis not meet to allow the young to do as they please."

"Keane?" Glenna shook her head. "Ach, nay. Keane is no' so much a boy," she disagreed. "Aidan himself led this clan when he was but a year younger than he."

Lili considered that. So Aidan must have been Sorcha's age when his father died, which meant that he could be no more than six and twenty now, for Lili had been nine when Padruig took his campaign into the Highlands, and then eleven when she'd learned about her curse. At the age of twenty-two, she felt as though she'd lived two lifetimes already.

Her gaze sought Sorcha. The girl was three and ten, she believed, so her father was dead the year before her birth... was she conceived before his death? Or was she another man's babe? The girl looked very little like her siblings.

A terrible idea needled its way into her brain, but she shoved it away, her thoughts returning to Aidan. For all his youth, he seemed so much older than his years, and she reasoned that it must be that cold, dark look in his eyes.

She was grateful to the womenfolk for taking her mind off the evening to come. The thought of it made something like doves take flight in her breast.

"Just the same," Aveline persisted, toying with a greasy curl. "Temptation must be avoided as the flesh is weak!"

Cailin lifted a brow, giving Aveline a shrewd look. "Mayhap in the Lowlands or in England men and boys will dip their wicks where they should no', but no' here. Anyhoo, I dinna see a hand fast ribbon about your wrist, and ye dinna complain much last night."

Her meaning was not lost to Aveline—or to anyone—and Aveline's cheeks flamed.

Lili tried not to laugh at Cailin's frank appraisal, but a tiny smile insisted at the corners of her lips, for it seemed quite likely that no one else had missed Aveline and Rogan's mingling of limbs. Ach, she wished Aveline would find a way to enjoy herself as well, for she, too, was far younger than she appeared. It was only her righteous attitude that made her seem as though she were fifty or more. Not even Lili's mother, so long harried by her father, seemed quite so old.

Thankfully, Aveline hushed her mouth from that moment forward, watching with a reproving frown as the womenfolk worked. When Lili's dress was complete, Glenna left her to gather up a blanket she had brought from beneath her pile of clothing. She returned, unfolding it, flicking it out to remove the grass, and it was only then that Lili realized what it was. She gasped with surprise, her heart tripping.

It was a new arisaid to replace her old one—the one Aidan claimed he had burned. But this one bore the colors of her new clan.

She felt instantly bewildered by the gift. Ambivalence wove its way through her heart, for it was both the best and the worst gift she had ever received.

She was playing a role, she reminded herself.

She did not deserve the cloak, but she loved it just the same.

Dinna allow yourself to love these folk, for you will only regret it in the end.

Still the gift touched her to the core of her soul. After she had taken Stuart's name, she had commissioned her own plaid, embracing her new life with a new people. Unlike that one, this one was a gift of the heart from these people, and they were embracing her as their own—as unlikely as that possibility had once seemed.

Glenna smiled at her expression. "'Tis my thanks," she said, "for saving my son."

Choked with emotion, Lili shook her head, disbelieving the generosity of the gift even as Glenna laid it out before her eyes. The intricate weave must have taken months to achieve. She reached out to touch it reverently.

Lili's voice caught. "I did nothing," she protested. And it

was true. She was certain the boy would have recovered on his own.

"Aye," Glenna contended, "but ye did." And then she disclosed with a wink, "I was making it for myself, but now 'tis yours." And before Lili could protest, she swung it about Lili's shoulders, and Lili's eyes filled with tears.

"Now ye will truly be our lady of Dubhtolargg!"

* * *

Aidan felt the tension mounting in his chest.

As the day wore on, the celebration moved closer to the tabled stone that would be their altar, and before the night was done, Lili would lie in his arms.

His enemy in his bed.

He had no idea whether it was because his clanswomen seemed to embrace her so easily, but he dared to think of her without the stain of her father's sins.

Even Lael seemed far less angry, and despite the fact that his eldest sister would not be so quick to embrace Lili, she handled the arrangements for the feast without complaint, overseeing the number of sheep they would slaughter for the pits, and making certain they had more than enough *uisge* and mead.

Even more important than his sister's cooperation, Aidan heard a note of hope amidst the anxious whispers of his clansmen. Mayhap they had gleaned it from their chieftain, for Aidan could not deny that a tiny thread of hope was weaving its way through his heart.

What if he was wrong?

What if once again, as his father had before him, he was leading his folk to a slaughter?

Keane was his age when he'd accepted the leadership if his clan, but with the sickness that haunted them now, and his brother's immaturity, Aidan wasn't quite as optimistic for their survival should he die.

Nay, but this time they would remain on guard.

And this time, there would be no feasting indoors at their

tables. His men would not sit idly by draining their cups so the bastards could rise up and slit their throats to the accompaniment of the reed and lute. Aye, and this time their *guests* were far outnumbered, unless...

He climbed upon the tabled rock—the place along the hillside that afforded the clearest view of the entire vale—and peered out over the horizon, searching for the telltale gleam of silver along the bluff tops. His Scots brethren were far too much like the English now. While no true Highlander would don helms and hauberks, the Lowlanders and Reiver lords could scarce be distinguished from dirty *Sassenachs*. David himself was encased in silver when he rode. But if he ever hoped to quell these rebellions, he needed to shed himself of his English ways.

No matter, for even if the enemy appeared in the dark of night, and all that was visible was the whites of their eyes, Aidan had men stationed along the only path that led down into the vale. They would sound horns the instant they spied anyone's approach. For the sake of his people, He had taken every precaution to reduce their risks.

Aye, though if this union be true, if everything was as David claimed, his marriage to Lili could begin to set them truly at ease, for by it, they would form an alliance and truce. Although Lileas' lineage was far from the Ailpín line, their marriage should make it clear that Aidan had little design upon Scotia's throne. His people only wished to be left in peace, to safeguard the stone for a time when a true king arose to unite these troubled nations.

As for the curse, he did not believe a word of it. If he died because of Lileas MacLaren, it would be because she plunged a dagger between his shoulders whilst he slept—that and nothing more. But his trust would not be easily won.

Yet he was not made of stone.

As the sun began to set, anticipation settled like a swarm of bees in his belly.

Mo chreach! He was no beardless youth to be stricken with nerves before bedding a bonny lass, but he could not deny that he suffered an attack of nerves all the same. He steeled himself, but nothing could have prepared him for the sight of his bride as she appeared over the rise of the hill…

For an instant, the gleam of silver tensed his shoulders… until he realized the twinkle arose from within the vale.

With nearly every clanswoman marching at her heels, Lili followed Una's bent form hobbling along the path. Aidan's colors flowed from her shoulders, fluttering in the breeze. Her hair, unbound and left to fly at her back, glistened under the last rays of golden sun. A circlet of silver—his mother's, he realized, even at this distance—sat atop her shiny dark head.

The sight stole his breath away.

Like the warrior queens of their distant past, she marched with shoulders straight and proud, advancing through the twilight.

Alas, but the battleground was his heart.

By the sins of sluag! The swiftness with which she had won his people over was a testament to how eager his clan was for peace.

God save them all if he was wrong.

There was no mistaking Aidan's silhouette standing upon a bluff.

His features were obscured by the sun in Lili's eyes, but she knew he had spied her by the way he shifted his stance, and his hands flew to his hips.

The man would give no quarter if he discovered her deception, and tonight her path would be writ in stone.

If she weren't such a charlatan and her husband didn't seem to loathe her, she might have felt joyful beyond anything she had ever experienced in her life, for as she rounded the hilltop, surrounded by the chieftain's womenfolk, she felt like a true Pecht queen, beloved by her kin. The sun lowered as they marched, for Una had told her that they would be wed in the hour between times, blessed by this world and the next. By now, the women who had not joined them at the loch, and the children all gathered up on the hillside, waiting with breaths paused as the procession passed.

As they neared the table stone where Aidan stood, the men all parted for them to pass, and those who did not comply quickly enough received a whack on the shins with Una's staff. That bejeweled stick seemed to reach the length between her and whomever she aimed it at and land a bone-jarring smack that sent more than a few men hopping back in pain.

Una had come to retrieve them from the loch, her face painted fully in blue and her one good eye smeared with black to match the dark patch she wore over her left eye. She looked like a demon with that face and her curly white hair, but Lili sensed an ally in her, much the same as she did with Sorcha and Glenna.

Aidan's youngest sister walked beside her though Cailin had disappeared into the throng... probably not quite prepared to stand at Lili's side and face her sister Lael, for Lael's absence had been duly noted.

As Lili neared the place where Aidan stood, her knees faltered. He loomed before her, larger than life, dressed in a fine blue tunic to match her blue gown. Wearing a breacan to match her arisaid, and leather boots that were laced up his bare legs, he stood fully armed, as though he met his foe and not his bride. Thankfully, he had eschewed the blue paint today, though the look upon his face, now that she could see it, was not tender at all, nor did his eyes hold any pride. He looked like a pagan god, and Lili resisted the urge to cross herself, despite that she was not the most pious soul.

Sixteen

"Great gods who create and bring forth life, we ask your blessings on this day of gathering!"

The clanswomen all dispersed into the crowd at the beginning of Una's prayer, and before Lili could follow anyone, Una took her by the wrist—her bony fingers strong and insistent—and pulled her along behind her.

Climbing adeptly and more agilely than her old limbs should allow, the old woman led the way up the stone steps to where Aidan stood waiting for them. As they passed, Una bade the priest to follow with a crooked finger, and the man recoiled. Rogan pushed him into the procession.

Taken aback by the piercing look Rogan gave her, Lili hesitated only an instant until Una turned to fix her with a one-eyed glare.

"Dinna tarry!" she scolded them both. But thankfully she did not wield her staff this time, and it was a good thing, for Lili was beginning to live in fear of it. So far, she and Aidan seemed to be the only ones the old woman didn't seem inclined to rebuke whenever it pleased her.

The sun was setting now, and a soft golden light fell across the vale, turning the grass a golden hue. A cool breeze lifted the cloak about Lili's shoulders, but her shivers were far more likely those of trepidation.

Once they had reached the stone dais, and before Lili had

a chance to wonder what she should do next—for this was unlike any wedding celebration she had ever attended, and far different from her first—Una positioned her next to Aidan and poked the priest in the back with the end of her staff until he was herded directly to the spot she wished him to stand. The man gave a startled little whimper with every stab.

A sea of faces stared up at Lili, expressions ranging from pleasant to curious to disapproving... and then there was Rogan. His blue eyes offered an unmistakable warning...

Lili turned away, grateful at least for the simple fact that soon he would leave Dubhtolargg, and then if she must sell her soul to the devil, at least she would do it without Rogan's rancor and evil black eyes. And if God had any mercy at all, once he returned to Keppenach, he would simply forget her son was in his care, and in the meantime Lili would find a way to do her worst—for the sake of her son.

Finally, once the four of them stood together, after the entire crowd fell silent and Aidan stood beside her, the priest cleared his throat to speak the words.

Like an asp, without warning, Una's staff snaked out at once, thumping the man hard upon the pate of his head, hitting her mark despite the fact that she was a good two feet shorter than the prelate. "I will apprise you when 'tis your turn," she reprimanded.

Rubbing the pate of his head, the priest frowned and stepped away, and Lili tried not to make a face—not even to smile—for fear that Una's staff might next call her name.

Aidan had yet to even look at her, which was just as well, for if he did so now, he would find her quaking in her slippers. For all the stature she might have enjoyed during the march uphill, her mettle was completely gone now, and she felt like a frightened babe set before a sea of faceless strangers. At the moment, she did not even dare seek Glenna's gaze for support, for this was all a lie, and her mother had always told her she could not dissemble to save her life. It was the very reason she could never win her father's favor, for she could not pretend when he made it so clear she was of little value to him. Even with Rogan, her eyes and mouth had always betrayed her.

"You will join hands," Una demanded.

Finally Aidan looked at her, and Lili's heart skipped a beat. He met her gaze directly, and more gently than she might have expected, and he drew her hand into his and held it so their wrists were joined and their pulses met.

Una carried in her hand a number of ribbons similar to the ones his womenfolk had pinned upon her dress, and she looped one now over their joined wrists, binding the two of them together. "Lileas and Aidan, do ye come voluntarily to make this union?"

"I do," Aidan said, his voice booming like thunder across the hillside.

Lili could not find her voice to speak.

He lifted a brow, challenging her. "Do ye?"

Lili nodded.

Una berated her. "Ach, child, speak the words, so all who see may also hear!"

Wincing, for Lili half expected to feel Una's staff on her shins, she said, "I-I do."

"Will you honor and respect one another?" the old woman persisted.

"I will," they said in unison.

David's priest cleared his throat and whispered angrily. "'Tis utter blasphemy! It is a woman's duty to honor her husband! This is not the way of Holy Church!"

Without even looking at him, Una's staff came up and popped him squarely on the chin this time. She then wrapped another ribbon around their wrists and continued as though nothing at all had transpired. "Will you forever aid each other in times of pain and sorrow?"

The priest groaned beside her.

Lili tried to concentrate on Una's words. "I will," they said again in unison once more, and once again, the old woman looped a ribbon about their wrists.

Lili peered up at her betrothed, wondering of Aidan's thoughts. His gaze revealed naught.

"Will you be true to one another that you may grow strong

together?"

"I will," Aidan said at once.

Again, Lili faltered. She eyed the priest, who was still nursing his newest wound, the words catching in her throat. The man's dark eyes were dilated with fear, for he understood better than many that she was bound to betray not only Aidan, but his people as well. Admitting it now would only see them all dead. Realizing that she would be damned to hell for saying the words, she hitched her chin, and said, "I will."

Aidan's eyes glittered. His lips curved ever so slightly. He watched her face—her eyes—not the ribbon as it was looped over their hands for a third time.

"As your hands become withered, will you reach out only for one another?"

Lili thought about all the mistresses her father had taken. Even Stuart had been said to have a few, and she wondered if any man could be true. But Aidan did not hesitate to answer.

"We will," they said together, and for a fourth time, the ribbon was looped about their wrists.

"Is it your intention to bring peace and harmony to this clan?"

Lili had the sense the question was directed solely at her, and Aidan did not answer this time. Swallowing, she lifted her gaze to him, and nodded as she said, "It is."

He remained silent, simply assessing her with those stark green eyes, and the old woman looped the ribbon a fifth time. Lili could feel it now like a noose constricting her throat, cutting off her breath.

The last of the sunlight winked off the blade of Aidan's claymore.

"When you falter—and you will—will you then have the courage—and loyalty—to remember these promises you have made to one another?"

"I will," Lili said and swallowed, hard.

"Aye," Aidan agreed.

The breath of the world seemed to pause in that instant as twilight succumbed to shadows. Una suddenly spun about, her staff raised to acknowledge the priest, the milky jewel of her staff glowing softly, as though it had swallowed the sunlight and held it trapped within. "Is there aught you would say now?" she asked the man.

The priest shook his head adamantly, his eyes fixed upon the staff she wielded in her hand, and Una dismissed him quickly, turning and declaring in a voice loud enough for all to hear, "Lileas and Aidan, now as your hands are bound, so too are you bound to one another. Aidan, will you bestow the kiss of peace upon your betrothed?"

Aidan's gaze slid to Una. He found the old woman's good eye twinkling mischievously. At once, he peered out at the crowd of faces and found their expressions questioning.

The look upon Lili's face was no less expectant. Her small hands quaked within his own. His heartbeat quickened at the thought of kissing her... and his palms grew sticky with anticipation. Her violet eyes darkened, her pupils dilating, and it seemed as though she would flee, like a terrified doe. Lest she do so, he pulled her toward him, peering once more out at the shadowed faces of his kinsmen. Then he tarried no more. He drew Lili into his arms and placed his lips upon hers only to find them trembling far worse than her hands. He thought to spare her, but his tongue did not obey. Eager for the taste of his new bride, he pressed his tongue between her quivering lips, but they were sealed like a virgin's, barring him entrance. But since she was no virgin, he assumed she did not welcome the kiss, and he drew back to study her face. There was only confusion there, not revulsion, so he offered her a bit of a smile and turned to raise their arms for his people to witness their hands bound together.

A cheer rang throughout. The exuberant sound startled even Aidan, but he was moved by it nonetheless.

"Behold my bride!" he said, his voice thick with emotion, and then he added, surprising himself with the veracity of the demand, "Respect her as ye do me!" His gaze immediately fell upon Stuart's brother, for that particular message was primarily for him. No matter their feelings about Lili, his kinsmen would never disrespect her, he knew. But if that man ever laid another hand upon his bride again, no matter the reason, he would skewer him through. And once the celebrations were done, he intended to see the Scots bastards escorted out of his vale.

Today they were welcome to make merry.

Tomorrow their welcome would be worn.

SEVENTEEN

U isge flowed aplenty. Herds of boys, gnawing on legs of lamb, chased after giggling girls, who wagged their tails, despite that they hardly understood what it meant to do so. Lili was mindful she did not do the same, for she knew very well that her flirtations would be answered for sooner rather than later.

The bonfire burned bright, sending tendrils of smoke high into the night sky, along with glints of glowing ash. The mood, unlike the night before, was festive, though as soon as Una appeared a hush fell over the gathering. She brought Lili and Aidan both wooden tankards filled with *uisge*, and then holding her own cup high, she gave them each a toast in a voice as ancient and rugged as the Highland hills.

Be the Maiden, Mother and Crone,
Be the Horned God, the Wild Spirit of the Forest!

And then she tilted her cup back, quaffing the contents without taking a single breath. Aidan lifted his glass in much the same manner, but he waited for Lili to bring her cup to her lips.

The scent of the *uisge* burned her nostrils, but she tipped the glass back for the good of Scotland and to the health of her son. She came up choking and hacking, for she had never in her life tasted a drink so stout. They did not make such a dreadful potation at Keppenach. It felt like liquid fire. Even before she ceased coughing, the warmth was already seeping into her breast.

An answering cheer resounded throughout the crowd, and Aidan gave a grunt of satisfaction and downed his own.

Somehow, thereafter, Lili's cup seemed to mysteriously refill, with Una reassuring her that she must "drink up," because she would "need it." Lili thought mayhap she had forgotten that Lili was not a first time bride, and considered reassuring her, but after awhile, Una returned with a tray that held what appeared to be two pulpy houseleeks, both covered in a brownish powder, and she wondered by chance if that was what the old woman had been referring to when she'd urged her to drink.

Aidan groaned at the sight of the plate, and his sister Sorcha clapped her hands with glee. So did a few others who spied the fare. Lili had the feeling that everyone but her knew precisely what was on the plate and it looked foul indeed! Was this a joke? Did they intend to poison her now and send her body back to David as a message of import?

"Joy of the ground!" Una explained at Lili's look of confusion. The old woman's eyes twinkled knowingly. "An' ye *must* take one. Eat it all and ye'll ne'er ha'e need of a hearth to keep ye warm at night!" She cackled at her own jest and slapped her thigh, holding the tray up with one hand for Lili to have first choice.

Understanding the ribald jest, Lili glanced up at Aidan. The look in his green eyes challenged her, and she reached out to seize the smaller of the two before he could chance to take it, hoping to save herself from choking on the larger one. Ach, but thank God for the *uisge*! she thought now, and glanced down into her cup to be certain she had enough to chase the rotten houseleek.

"'Tis a lusty bride ye wed!" someone jested from the crowd as Una pushed the tray toward Aidan. The crowd answered with a bawdy laugh and Lili's cheeks flamed as Aidan accepted the remaining *delicacy* with a smirk, eyeing her over the *treat*. But then he faced her as though waiting to see what she would do with hers.

Lili held up the foul-looking houseleek between them, taking some small comfort in the fact that if they had wished to poison her, they probably wouldn't have gone through so much trouble to dress her before the ceremony. And yet, upon closer inspection, she was horrified to spy something moving.

"To wedded bliss," Aidan challenged, and the slow grin that spread across his face transformed his features before her eyes, giving him a rather boyish appearance.

The sight of his smile, meant only for her, fairly stole Lili's breath away. Sucking in a breath, she held the houseleek up, and thought for certain she felt something wriggle against her thumb. She tried not to grimace. "And this will provide wedded bliss?"

His grin widened, revealing the white glint of his teeth. "If ye dare?"

Betrayed by her woman's heart and her body, a tiny thrill tickled down her spine. God forgive her, but she could not claim she did not anticipate his touch. A more handsome man she had never known. *What would it be like to lay with him?* Without thinking, she peered down below his belt and shivered, and she looked up to find Aidan staring at her, waiting... smiling...

She peered at the foul houseleek, mustering her nerve. By God, if it was proof he needed of her willingness to wed him, there could be no greater proof than this. Taking a deep breath, she swallowed the houseleek whole, and then drained her cup behind it, not daring to linger over the taste or texture. Ach, but it was pickled, and something did indeed squirm upon her tongue!

Aidan swallowed his leek whole, and another cheer rang through the gathering.

Once they were done, Una smiled and hobbled away with her staff and her empty tray, nodding her head in approval.

Lili felt heady from the drink, her body warmed despite the chill of night in the air. But from that moment on, she could no longer put the bedding out of her mind. Thoughts of lying in Aidan's bed filled her with a titillating warmth that transcended the effects of the *uisge*, for while the *uisge* warmed her breast, the thought of lying beneath his warrior's body, warmed her in far deeper places. Now despite that she told herself it was part of the role she must play, she could not bring herself to think beyond that moment when he would make her his own.

To her surprise, instead of joining his men to share bawdy jests, Aidan remained by her side, introducing her to kinsmen she had not yet met. She spoke to them politely and with a sense of confidence she scarcely felt.

Glenna's son came wrapped in a warm plaid, on the shoulders of one called Lachlann, with Glenna accompanying the brawny warrior.

"Lachlann says the faeries left auld Morag's cheese only for me," the lad bragged. "To make me strong again, and look!" He fortified his muscles, looking fierce, although his face was still wan, and there was a fine sheen of sweat upon his upper lip despite the cool night air.

Lili was certain Glenna had read her thoughts. "We brought him only to pay his respects to his new lady," she offered with a smile, and a curtsy, though it was not a gesture of obeisance—more a playful show between friends, which it seemed they were fast becoming.

Lili could not allow herself to feel guilty. To save her own son, she had no choice.

She smiled at the boy, and reached up to feel his forehead, an automatic gesture. It was cool to the touch. "Ye are braw, for certain," she told him, grinning back at him, "and one more night of rest will see ye e'en more so."

The boy nodded, smiling. "That's what me minny said, too, but Lachlann said he dinna mind the load e'en though I am big for eight!"

Glenna touched the warrior gently upon the arm, a tender gesture of thanks, and the man did not miss it. He peered down at the child's mother, his look gentle, despite his size, and then looked toward Lili and winked and said, "'Tis glad I am no' to have the chief competing o'er the lasses anymore."

Acutely aware of the way her new husband observed her every move, listened to her every word, Lili laughed nervously.

Aidan suddenly bent to whisper into her ear as Glenna, Lachlann and her son moved on. "My kinsmen crave ye to be true," he said. "See that ye dinna play them false."

It was a swift reminder that no matter how real it all seemed, this was no true match and her husband did not trust her. "I wish only for peace," Lili insisted, and it was true, for she wished with all her heart that peace would be their conclusion.

But it would not. She knew that only too well.

The look in her eyes gave Aidan the impression she meant every word she spoke, and in that instant he wanted desperately to believe her.

Despite that it was his wedding, he knew there was much he should be doing, aside from standing here ogling his bride, but he found himself entranced by the sight of her, the subtle movements of her brow... her mouth... the gentle turn of her lips. And when she smiled, he liked the way she turned her head ever so shyly—like a sweet child.

But she was no child.

With the advantage of his height, the view he had of her lovely breasts was unbearably delicious—particularly for a man who had not lain with a woman in far too long. The neckline of her gown was not nearly as revealing as the one she had arrived in, but it taunted him just the same. It seemed every move she made, every word she uttered, only served to undermine his resolve to resist her, and that truth settled poorly in his gut.

Or mayhap it was simply Una's pickled houseleek—nasty fare!

By the gods of his ancestors, it was his duty to remain strong and vigilant... but at this moment, Aidan had no notion where Rogan was, nor the milksop priest, nor the men who had escorted them. For that matter, he hadn't seen Lael all evening, although it was certain she was somewhere in the vicinity. He had eyes only for his bride. For all he knew, Cailin and Keane could be preparing to blow the kegs once more, but he couldn't bring himself to care.

Lili had come to him, not in her lavish *Sassenach* gown, but in the simple woolen dress his mother had worn when she'd wed his Da. Gone was her MacLaren cloak, and in its place she wore an arisaid woven solely of his colors—a gift from Glenna, no doubt, which only served to illustrate how much Glenna's heart had turned toward the lass.

Forsooth, his wife was a bloody sorceress, it was true, for she was bewitching him even as she stood beside him in utter silence. And she did indeed share Sorcha's freckles, though Lili's were barely visible, as though she'd outgrown them. The elusive scent of roses drifted to his nostrils, and he yearned to bury his nose in the lustrous strands of her hair to see if that's where the scent originated. "I ken that David's hand is well played," he told her. "In truth, I dinna believe in sorcery, Lili, but your beauty is no less a curse."

Lili peered at her husband in surprise.

The tone of his voice was not rude at all but his words seemed intended to be. And judging by the look in his eyes, she thought mayhap his own words had taken him a little by surprise, and that he had merely spoken his mind, for if aught, his tone and expression now seemed more plaintive than anything else.

Could it be his backhand way of complimenting her perhaps?

The thought that he might actually desire her sent a tiny frisson of both fear and excitement racing down her spine. Never mind that she had convinced herself she dreaded their coupling. The fluttering in her breast named her a liar. Aye, for considering his dismissal of her yesterday and his angry words this morning, she had thought him completely immune to whatever it was that other men seemed to find attractive about her. She had not even felt such a heady rush over Stuart's flirtations.

The sound of the reed lifted somewhere in the night, haunting and melodic. Her senses were dimmed and heightened both at once—the *uisge*, no doubt—or mayhap 'twas the pickled houseleek, for while it seemed that Lili only played at magic, she sensed the old woman harbored ancient secrets in those unnaturally green eyes.

Why she was driven to answer as she did, Lili had no idea, but she dared to flirt with her husband. She arched a brow. "And here I thought ye were brave to wed a cursed lass... do ye tell me now, Husband, that ye dinna believe your own wives' tales?"

His green eyes reflected the flames, turning more gold than green... like those of a wolf's, and a tiny, feral smile turned the corners of his mouth. He said, without much heat to his words, "The only tale *my* wife should tell is the truth, and if that not be the case, she will find herself accursed in truth."

Lili turned away.

How quickly they veered from compliments to threats. And yet somehow she felt a little less nervous with the knowledge that he was not immune to her. Still... her purpose here was becoming all the more confused, for despite that she told herself she was simply playing her role, nothing in her life had ever felt more real than this—from the desire she spied in his gold-flecked eyes, to the danger she sensed lurking just beneath the gentle warning. Something compelled her to warn him as well, for what if it were true? What if he grew to love her? What if she buried yet another husband? Then again, she would bury him anyway. At least this way she could lay the blame at someone else's feet.

"Tisna me who ever claimed I was cursed," she reminded him, meeting his gaze once more. "Still, I have already seen one husband put beneath the ground."

"Is that a warning, *mo cridhe?*"

Aidan watched her expression, trying to read her.

Her lovely breasts rose with the catch of her breath and her eyes flickered with recognition of the affectionate words he used. *My heart.* For, aye, it seemed she was weaseling her way into his, despite the careful guard he kept.

And yet ... strip away their associations, and they were

much the same, he mused. They both hailed from the same past, the same proud nation. Only her kinsmen took another path, while his yet another. Dressed now as she was, with her hair adorned by a circlet of silver, bearing his howling wolf's head device, there was nothing left to remind him of her ties to Scotia, and certainly not to England. How much of her heredity was gone by now, he wondered, supplanted by *Sassenach* customs? For what else was Scotia now but an arm of England? He wondered: Was there aught left of her Pecht heritage? In truth, she might have been fully Gael, but cloaked in his colors, with her dark hair sweeping into the night, and her face kissed by the firelight, she looked more like a Pecht queen.

"Nay," she replied finally, her voice no more than a whisper. "No warning."

God's truth, but he had forgotten that he'd even spoken so enraptured was he with her beauty. Her violet eyes sparred with his, challenging him at some deeper level, unknowingly feeding his carnal hunger, for the desire to possess his wife, body and soul, became tangible in that instant. The need to hear his name whispered upon her lips was undeniable. Only one thing was certain: He desired her with a hunger that he wondered could ever be sated.

All sounds faded for the space of a breath, and it seemed the world paused. Even the breeze broke, as though the gods themselves held their breaths to see what he might do... and still she would not look away.

"Take heed, *sùilean gorm*, if you continue to look at me just so, I will take it as an invitation."

He'd called her *Blue Eyes*.

Lili blinked, unable to look away.

The beat of her heart quickened and her palm felt sticky against the cup in her hand. Suddenly, as though fed by the passion ignited between them, the fire beside them seemed to surge, burning hot, dancing wildly. Flecks of golden ash rained down from the night sky.

"Drink up," he said softly, eyeing the wooden cup in her hand.

He quaffed the rest of his own, and called out to the crowd, "*Slàinte mhòr agad!*"—*Great health to you all*—and then he tossed his wooden cup into the writhing flames and looked into her eyes.

Lili shivered, but held his gaze.

There was no way to avoid what she sensed was to come, though come what may, she vowed to do this on her own terms. Shuddering at his intense look, she did as he bade her, drinking full half a cup, and then she too threw her cup into the bonfire.

Suddenly without warning, Aidan lifted her into his arms and raised her high, exclaiming to one and all. "*Oidhche math!*"

Just like that, he bade them all good night.

EIGHTEEN

The night grew dark as they slipped away from the bonfire.

The sound of revelry faded behind them and Lili's heart beat a staccato in her head. With every step her husband took, she imagined herself closer to the black sin that would condemn her soul to hell.

Aye, but dinna think of that just now.

Aidan spoke not a word as he whisked her down the long pier toward the *crannóg*. In the darkness, the pitch torches roared past her ears, the winking of flames scant competition for the glowing stars in the clear night sky, although were it not for the torches, the hall itself would have been immersed in blackness—swallowed by the bottomless darkness of the loch.

Silent and surefooted, Aidan bore her inside the hall, passing through the dimly lit room, and toward the laird's chamber, where she had slept the night before. And then, once inside the laird's bedchamber, he set her down upon her feet.

She felt dizzy and cold, her fingers icy and trembling.

In anticipation of the bedding perhaps, the brazier had been lit and the fire gave off a tawny glow but failed to warm the room. Unattended fires were not prudent in this wooden fortress, and this one was barely a flicker.

Tonight, the shutters were closed against the night sky—as though he would keep all that transpired in this room a secret wholly unto themselves. The thought gave Lili a shiver of trepidation, for now was the moment when she would discover whether her husband was a savage or a gentle man. There were dark promises in his eyes that she could not read.

He closed the door gently and went to the brazier, stoking the flames, and for a long moment, silence permeated the room, the pop of green firewood the only sound that dared to defy the quiet. Her head swam a little—the effects of the *uisge* no doubt, but she was glad for the heady brew for it gave her a courage she might not otherwise feel. No matter that she told herself she was not afraid, her shivers betrayed her.

Divesting himself, he hung his claymore on two pegs upon the wall—clearly, he did not sleep with it. And with quiet precision, he set his dirk aside as well, and proceeded to remove his breacan and tunic, tossing them to one side upon the floor, away from brazier lest they catch a spark from the flames. Then he lingered by the fire to stoke the embers, completely naked save for his boots.

Silhouetted by the firelight, he stood with his back to her, unashamed. His shoulders were wide and muscled and the firelight danced upon his swarthy skin. Lili had certainly seen him bare-shouldered before, but unpainted in the soft light, this was far more intimate. One long scar ran across his left shoulder and another lower at his side. His buttocks were strong and lean, the muscles flexing as he moved the poker about the brazier.

Shivering softly, Lili told herself it was the cold, but even now she was growing warmer as she watched. And then he turned to face her suddenly, and she gasped, her eyes widening of their own accord, for he was somewhat *larger* than she had anticipated, despite that he was not yet fully aroused. Lili swallowed convulsively.

"Now, my little dove, we will discover how willingly you come to me."

Lili tried hard to still her tremors. "W-why must you doubt me? I spoke the same vows as you."

He chuckled low, but there was little mirth in the sound. "Why indeed."

It wasn't a question.

He strolled to the bed while Lili remained precisely where he had set her down by the door, and he sat down to unlace his boots. All the while, Lili watched, wide-eyed and shivering every so oft as he made quick work of unlacing his ties. She blinked, and one boot came off. He tossed that aside with a thump, and began to unlace the other, eyeing her all the while. "In all my years I have ne'er taken a woman unwilling, Lili. I'll na begin now."

By all that was virtuous, she was quaking like a virgin, and he sought to put her at ease. "Tell me true... did you wed once and bear a child?" Since she had arrived without her son, there was no proof of that, save the word of men Aidan did not trust. To look at her simply belied the fact, for even wrapped in her new arisaid, he could make out the lithe form of her body.

She lifted her chin and pulled the arisaid more tightly around her shoulders. "I-I did."

Aidan frowned, for the gesture meant she either feared him—although he'd given her no true reason to as yet—or she did not wish to lie with him.

Both scenarios displeased him.

She was his wife now, but Aidan would never force himself upon any woman, not for any reason. Not for peace between nations. Certainly not for any alliance with David. Not even to prove to himself that he was immune to the plea he spied in those violet eyes.

"I will ask you only once more... is this..." He gestured at the bed, lest she mistake him. "... your will, *mo cridhe?*"

Her eyes darkened to black in the shadows of the room, and her voice trembled but she answered him at once. "I have said... many times now... aye." And yet she clutched the arisaid more tightly to her breast, her knuckles whitening over the effort of holding the wool closed.

"Then prove it," he demanded.

She seemed startled by the challenge, but Aidan merely sat,

waiting for her response, determined to make her show him. "W-What would you have me do?" She swallowed visibly.

Like a poppet on a string, his cock stirred between his legs. "To begin with, you might speak my name... once... so I may cease to think of this as a business arrangement."

"I f-fail to see why one should preclude the other," she told him. But despite the mettle in her words, she stammered, and his lips curved a little, admiring her.

He considered her answer a long moment, and then nodded, acknowledging the fact as truth. In this, he must give her leeway, for he could not expect her to declare affection for him in the meager time since he had known her. As yet, there had been little enough tenderness between them, but he would remedy that at once. His own vow to steel his heart against his Scoti bride was forgotten for the instant.

Even frightened as she seemed, her eyes challenged him and her posture remained proud. He sensed something in her that sent his pulses racing and his blood singing through his veins. She would not be easily won, but she would be worth every ounce of patience he could muster.

He had been told he was a tender lover, and if he was, it was because he could not rouse himself with unrequited passion. Whatever war they might be waging outside this room, he would not carry it within his bed. "I would see you," he demanded. "Let go of your shield, warrior maid."

Lili blinked in confusion. "My shield?"

He smiled darkly, and said, "The arisaid. If you come to my bed of your own free will, I would see you walk to me in the glory you were made."

Lili's head swam. Forsooth, it seemed his entire demeanor had changed once he'd closed the bedroom door. Drawn to the heat of the fire, she moved closer to the brazier, unmindful that by doing so, she would offer him a clearer view.

But something in his gaze compelled her.

The hunger she spied in his eyes emboldened her. Whether it was the *uisge* or something else, she didn't know, because she had never been so immoderate even in Stuart's presence, but she suddenly loosened her hold upon the arisaid, her breath catching nervously. Something about the appreciative gleam in his eye persuaded her to drop the cloak more effortlessly than the hot fire blazing at her back. It fell to the floor with a soft whoosh, and then she stood there for his appraisal, her breath trapped painfully in her breast.

And still he waited, not stirring from the bed where he sat, apparently unwilling to breach the distance between them. She might have thought he was displeased, save for the look of desire in his eyes. Seduced by that look, she reached for the hem of her gown and pulled it up and over her head, allowing the soft wool to float down to the cloak at her feet. And then she stood there, cool air kissing her skin, pebbling her nipples. The fire warmed her bottom.

It was the longest seconds of her life.

Aidan sucked in a breath at what she had revealed to him.

His eyes, greedy for the sight of her, swept the length of her body, and his breath caught in his lungs.

Her limbs were limned by the firelight, her hips painted with tawny light. And though he could not quite see her eyes now for the firelight blinding him, his gaze was drawn at once to the apex between her thighs, where the golden flames licked between her legs. His mouth watered as he thought of putting his tongue there, and his cocked stirred once again, stiffening against his thigh. "Ye are lovely," he said at last, lest she mistake his reluctance to go to her. He needed to know beyond a shadow of doubt that she accepted him of her own accord.

"As are you," she returned, and it took Aidan a little by surprise. He chuckled low, inordinately pleased that she thought so, no matter that he had never considered his countenance before now. Her nipples hardened before his eyes, and points of light danced before his eyes, but not even the *uisge* could have kept him from hardening fully at the sight of her tentative smile. His shaft sprang forward like that of a beardless youth's, ready to pounce.

Still he didn't move.

He waited.

The circlet of silver remained in her hair, and she looked like a princess standing there with her chestnut waves shining by the firelight.

"What more must I do to prove myself?" she asked softly, and Aidan could not help himself. His hand sought his shaft, craving her touch, but he stroked it merely once, and shuddered, holding it firmly within his fist as he enjoyed the sight of his lovely bride naked by the fire. "Come here, Lili," he said, and shuddered with barely restrained ardor.

Lili's heart thumped like drums beating against her ribs.

She saw where his hand went, and was shocked by the complete lack of inhibition. There was nothing diffident about her husband's manner. And yet, he seemed completely restrained, hardly showing any reaction save for that small gesture.

The fire warmed her bottom, but the desire in his eyes started yet another flame, one that flickered in the deepest recesses of her body. Even before she took a step, her body convulsed in secret places, startling her with the reaction, for this was not anything she recalled from her first coupling with Stuart. Her first husband had been a mass of groping limbs in the cold darkness.

Nay, this was something far, far different.

As though carrying her with a will of their own, her feet padded across the wooden floor, closing the distance between them. And then she stood before him, and still he refrained from touching her, until the tips of her breasts ached from the cold... or more... with the need to be touched by his warm, strong hands.

After a moment, he reached up to pluck the silver circlet from her hair, gently working it free of her pins. He tossed it on the far side of the bed. His eyes pierced her and he spoke low and soft, full of calm. "If 'tis your will, you may turn and walk out that door, Lili—this moment—and I would gladly send you home with men aplenty to see you safely to your door."

God help her, but Lili didn't wish to go.

"If you do not," he warned. "If you stay, if you lie beneath me... I will never ever let you go. Do ye ken?"

Like a flash of lightning, Kellen's face appeared before her. Rogan's threats accosted her, along with all the promises she had made. There was no doubt by the look in her husband's eyes that he meant every word he spoke.

"Do ye ken?" he persisted.

Lili nodded, her heart hammering.

But there was only one path for her to take now. Precisely where it would lead she could not know. For answer, she dared to reach out, setting her hand to his cheek and he turned his face into her palm, groaning deep in the back of his throat ...

NINETEEN

Aidan could not see her eyes to know how she took his warning.

He half expected her to dress herself and leave, half expected her to respond with practiced words of reassurance, but he did not quite expect the response she gave.

Ach, he'd meant to let her set the pace tonight, but when she touched his face, all reason fled. His arms went about her waist and he drew her into his embrace, pressing his lips against her warm, sweet breasts. The scent of her was intoxicating—clean woman and flowers.

His tongue ventured out of its own accord to lap the salt of her flesh and he found her skin sweet and soft. "I am bewitched," he murmured beneath his breath. "I have never desired a woman so much…"

Hearing the passion in his words, Lili shuddered against the warmth of his embrace. His fingers splayed across her back, pulling her toward him eagerly to suckle at her breasts. The intimate gesture shocked her for only her babe had ever suckled there. Her cheeks flamed, the warmth pale in comparison to the heat that was now growing in her womb. She made some keening sound that was alien to her own ears, and her head fell back in abandon. She cried out softly as his teeth gently nipped at one nipple, pressing gently but greedily.

Confusion muddled her brain, for his touch was far too

gentle to be that of her enemy—and yet that was how she *must* see him, or she was truly doomed to fail.

Suddenly he lay back upon the bed, pulling her atop him.

Gasping in surprise, Lili let herself go.

Was she such a wanton that she could desire her enemy so much? That she could grow wet for his touch? To her dismay, she felt the dampness between her legs as he positioned her so that she straddled his belly.

Behind them, the firelight provided the only light in the room and the bed dwarfed even her husband. She blocked the light from his face, but she could still spy the gleam in his eyes, until he closed them again, groaning as his head fell back, baring his neck to her. Were she a practiced assassin, she might have slit his throat right then and ended it all, but she was not, and she was beginning to doubt that she would ever be so bold. Nor could she find it in her heart to wish to carry out such a sin.

Aidan tried in vain to constrain himself.

He willed his heartbeat to still, but his breath remained imprisoned in his lungs and he groaned as her hand splayed gently upon his chest. He laid his head back and peered up at her, bemused, holding her wrist firmly in an attempt to clear his lust-fogged brain. But then he felt her wetness kissing his belly and his shaft hardened completely, rising up against the warmth of her buttocks. He was lost then, from that moment forward.

If he hadn't already been so mindful of his response to her, he might have spilled his seed then and there. But despite that it had been so long since he'd lain with a woman, or since he had pleasured himself, he was not a boy and would not allow himself to relieve himself as one.

Nay, but when he found release, it would be within the depths of her sweet body and he wanted to feel her womb embrace him as a lover. He wanted to plant his seed there. And aye, he'd meant everything he'd said, for the instant it became a possibility that she might carry his bairn, he would never release her from their vows. If it be within his power, no babe of his would make their way into this world without him to protect and guide him.

"Ride me, Lili," he commanded.

For an instant, Lili had no idea what it was he was asking of her. But his shaft twitching insistently against her backside was an immediate clue. Her heart hammered in her breast as she realized what he meant for her to do.

It was utterly shocking—nothing in her wildest dreams could have prepared her for this coupling. But there was a part of her that reveled in his request, knowing instinctively that he was offering her control over the coupling—over him.

He shifted beneath her, and Lili swallowed, feeling suddenly as brazen as she had ever felt. Her heart beat mercilessly as she repositioned her weight, rising to allow his shaft beneath her, and then, although she had never done this before, she followed her instinct, shifting her weight forward again so that she lay as though over the withers of a mount. She didn't give herself time to think about the size of him, or the feel of him begging entrance. She tilted her hips to accept him, and pressed down, sheathing him fully and crying out at the delicious feel of his hot, soft flesh within her body.

Aidan too cried out, a guttural moan, and closed his eyes only an instant, but he reopened them, and demanded once more, "Ride me, Lili."

Lili did not need to be asked again. Feeling heady in a way the *uisge* alone could never have accomplished, she rode astride his body, arching over the thickness of him caressing her from the inside. He filled her so completely, his body tensing as she rode him, and in that instant she sensed the dominion he had given her over him—as a woman—as his wife.

His gaze glittered like green diamonds through the shadows, and his eyes were dazed and filled with pleasure as she continued to stroke him with her body, coaxing his male gift into her womb. Her skin prickled with pleasure and her body convulsed around him, conveying promises of something more... something mysterious... something magical. Seated atop him, bared to his eyes, with the firelight dancing upon their bodies, she felt transformed somehow, no longer a pawn in the games of men. And in that instant, she dared to think of nothing more than the man who lay beneath her, not the sins she must somehow commit, nor of how she might feel tomorrow. In the instant, she only cared about how she felt... how he made her feel... how she might please him.

His hands crept up her waist, cupping her breasts, kneading softly and arching into his hands, Lili rode until her body was covered with a thin sheen of sweat. From somewhere deep within her, a thread began to uncoil and suddenly she was no longer concerned with the sway she held over Aidan, for his pleasure gave way to her own.

In all her life she would never have imagined that it could feel so good to be filled so completely by a man.

She looked like a goddess atop him, her body writhing before the firelight, a pagan dance as old as time. A lustrous sheen of sweat covered her creamy skin and Aidan could suddenly not bear to allow her to keep her pace. In one swift motion, he repositioned her beneath him, and pulled his shaft out far enough so that he could peer into her eyes.

She cried out, her nails digging into his flesh, urging him back and his heart hammered in his ears. The tip of his shaft throbbed but he held back nevertheless, wanting her to open her eyes and see him first.

Once she realized he would not budge, she lifted her hips into his pelvis, seeking him, throwing her legs around his thighs. She opened her eyes and Aidan reveled in the feel of her legs wrapped around him.

This was the moment he had been waiting for.

Though her eyes were glazed with passion, he wanted her to know beyond a shadow of doubt who was taking her now. He wanted her to realize that from this moment forth she was his, and his alone. "I will give you sons," he whispered hoarsely, surging down against her, the motion slow and calculated.

"Aye!" she cried softly.

"And daughters," he said, withdrawing a bit to tease her.

"Oh, nay!" she cried again, and dug her nails into his shoulders, as though she would prevent him from leaving her.

"*Buin mo chridhe dhuit!*" he whispered, and then words were no longer welcome.

She cried out once more as he thrust deep, seeking her womb. Mindless with the need for release, he rode hard, filling her completely. She met his every thrust as though she understood his words, accepting him fully and with equal passion. Their coupling was fierce, neither relinquishing control, their bodies battling for that heady thread of pleasure. When at last Lili's body convulsed beneath him, and she cried out, Aidan spilled his seed into her womb, though even then he did not stop. He rocked against her gently, taking immense pleasure in the way she spread her legs for him, like a flower opening to the sun.

Lili's senses scattered, her inhibitions completely swept away by the pleasure his body provided. She wanted him deeper still, deeper despite that she had already discovered the mysteries he had promised. She moaned softly, marveling that even though she'd already felt the heat of his seed inside her, he would not stop. He groaned as though in pain, but continued, as though taking pleasure in the simple act of loving her.

Sated, she released him, letting her arms fall to the bed, enjoying the way he loved her so thoroughly...

She sighed contentedly for his words still rang in her ears... words not even Stuart had uttered—not in any language.

My heart belongs to you.

She didn't say it in return, but in that instant, everything changed... *everything.* For no longer could she be his enemy. He was no longer hers.

TWENTY

The chances of the boy surviving the fall off the cliff were minimal, but the urge to slip away to make certain he was dead was unbearable. Still, Rogan resisted, unwilling to undermine his own efforts.

He had taken great pains to be noticed all evening by Aidan's clansmen, knowing that the instant they found the lad's broken body they would naturally seek someone to blame. They would look first to their unwanted guests. Lili's whereabouts had been accounted for all day and night, so she would not suffer their accusations. His own men, all of them, had remained by his side, and Rogan had slipped away barely long enough to follow the boy and shove him off the cliff, then he had returned straightaway. Not even Rogan's own men were wise to him—they thought he'd gone to take a piss. Stupid Aveline had been with Lili and the women.

If the boy should survive, he doubted the lad could name him, but with long hours gone now since he had pushed him over the cliff, his survival seemed every moment more doubtful.

Arrogant little twit.

He'd caught the boy watching the women—so intently that he hadn't even realized he had an audience himself... not even in the end. It had been far too simple. All Rogan had had to do was slip up behind him and give him a good shove.

The lad had been standing by the edge, watching the women walk up the hill. His cry of alarm had been muffled by the roar of the waterfall, and not even the lass whose arse wiggled for the boy while she'd walked away had realized. By the time she had turned around to see if he was still watching, both Rogan and the boy were gone, and for all Rogan knew the lad had drowned instead of breaking his neck. He hadn't even taken the time to peer over the cliff side to see where the bastard had landed.

With eyes that burned from standing too close to the fire—so that everyone would see him clearly—he watched Aidan bear *his bride* away, unmindful of anything but the woman in his arms. He watched until they disappeared into the black hole that was his hall, rage threatening to snap his ribs and rip his chest in two.

Once they were gone, his gaze returned to the fire where he watched the last of Lili's cup be devoured by the flames.

The whore had had eyes only for the dún Scoti all night, not once looking in Rogan's direction—as though she'd all but forgotten his presence here at Dubhtolargg. He felt his control of her slipping quickly away, and his gaze fell to Aveline at his side.

Mute, for there were too many ears about, he waited for Aveline to look at him and pierced her with a glare, warning her without words to stay true to his plan. God's teeth, but he could not even afford to step away into the shadows with her, not even to relieve the terrible anger that was welling up within his breast. He plucked the wildflower out of her greasy hair—the same flower all the women wore as well—and crushed it within his fists.

"You are not one of them," he apprised her, whispering near her ear. "You'd do well to remember that when I am gone."

Aveline nodded, peering down at her feet.

Still Rogan was not appeased, because no matter what he might gain after all was said and done he could not bear the simple fact that Lileas MacLaren would sooner open her legs to a savage than to share his bed or name. With barely restrained violence, he tossed the crushed yellow blossom from Aveline's hair into the flames.

Aye, but in the end, victory would be his.

* * *

Sated and comfortable lying beside his bride, Aidan closed his eyes, remembering the way it had felt to move inside her. He continued to brush his fingers across her belly, reveling in the feel of her soft skin against his callused fingertips. She had given equal measure, rising to his every challenge, and he was pleased to the core of his being.

She lifted sleepy lids. "You have scars on your back … what are they from?"

Aidan smiled softly. "I learned not to anger Lael at a verra young age," he lied. Now was not the time to reveal that he had earned them the night Padruig Caimbeul had murdered his father and raped his mother. Padruig's men had restrained him, forcing him to watch her father defile his mother. And then when Padruig was finished, her father's men had plunged their daggers into his back—two at once—then left him for dead.

"I fear she doesna like me much."

He spied the worry in her gaze and knew it was genuine. "Gi' her time," he advised. "My sister's loyalty is no' so easily won, but when she gives it, she will give it wholly."

He lifted a hand to her cheek, caressing her face with a thumb. "Ye truly are beautiful, Lili—particularly when ye smile. I would see that ye do so often."

She turned to face him, lying on her side, her violet eyes glistening. Though her words did not match the touch of sorrow he spied in her eyes. "If ye love me often as ye did tonight, I willna be able to help it. They'll think me mad and call me a *loon*."

Aidan laughed. "There are many things they may call you, *mo chridhe*, but *òinseach* is not one."

She nodded, and then closed her eyes. "Do ye truly believe peace is possible betwixt us?"

Aidan considered the question, and the woman cozied in his bed. She was hardly what he had expected. He didn't fool himself into believing the man who had stood smirking over his father's body with a bloodied blade slung over his shoulder, could regret his betrayal and deception of a people he clearly despised, but mayhap there was hope despite everything?

He waited so long to answer that he thought she might have fallen asleep. "Aye," he said finally, and her lips turned upward at the corners and she sighed and relaxed.

After awhile, Aidan dared to relax as well, and consider that mayhap, in truth, this marriage could buy his kinsmen peace for a time.

Could he afford to take David at his word? Even after David had stolen his sister Catriona and spirited her south? In the man's defense, he had intended, he'd said, to wed Cat to an ally in the name of peace. But Catriona would never have been happy as the wife of an Englishman, or even a border lord. In truth, she might have cut off her husband's bollocks and served it to him in his soup. None of his sisters would easily accept such a fate—least of all Lael or Cat.

He lay in the darkness, thinking that it was past time to get up and stoke the fire lest his lovely wife perish of cold while lying naked in their bed. But he lingered, contented and languorous, thinking in that moment of his sister Cat and the man she had wed: Gavin mac Brodie... brother to a chieftain with fealties to no one but his immediate kin. At least he was a Highlander. Aidan's people had never crossed swords with anyone from that region of the Highlands. Like his own kinsmen, the mac Brodies and MacKinnons kept mostly to themselves, despite the fact that the MacKinnon had blood ties purer than most to the Ailpín line. Like Aidan, he simply seemed to wish to live his life free of strife. Still, the MacKinnon called himself a Scot. So did Gavin mac Brodie, for that matter.

So did his beautiful wife.

What of their babe? The children of their union. Would they any longer be worthy of the Pecht name?

They were saving the real stone for a rightful king, but what if their time had passed? By accepting Lili as his bride, he had, in effect, put an end to their pristine bloodline. Unless he relinquished leadership to Keane when the time came... His people had become a final bastion in a world that was quickly coming to an end. If he felt ambivalent about their purpose, it was mostly because of that, he supposed. The customs of his people were going the way of his faith.

Una claimed this woman at his side would be their salvation... could she perhaps be his as well?

As he lay there studying the perfect arch of his wife's brow and the fullness of her lips, he was startled by an urgent knock at the bedroom door.

The sharp sound of rapping boomed through the chamber.

Startled as well, Lili bolted upright.

The hour was late, and the urgent sound could only mean one thing: Something terrible had happened. She gave Aidan a questioning look.

Aidan arose from the bed and Lili scrambled for the covers. Without bothering to dress himself, he went straight for the door, cracking it open to peer outside. She heard a fervent female whisper, but couldn't make out the voice or comprehend the fevered words spoken so low. Her husband turned to pierce her with a look that sent a cold shiver down her spine. "Dress yourself!" he commanded, and then threw open the door, completely unmindful of the woman who stood outside—or the one in his bed.

But his sister Lael was hardly concerned with her brother's state of dress. Her gaze sought Lili's and the fury Lili spied there shriveled her tongue. She might have asked what was wrong, but before she could even pull herself together, Lael spun and walked away.

Aidan dressed quickly, eschewing the tunic and simply wrapped himself in his breacan. He followed his sister out the door, but not before retrieving his claymore from where he'd hung it upon the wall. "Get dressed," he demanded again, this time without bothering to look at Lili. Neither did he bother with his boots, or spare Lili another glance to be sure she complied. He left her there with the door open wide to the cold, wondering what could have possibly happened. Apparently, he intended for her to follow, so she hurried to retrieve her clothing and dressed as quickly as she was able.

TWENTY-ONE

"They discovered him near Caoineag's Pool," Lachlann revealed when Aidan entered his brother's room.

Una was already at Keane's bedside, examining the wound on his head. "He is quite fortunate," she said gravely. "He has already awakened once, though just for an instant."

"Did he say aught?"

Lachlann shook his head.

"Who found him?"

"Meara," Lael replied, entering behind Aidan. "She couldn't find him at the bonfire, and went searching where she'd spied him last."

Aidan frowned.

"Apparently, he was watching the women bathe," Lachlann added.

Aidan shook his head and sighed, blaming himself for being so pre-occupied with his Scoti bride that he had completely neglected the safety of his family. He sat at the edge of his brother's bed, setting the claymore down at Keane's feet. "Where is Cailin?"

It was Lael who answered. "I sent her home with Fergus and Meara—to question the lass if she could. Meara was beside herself with grief after seeing so much blood, and since she saw naught, I dinna believe it was in her best interest—or

Keane's—to allow her in his room."

Aidan sighed again, the sound weary, as though he carried the burden of the world upon his broad shoulders. "What else do we know?"

"No' verra much," Lachlann replied. "I took Glenna and her son home. As I returned, Meara came shrieking like a banshee from the direction of the loch."

Aidan stared at his brother's still form, trying not to allow fear into his thoughts. Keane's body was bruised and bleeding, and he had a cut and whelp on his forehead nearly the size of Una's *keek stane*. But his breathing seemed stable. Keane was his only brother, but more than that, for the time being, he was Aidan's sole heir as well.

Aidan raked a hand through his hair, considering the tale Lachlann relayed. His brother had always been surefooted. That he would have slipped and fallen down any cliff was certainly possible, but not probable. "No one saw anything more?"

He was vaguely aware that all eyes turned toward the door, and no one answered him at once. He turned to see that Lili stood in the shadows of the hall, wringing her hands. She didn't speak, and for an instant, she didn't seem able to make herself enter the room, though thankfully Aidan didn't read any guilt in her vivid blue eyes, only dread and confusion. That fact eased him somewhat. He didn't want her to be involved in this.

Lili lingered in the doorway.

Even before she saw who it was in the bed, she feared the worst, realizing it must be one of Aidan's kin to have been brought within the *crannóg*. Even after her husband waved her inside the small room, she hesitated.

His eyes did not accuse her, but the energy in the room was black. Lili was very sensitive to the auras of others, for she was often sustained or diminished by them.

Una stood at the bedside, mumbling in the old tongue as she traced circles upon the boy's forehead. "Mother of all, we are One," she whispered. "Cease his pain, gi' him none."

By the light of a single fat pillar that was seated in an iron brace above Keane's bed, Lili spied a glimpse of his bloodied face, barely recognizable for the swelling.

If they would allow it, she might be able to help. She had worked very hard all her life to become more than simply a lovely face—the victim of some silly curse. She was well versed in the simples, but she had also studied the old ways and even had a rare manuscript of Byzantine medicines brought back by her grandsire from the Crusades.

"May I help?" she asked.

Lael's head turned in her direction. "I believe ye may have helped quite enough already!"

Aidan threw up a hand. "Enough! She has been with me all this night."

"Aye, and what of her companions?"

Aidan's gaze swept up to meet Lael's, one brow lifting. "What of them?"

Lachlann shook his head, denying the accusation. "They have all been accounted for all day and all night as well. Between the lot of us, we havena let a one out of our sight."

Aidan peered up at his sister, his voice brooking no argument. "Never make accusations without proof, Lael."

"Somehow I *know* they are responsible!" Lael persisted. "Keane is not a clumsy dolt, Aidan! He has climbed those bluffs a hundred times and more!"

Aidan turned to wave Lili into the room again, peering up at his sister, his mouth set in grim lines. "Nevertheless, I'llna allow ye to gainsay me. Show me proof, or gi' my wife the respect due her."

Lael threw her hands into the air. "Ach, ye're thinking with your willie no' your head, Aidan! One night spent in that witch's arms and already she's turned your brain to mash!" Clearly angry, she marched past Lili and out the door, bumping Lili's shoulder angrily.

Lili said nothing. She let the girl pass, and all the while Una listened quietly, watching everyone. Now she too urged Lili to come closer to the bed. This time Lili did as she was asked.

At the sight of Keane up close, she gasped. The left side of his head was distended and purple. His left eye was swollen closed and his hair was caked with blood. More blood was seeping from his nose.

"The injury to his head is grave," the old woman said softly. "I dinna believe he cracked his skull, but he has lost much blood. Come," she demanded. "Your healing skills are far greater than mine."

Lili wondered how the woman could possibly know such a thing.

Una merely smiled as though she'd read Lili's thoughts, and waved her closer still. "Take a look, lass. Tell us what must be done."

Lili hesitated, uncertain. She looked to Aidan first, to be certain he approved. Once he nodded, that was all she needed to know. As though she were suddenly possessed by someone else, she immediately set to work. Gone was her apprehension, all her timorous thoughts. In her place was the healer who had seen far worse than a boy with a bloodied head. She had seen a husband with an arrow through his eye, clear through his skull. She had sawed off arms and legs and had watched babes die whose bodies were covered with bulbous. She was hardly squeamish. She demanded hot water, blankets and needle and thread. She ordered the hefty Lachlann to help her strip Keane's clothing, and she urged her husband out of the way, making mental notes of all the herbs she must retrieve from her chest.

Aidan watched his wife work, marveling in the sudden change in her demeanor. She was suddenly far bossier than both Lael and Una put together. But he realized she was trying to help and she clearly knew what she was doing.

There was little he could do here but be in the way, so he left his brother's care to Lili and to Una, bidding Lachlann to come along once he was through divesting Keane. Finding Sorcha worrying in the hall, he sent his youngest sister into Keane's room as well, determined now to find out what had happened to his brother.

Lael was standing out upon the pier as though to bar the entrance within to any who might dare try. Her back was rigid and tense, and he made himself known as he came up the walk behind her, lest she spin about and cleave him in two with one of her angry blades. Her eyes slayed him though her hands remained clenched at her sides. "How can ye leave that woman with our brother?" she demanded at once.

"*That woman* is my wife and ye'd best come to terms with it."

"Ach, Aidan! How can ye trust her?"

"Una trusts her," Aidan countered, "That is enough for me."

And yet it wasn't, he realized, for if that were truly the case, he would not have sent his sister Sorcha into the room to watch over them. Despite that he had witnessed with his own two eyes what Lili could do—what she had been willing to do for a stranger on the first night of her arrival—he still did not trust her explicitly.

Doubts crept into his head, but he shoved them away.

On the beach, the bonfire raged, and many of his kinsmen lingered, despite that the revelry had long ceased. Now it seemed they were huddled about the fire, simply waiting for word from within.

Aidan ordered Lachlann who walked out of the *crannóg*, "Set guards upon the hall, then *escort* our *guests* to their beds. Assign as many men as can be spared to guard their door. Wherever they go—whatever they do—I want to know. I dinna want any o' them pissing without my knowledge!"

"What of the maid Aveline?" Lachlann asked.

"The *siùrsach* as well!" Aidan snapped, slipping past his sister. "You come with me, Lael!"

Grudgingly, his sister left her post and followed him down the narrow dock. With his sword, he snuffed the torches one by one as he passed, leaving the *crannóg* in utter darkness save for the faint light that emanated from within. From the shore, unless you knew precisely where the dock entrance was, it was impossible to find it without revealing your presence to the guards. "Where are we going?"

"To inspect the pool where Keane was found. I would know from whence he fell—and how." And aye, superstition or nay, some part of him must know if he could hear the

Weeper's wail. He could not bear to lose Keane now.

He was just a boy.

Sensing Aidan's distress, Lael's temper eased, trusting him to do what he must. She grudgingly admitted, "I too was watching the Scots. 'Tis true enough what Lachlann says. They were all accounted for, but one of them could have slipped away during the games?"

"Unless we can prove it," Aidan persisted, "we cannot risk the consequences were we to accuse one of David's men."

"Since when do you care about alliances with David?" Lael asked, keeping pace behind him as he left the dock.

His eyes cut through the darkness, spearing her. "You mistake me, Lael. I care no' one whit about alliances with David or anyone else. But I do not intend to bring war into this vale. There is too much to lose, lest ye forget?"

The stone.

They both understood that's what he was speaking of.

It had been their duty all these years, not to rise above other tribes, but to safeguard the stone, for inasmuch as it held the power to unite nations, if it fell into the wrong hands, its possession would only lead to more bloodshed. Many would covet it, only one could truly wield it.

Lael fell into silence at his side.

TWENTY-TWO

With Sorcha and Una's help, Lili cleansed Keane's wound as best she could, then stitched it and applied salve. As she had for Duncan, she burned juniper to ward away infection in the air, and then she sent Sorcha after *vin aigre*. Leaving Una alone with Keane, she went after her medicines herself, wholly aware of how close she had come to being discovered last time. Particularly now with suspicion hovering like a shadow over them all, she could not risk that someone might discover the ring. Returning to the room, she overheard a snippet of conversation from the hall.

"Mayhap the one to follow me, Sorcha, will not be you."

"Lili? But she's Aidan's—"

"Aye, but I had a husband once, too."

They might have said more, but Lili came hurrying through the door, mindful that she could not waste any time, even for eavesdropping where it might aid her. But she wondered what Una could have meant. As she prepared her herbs, she couldn't help but consider the old woman with a husband and children and the image completely escaped her. Somehow, Una seemed as ancient as time itself. But that was a ridiculous notion, for she was clearly flesh and blood—why would the woman lie? If she said she'd once had a husband, then certainly she must have had a husband.

One thing was certain, however: If Keane died, Lili would

not be the only one to come under scrutiny. So whatever she could do to prevent it, she must. And as soon as she had a few moments to herself, she must find a place to better hide the ring until she had need of it. She didn't dare consider the simple truth... that she would not use it. God's truth, if she had wondered before tonight, she no longer did. She could no more murder Aidan—or any other human being—than she could allow this boy to die. What that meant for her own son she didn't know, but as she stitched the cut on Keane's forehead, she realized the truth.

There must be some other way.

When she had done everything she knew to do, save one last thing, she hesitated but a moment. She had recognized the strange gestures Una had made when she'd first come into the room, and knew the old woman would not question what she was about to do. But this was not a thing she risked doing before others—certainly not before her father or Rogan. And yet she trusted both Sorcha and Una to understand that she meant Keane no harm. It might be little more than ceremony, but where there were lives at stake, Lili would employ all avenues available to her, even those of a more spiritual nature.

She sat down on the bed beside Keane, placing a small candle she'd found in Keane's room on the right side of the boy's bed. And then peering back to see that both Una and Sorcha were watching her closely, she nevertheless placed her hand, palm up, and closed her eyes to concentrate, visualizing bright white light forming within her hand—the light of healing—drawing out all pain, impurity and injury. Behind her lids, she concentrated hard, forming the brightest glowing. After a moment, Lili's hand began to tingle and she turned it upside down and covered the wound upon Keane's head. And then concentrating again until she felt the light wane, she then closed her fist and placed it over the unlit candle, and whispered, "I consecrate this candle as a tool for healing." Then she lit the candle and without daring to turn to look at the expressions upon the faces of her audience, she whispered, "Mend as the candle burns, sickness end and health return." She took a pinch of rosemary from her sack, sprinkling it onto the candle flame. The flame popped, surging and burning black for an instant before burning true once more.

For a long moment, not even the sound of breathing breached the silence in the room, and then Una whispered at her back, "Lo... the child I once cursed has become a blessing. Well done, Lili. Well done."

* * *

Aidan discovered little evidence by the pool.

As best he could determine, it appeared to him that Keane had somehow fallen from the edge, just above the gully where the water flowed strongest. There was a bloodstain on a rock nearly fifty feet up, but hitting it would have placed Keane squarely in the water at Aidan's feet. From there, Aidan searched the immediate bank and found a trail of blood leading from the edge of the pool to the spot where his brother's body must have been recovered.

Lael had not been the one to find him. By the time she had rushed to the loch, Lachlann was already carrying him away, but she knew whereabouts Lachlann claimed he'd discovered him lying unconscious.

His sister had climbed to the cliff top to inspect that area as well. She peered down at him now, with one hand upon her hip, her lithe form silhouetted by the half moon. In her left hand, she held up a torch that illuminated one side of her face, wreaking havoc with her angry features. She was a hellion, his sister, and Aidan suspected she would never soften enough to wed. But if she ever did wed, poor soul the man who must deal with her. "D' ye find anything?"

"Nay. Not even a scuffle. He must have gone straight down with nary a stumble."

Aidan swept his own torch across his brother's blood where it soaked the ground. The torch roared as it passed, casting spots before his eyes, but he saw well enough to note that there were no scuffles here either—naught save what appeared to be his brother's struggles to reach higher ground.

He must have been aware enough to get this far, and must have lost consciousness once he'd climbed safely out of the pool. That gave him hope.

"What now?" Lael shouted down at him.

Aidan shrugged. "Now we hold the bluidy Scots in their huts til Keane awakes."

"*If* he wakes!" Lael countered.

"Aye, he will," Aidan reassured her, though he knew not why. For reasons he could not explain, he somehow sensed Lili would see it done.

Or mayhap it was simply a brother's hope.

* * *

For what remained of the night, Lili watched over Keane. She, along with Una and Sorcha all sat waiting for him to reopen his eyes. Finally, Sorcha was brave enough to ask, "Will my brother live, Lili?"

The worry in the little girl's tone gave Lili a pang of grief. She peered down at Keane's face, wondering what it must be like to have brothers and sisters who loved you so much. She must believe it wasn't much different from the way she felt about her son, but she could not find that same affection in her heart for her parents.

"I canna say," she told Sorcha honestly, "but I think he will."

Because of the bruising, it was difficult to determine whether a healthy color had returned to the boy's face, though it seemed to her that his movements had increased since she'd come back into the room. He was wincing every so oft now, and twitching his brows as though in pain.

"When my brother awakes, he will tell us what happened," Sorcha said with conviction.

For her part, Una merely grumbled, shifting in her chair as though she struggled with her private thoughts. She lay her staff across her lap. "Let us hope, for once, your brother was simply a clumsy dolt!"

Sorcha nodded, and Lili nibbled her lip, praying to God

the old woman was right, and that Rogan had naught to do with this.

God help them all if he did, for she knew Aidan would kill him... and for her part, after what they had shared, she could suddenly not bear the thought of him looking at her with anything less than the tenderness he had shown her tonight.

* * *

Fully dressed, Rogan sprawled upon the bed they had given him, staring out the chimney hole in the thatch ceiling. It was dark outside.

These people lived little better than peasants. Their homes could all be burned with little enough effort and without any loss. The trouble was, he would never leave the vale alive if he burned them down. There was only one way out of this vale, and their weapons and horses had been confiscated upon their arrival.

The dirty bastards had herded him here, as though he were little more than a dumb goat. All three men, along with the priest, had been shoved in behind him, and although they hadn't locked the door, he could hear them standing guard outside. He had no idea how many there might be, for the only window in the hut faced the west, and it was shuttered with a man guarding it from the outside. But no news was good news, in truth.

It seemed the boy lived for the moment. He knew they had discovered his body, and knew they suspected foul play, but he also knew Aidan dún Scoti was smart enough not to execute guests in his home without evidence. It would hardly be much different from the atrocity Padruig had committed when he'd supped at their tables as friends, turning on them in the middle of celebration.

Besides, Rogan sensed Aidan dún Scoti's honor was far too great to kill an unarmed man. If he found Rogan guilty, he might give him a sword, and even if they cut him down after, Rogan vowed to take a few of the bastards to hell with him first. He was as skilled a swordsman as any.

However, if he died, he stood to gain nothing, so he considered another plan.

The priest was asleep in the chair, snoring. The old fool had probably not slept since they'd arrived for he was a cowardly dolt who could scarcely bear the sight of his own shadow. The Pecht priestess—if that's what she was—had given the prelate a knot upon his pate and a cut on his chin that made him look like a twelve-year-old lad fresh from a fight. If he was sleeping now, it was only because his energy was depleted. Nay, he could not cast blame there, for the man would reveal aught he knew with a simple threat. That he had not done so already was a miracle equal unto the birth of Christ.

Of the other three men, one was David's spy in much the same way Aveline must be his once he was gone. He could lay the blame there, he supposed, but that man was no fool and Rogan would prefer not to match wits with anyone at a time such as this.

Of the remaining two, one was a bigger lout, and though he'd been with Rogan the longest, that might actually work in Rogan's favor, for he would understand precisely what Rogan would do to him if he dared to challenge him. And the man had nowhere to go—though he might prefer to take his chances with Aidan.

That thought made him smirk, for he knew better. All three of his men thought Aidan dún Scoti the spawn of the devil himself, and with that settled, his mood lightened considerably, and he closed his eyes to wait.

TWENTY-THREE

It was near dawn when Aidan returned to Keane's room.

All three women had fallen asleep, but his brother's eyes were open—at least one. The other he could barely crack for the swelling. Nevertheless, a grin broke across Aidan's face at the sight of him awake.

Keane moved his mouth to speak once he saw Aidan, but the gesture was wholly unfamiliar for the monstrous swelling. "Di' we win?" he asked, in a weak attempt at humor.

"Ach, ye randy lil bastard!" Aidan scolded. "Ye gave us a fright! Nay, the ground won, and 'tis lucky ye are that Caoineag didna feel like weepin' tonight." He peered at his wife, who was curled at Keane's feet.

"I didna wish to wake them," his brother said.

Lili was the first to open her eyes. She blinked and smiled at the sight of Keane's open eyes and Aidan felt a surge of gratitude clear to the core of his soul. He wanted to kiss her in that instant, with all his heart.

Sorcha awoke next and went squealing to the other side of the Keane's bed. Keane lifted his hand and tried to ruffle her hair, but the effort lacked much strength.

Una snorted awake, her hand tightening around her staff in her hand. She thrust it out, and gave a little gasp, and Keane's eyes sought the sound. "I dinna suppose Meara sleeps none the wiser?" his brother dared to ask.

Aidan lifted a brow. "If that is all ye have to say, I ken ye'll be just fine, but nay. Meara, the poor lass was the one to find ye."

Keane nodded almost imperceptibly and tried to wet his lips as Una finally came to the bedside.

Lili reached behind Aidan's back, to retrieve a small dish she had set there. "She dabbed a cloth inside the dish and set it upon Keane's lips. He grimaced. "'Tis bitter," she advised, "but the *vin aigre* will work its magic both inside and out if ye can but bear the sting."

Keane grinned a hideous grin. "Ach, I'm a mon now," he bragged. "Suppose I can stand a wee bit o' pain." His glazed eyes sought Aidan's and Aidan realized he was referring to the toast they'd shared yesterday morn. He patted his brother's shoulder. When Keane tried to move, he pressed his hand down to prevent him from rising. "Later," he said. "Rest." Later was soon enough to have a talk with the boy as well. He needed to grow up for the sake of the clan.

His sister Lael walked into the room and seeing Keane awake, she too gave a little joyful squeal and ran to the side of the bed where Sorcha stood. For a moment, Aidan studied his sisters standing side by side and realized how disparate his oldest and youngest sisters were. Sorcha was far more like Lili in more ways than simply the color of their hair and the freckles on the bridge of their noses. She had very little in common with either Lael, Cat or Cailin.

Concealing her thoughts even from Aidan, Lael spared a glance for his wife but held her tongue, acknowledging neither gratitude nor contempt before her gaze returned to Keane.

For her part, Lili remained silent, but she remained exactly where she sat, neither cowing to nor confronting his sister, and a thread of pride wove its way through Aidan's heart. Indeed, the lass would find her place amongst his kin.

"Have you any memory of what happened?" Aidan pressed his brother.

Keane shook his head, his pale green eyes hazed with pain. "Only that I stood one moment watching Meara's sweet—"

His gaze danced around the bed, at the faces surrounding him, remembering himself—"er, the next I was face down in Caoineag's Pool."

"Was there no one else near?"

Once again, Keane shook his head. "I canna clearly recall, but I dinna think so. My eyes were pre-occupied," he confessed, and tried again to grin. The effort cost him. He groaned in pain.

"Serves ye right!" Una announced suddenly, smacking the end of her staff so loudly upon the wooden floor that it echoed below. No doubt she would have preferred to abuse Keane's head instead. "Despite that ye like to think so, ye're no mon," she declared. "Ye're as much a wee babe as the day I dragged ye kicking and screaming out of ye're minny's womb. And if ye dinna mind yourself, ye'll ne'er see the day!" She turned away, but Aidan noted her glazed eyes, and he knew that she did not intend to allow anyone to see her cry. "Ach," she groused, "a growing boy indeed harbors a wolf in his belly!" And she stomped out the door.

* * *

No matter that Keane did not recall what happened at the waterfall, Aidan would not rest easily until their guests were long departed. They had come to see Lili wed, and now that the deed was done, there was no reason for any of them to remain. Their presence here only threatened discovery of the stone. So whilst his brother continued to recuperate, he rounded up their Scots guests, returned their weapons, and sent them on their way.

Lili stood upon the pier, worrying her hands, but otherwise said little. If Lael had had her way, they would have sent the Scots off with nothing more than what they'd arrived with, but his sister nevertheless arranged a basket of food that would see them to their destination—as long as they did not gorge themselves during their meals.

Aidan insisted Aveline go along with them. As far as he was concerned, his wife didn't need a maid, nor had Aveline shown much interest in performing any of the duties for which she had been employed.

"She is not my charge," Rogan complained, speaking up at once.

Aidan lifted a brow, a scornful retort hovering upon his lips, for only now did the man suddenly not have any use for the girl. He could easily imagine the woman's belly distending three months hence, and Rogan clearly did not care. The fellow had done little to change Aidan's opinion of him, and Aidan would be glad once he was gone. "Neither is she mine," he maintained.

"Alas, but I do not have a place for her under my roof, and it will displease David immensely if I send her home to Teviotdale."

David could hang himself on the laces of his boots, for all Aidan cared. "'Tis a bluidy shame," he said.

Rogan gave the maid a weary glance, and she visibly cowed. Aidan had a sudden shred of compassion for the lass and wavered. For her part, Aveline seemed torn. She clearly did not feel at home here, and yet she seemed to be gazing at Lili anxiously, silently pleading with his wife that she speak in her behalf.

Lachlann handed Rogan his weapons. The man placed his sword in his scabbard and his knife in his satchel. His men were already prepared to ride, none daring a glance at their lord. "Would you truly send the lass to travel unchaperoned with five men?"

"Four," Aidan countered stubbornly. "Seems to me the priest dinna retain possession of his balls."

The sour-faced prelate made a choked sound, appearing affronted. He shifted from foot to foot, his face turning pink, but said nothing, especially after sending Una a wary glance. With a bit of the devil in her one good eye, Una smirked, digging the end of her staff into the ground, needling the man, and Aidan nearly laughed.

"Aidan…" Rogan used Aidan's name as though they were long time friends. "Come now… ye canna mean to leave your wife without her maid? The two have been together far too many years to separate them now."

Surprised by the claim, Aidan glanced at Lili. Her brows knit softly in response, though he could not tell if it was in surprise at Rogan's words, or consternation. Mayhap she didn't wish to gainsay him? *Mo chreach,* she might well become a bossy warrior wench when she was asked to ply her healing skills, but one night in his bed clearly had not given her the nerve to speak up now if she disagreed with him. "Is this true?" he pressed her, wanting to give her her heart's desire... not simply in gratitude for helping his brother, but because she was now his wife. He wanted her to speak up for the things she desired. Despite his bluster, Aidan's heart was softening toward her... and he scarce hid the desire from his gaze or the twitch of his shaft when he thought of her lying naked in his bed.

"'Tis true," she confessed, and nodded.

Aidan turned once again to examine the maid. The woman looked far more like a *Sassenach* than any lass he had ever known. Just the sight of her gave him heartburn.

Rogan persisted. "I fear if I take her with me, ye will subject the lass to the discipline of her father for having failed at her duties."

Aveline looked a bit like a terrified, abused puppy in that instant, Aidan thought. He truly did not consider her a threat. "Verra well. Stay," he relented. "But you'd best apply yourself to the duties you were assigned."

Her eyes were wide. "R-right n-now?" she asked, and looked a little bit as though she might swoon.

Aidan gave a growl of displeasure and turned away. He could not stomach weak women. He was aware that the lass ran to her mistress straight away. He cursed beneath his breath, but with that settled, he could not see the Scots gone soon enough, while all his kinsmen were still in one piece.

All four armed men mounted quickly, but the priest seemed to stumble over the hem of his stupid gown. His crucifix caught in the horse's reins, and Aidan could scarce take it any longer. He closed the distance between them and in one swift movement, without asking permission, or even hesitating over the man's weight, he plucked the offending prelate off the ground and sat him atop his mount. The priest shrieked like a woman.

"T-thank you, my lord!" he said, looking down at him, squirming uncomfortably in his saddle.

"Aidan!" he roared back at the man. "*Dia leat!*"

"W-what?" the priest stammered.

"I said go with God, ye lout! And do so quickly before I change my mind and whittle your bones down to pick my teeth!"

The man's face blanched, turning nearly as white as Una's hair. He found his nerve in that instant, or mayhap he lost it entirely, for he spurred his mount and headed toward the mountain pass before his companions could take their reins.

"I'm certain we shall see ye again as my nephew is certain to follow," Rogan said, and he lingered a moment even after his men had ridden after the retreating priest. His gray gelding danced impatiently beneath him, clearly confused by the signals his master gave him. His gaze sought Lili's then, and Aidan was certain he read in them a warning. "I shall give Kellen your best," he said to her.

Lili nodded. "Please…"

And then he rode away, leaving Lili staring after him, her body language unreadable though her eyes revealed far more than she realized.

TWENTY-FOUR

Fortunately, aside from the injury to Keane's head, there were no major wounds for him to mend from. Even the wound on his head, with all the swelling and bruising, looked far more hideous than it truly was. The fall into the water had kept him from breaking any bones. If it weren't for the smack to his head on the rocks on the way down, he might have walked away with naught but a grin as his reward for having braved the falls. Thus, he mended quickly, and for that Lili was thankful. He was a terrible patient, unable to remain abed for more than a day. His boyish head was filled with thoughts of "Meara, Meara, Meara!" The lad was certain the girl would consider him heroic now that he had "conquered death."

Lili merely shook her head, smiling at his impertinence, for behind all his shocking declarations and his defiant manner, he was still a boy at heart, not so much unlike Kellen. At least to some degree, she was able to ease her terrible longing for her son by caring for Aidan's little brother.

Judging by his first rude words to her—offering to show her where to piss—Lili might have thought Keane would remain as recalcitrant as his sister Lael, but the boy seemed hungry for a motherly figure in his life, and from the instant he'd opened his eyes and understood that Lili had been the one to heal his wounds, his gaze had softened toward her. Though he rarely held his tongue, he certainly did not use it to spit vitriol any longer.

Of course, neither did Lael. She was a prideful woman, who would never settle easily with Lili. But Lili would not force her to do so, for in the end, if Lili could not find a way to disembroil herself from this political mess, Lael would be justified in all her thoughts of Lili. And in truth, that was one reason Lili also did not attempt to wrest the care of Aidan's home from his sister, for as the lady of Dubhtolargg, she should be expected to manage the running of Aidan's household. It was no different at Keppenach or her father's keep. A woman's place was as chatelaine, no matter whether the keys she held were for a small pantry in a tiny cottage or a stone fortress the likes of which Maud of Huntingdon kept as David's wife. Of course, Lili had never been a guest of Scotia's king, but she didn't need to see their massive holdings to know how much power the man had seized for himself. He had King Henry of England's ear, and he was Earl of Huntingdon through his wife, and with that title, he had assumed control of Cumberland and Westmorland, Northumberland, and overlordship of the bishopric of Durham. Upon his brother Edgar's death, he then inherited all of the lands of Southern Scotland and thus crowned himself as King of the South while his brother Alasdair had claimed kingship of the North. Now that Alasdair was dead as well, David would not rest until all of Scotia was under his rule. But the Highlands would never easily bow to a king whose history lay in an English court. The husband fate had given Lili was no man to trifle with either... but he was just a single chieftain... one that remained isolated from the rest of the Highlanders. She could not seem to find a way to remove herself from the shackles of her duties. She was trapped, for the sake of her son... and Aidan was doomed regardless.

Aye, it seemed she was bound to mourn yet another husband. But this time she would truly mourn, for she was coming to know Aidan and she was growing to love the tenderness and respect with which he treated her—despite how she had come to him. It was much the same respect he accorded his sisters, allowing them a position of strength in his home. He was hardly diminished by their will, nor did he seem to feel threatened by it in the least. He was a man who was at ease with a woman of substance, and she admired him greatly for that.

He called her his flower.

The thought of it gave her a private smile, and her head warred with conflicting images. The only thought that seemed to clear her brain of the melee was the thought of her son. Kellen was her first duty. He would keep her path straight, even if in the end she would weep tears of heart-wrenching grief.

But how could she bear to betray Aidan and see him fall? How could she watch them put him beneath the ground... those fingers that loved her so sweetly.

More and more, she feared she would fail.

Once Rogan had gone, Aveline was given a choice. She could either remain within the *Crannóg*, in a small room near the lord's chamber, or she could choose the cottage she had been assigned. She chose the cottage, and Lili was glad she was not underfoot, not simply because the girl had taken to weeping half the day, but because it would be easier for Aveline to do her duty—not for Lili, but for Rogan—without so many eyes scrutinizing her. Lili could already tell that the *crannóg* itself remained fairly well guarded, for it was where Aidan and his family slept, in rooms that encircled the great hall.

The *crannóg* was big, but a fraction of the size of Keppenach, or her father's well-kept donjon and motte. Yet there was something very cozy about the way these folks lived, where the walls were not so thick it muffled all sound. But that simple fact gave Lili reason to blush, for Aidan was insatiable, and it seemed he'd awakened something in Lili that she had never realized she possessed: Desire, like her wretched conscience, was a constant companion. But only one of the two made a better bedfellow.

With Stuart, the act of procreation had not been so unpleasant, but that had been all it was—a means to get a son. He had been a good, pious man who took his duties as lord far more soberly than those of being a husband. He had been kind to her overall, doting, but not in the bedroom quite so much. There, he had been reserved, uncertain, leaving her to wonder what she was supposed to do, and that was precisely the problem, for while Lili understood medicine very well, she understood nothing at all about pleasing a man.

But she was learning.

Thinking of Aidan, she shivered softly, for he was a man who knew exactly what to do, and he rarely extinguished lights. Lili thought perhaps he knew every inch of her body by now, for he had kissed every hair and every freckle under the warm glow of their brazier. In fact, the thought of some of the places he had kissed her now burned her cheeks. Thank God he did not inspect her coffers in the same manner!

Somehow, without diminishing his manhood, Aidan gave her obeisance while in his arms. And more every day, she could not bear the thought of what she had been brought here to do.

Still, her husband was a mystery, for while within their room, he was tender and loving, outside their private quarters he was kind but aloof, occupying himself primarily with the training of his men.

Days went by and Lili avoided all thoughts of the vial and the ring in her chest, and subsequently, she worried and fretted about Kellen, her heart nearly bleeding for wont of the sight of her sweet son.

In the coming weeks, summer gave way to fall, and the leaves on the trees fell. The grass turned gold and the loch turned silver to match the sky.

The vale prepared for winter. Butterflies vanished along with the wildflowers. Squirrels hoarded nuts. Entire flocks of birds darkened the sky with their sojourn south, and Sorcha discovered a lone wolf pup, abandoned by his mother along the hillside forest behind Glenna's home. It was weak and skinny. Without help, the beast would be dead long before the first snowfall. Weeping, she brought the pup to Lili, and Lili treated it the same as she would any man or woman. Within a few days, the little beast was up and following Sorcha about like a dog.

"Where came you by the knowledge of the old ones?" Una asked one day, catching Lili on the way to Glenna's cottage. The old woman hobbled along beside her with her staff, keeping pace despite her awkward gait.

"Some through a midwife I knew, though much was gleaned through my years—wherever I could come by it, in truth. I had quite a thirst for the knowledge, you might say."

Unspoken was the reason Lili had been so driven to learn, for both Lili and Una understood precisely why she would be compelled. Una's head bobbled, and for a few paces she said nothing more, then offered, "One day when you are settled, I have a *leabhar* you may like to see."

Curiosity, like a famished beast, raised its hungry head. A book was a very rare thing. Lili had never expected to encounter one here. "A book, ye say?"

The woman winked at her, her white hair blowing in the soft breeze. "A verra auld book!"

"Ach, that would please me immensely," Lili confessed.

The old woman smiled and said, "I ken, lass. I do ken. Only tell me... would you take the advice of a doddering auld woman?"

Lili could not shake the feeling that, in truth, Una was her greatest ally here at Dubhtolargg, even more so than her husband—aye, even despite the burgeoning suspicion that the old woman was also the author of her curse and thus her misery. "Of course," she said.

"Trust your instincts, Lili, and whatever ye do, ye do it with your soul." And having imparted that, they parted ways. Una veered up the hillside path to where she so often disappeared. On many days Lili simply watched her wander up the hillside, wondering where she went, but she didn't ask.

As the days passed, one by one she came to know each of the villagers. Some sought her because Una urged them to do so, so she could treat their ailments, and others she came to know because she stopped to inspect their crafts. It seemed naught was sold here, rather they lived as one family, sharing what they had with one another, and everyone played some part—except Aveline, of course. The maid was lost and out of sorts.

Not far from Lili's thoughts remained the vial and the ring. She imagined them so often burning a whole in her coffers, but as yet, she had not moved them because it seemed the most natural place to hide them. Still, she wanted to take the ring and toss it into the loch. Thoughts of Kellen were the only thing to stay her hand.

One day while she stood at the window in her room, believing she was alone, she had unshuttered the window and stood looking out over the loch, the ring clutched in her fist, cutting into her flesh—the same way her guilt was cutting into her joy. God's truth, she was ready to toss it... but then she recalled her son holding out his little talisman and lost herself in the memory of Kellen running so excitedly from her garden to show her his newly discovered treasure.

He needed her to remain strong. He believed in her. He'd kept his little talisman because he wanted to believe whatever she told him.

Ach, but he would love the view from this window, she thought.

What she wouldn't give to kiss the pate of his head while he stood here right alongside her to enjoy the sight.

Despite that summer was gone now and fall was well into its days, the glen never lost its beauty. The surrounding corries were a string of white-tipped pearls, and the loch itself was a multifaceted jewel, reflecting the silver-gray sky.

Aidan approached from behind, slipping his arms about her waist. He kissed the back of her neck. Like a dagger, the ring dug into her palm, and she couldn't bring herself to turn around and face him. Though he didn't force her to. He simply embraced her.

"Ye've been standing here for nigh on an hour, Lili. What thoughts occupy your mind?"

Lili told him the truth—half the truth, at least. "My son," she said and sighed. "By the time I see him next he may be a man grown."

"Nay," he said. "Ye have my word, Lili. We will bring

Kellen home."

Lili nodded, the ring in her fist burning like a fiery ember. For once, she hoped he would not attempt to coax her into the bed, because then she would be forced to let the ring drop into the water, and her decision would be made once and for all.

He kissed her once on the cheek, sensing her withdrawn mood, and then he gave her the space she both prayed he would give her, and prayed he would not, for if he took the decision out of her hands, then she would know which path she was destined to take. But, nay, he left her alone with the ring and her dark thoughts, and went along his way, none the wiser.

In very little time, Lili's heart had completely softened toward Aidan and his people.

She no longer saw them at all the same. They were a peace-loving clan, and far from being the fearsome, pagan warrior with bloodshed on his mind, she understood now that Aidan only raised his sword to defend his vale. Indeed, her father had likely come into their midst as friends, and must have betrayed their trust, for naught else would explain their coming to blows.

She only wondered how they had survived all these years in the Mounth, living among warmongering tribes ... but she knew ... she knew it was because they kept themselves apart, defending themselves against outsiders.

Because her husband had embraced her, so too did his kinsmen, and for the first time in her entire life she understood what it truly felt like to be a part of a clan. How ironic was it that it was the one time in her life that she should not be?

She felt like a snake in their grass.

One morning she was tending to Aveline, trying to cheer her. With Glenna's help, she had found a dress and convinced the lass to rid herself of the faded green samite English gown she seemed to believe was so grand—it was not!—and she was plaiting Aveline's hair in the fashion the girls in the village wore, when she heard the blast of a horn.

At once her heart stopped. Kellen's face flashed through her thoughts and she abandoned Aveline's hair and hurried out of the cottage.

Could it be that Rogan had had a change of heart? Could it be that he was delivering her son? She could not imagine who else might come here. And then her heart twisted, for mayhap there was simply news and something was wrong?

With baited breath, Lili peered up into the hills, and then she spied the men on horseback coming down the mountain pass. Their colors were not that of Keppenach's, nor David's—nor any she recognized. With cloaks flying at their backs, their horses came thundering into the vale.

* * *

"Aye! Well take a look at that one!" Keane said proudly, pointing down at the ground. His face was nearly healed now, back to its normal size, but his ego had returned and inflated to twice the size before.

Precisely at this moment, he wasn't alone. Lang Glen, who was far too old and far too big to be competing with a lad half his age, climbed atop the boulder where Keane had stooped only moments before and peered behind it. "'Tis a puny log," he told the boy, guffawing. "Mine is full half a foot longer than yours, anyone can see!"

Aidan continued repairing the fissure that had appeared all too suddenly, piling stones atop it, examining the area around it, and he rolled his eyes at the exaggeration. This was a *tradition* he did not relish, although he could find little harm in tolerating it. Some boys were consecrated to always remain simply boys, and mayhap his brother was one of those. The thought of that displeased him somewhat, but he had begun of late to imagine what sort of child would come of his union with Lili. He dared to hope his first would be a boy, but couldn't begin to contemplate what that might mean for the future of his clan or the stone.

Damn, Una, for she had been the one to embroil him in this, and now he was beginning to feel great affection for Lili, no matter that he had tried to harden his heart. It was soft already, he realized—as soft as Lang Glen's head.

The land beneath his feet seemed solid enough, and the fissure was not even wide enough to see into so he could better determine the lay of the caverns below. He worried that this spot on the hill might be too close to the vaulted stone. At least he knew his men would keep an eye on it, for it was right in front of their godforsaken toilet.

"My turn!" exclaimed Hob.

"Nay mine!" called another, and the rest of the daft men all climbed up on the rock beside the two gloating fools, clamoring to peer down at the log of shit his brother had given birth to, vying to see whose was bigger and then to see who was next to try.

Somehow, it had become an agreed upon notion that all the greatest wisdom was gleaned in that instant—that somehow, the rapture of giving birth to a solid load of shit was a religious experience. If anyone asked Aidan, he thought the lot of them were far too preoccupied with defecation and he'd like to shove the silly bunch faces first down into their own dung. He loathed to think of the two-hundred years of shit lying down in that gully behind the rock.

A horn blasted, and he was suddenly grateful for the fact that not all his men were so witless as these. He recognized Fergus' windy blare the instant he heard it and knew at once they would be receiving guests. Twice the horn sounded, which set Aidan immediately at ease, for he realized these must be friends.

TWENTY-FIVE

B roc Ceannfhionn, they called him. *Broc the blond.*

If Aidan had considered Lang Glen a tall man, Broc was taller yet, with legs as strapping as tree trunks and arms the size of Keane's legs. Aidan was hardly a diminutive man, but he felt dwarfed by Broc's size height and breadth. But there was little guile in the behemoth's kindly blue eyes.

To celebrate their arrival, Aidan sent Keane after the *uisge* and tankards. His sister Lael continued to manage the kitchens, and his wife did not seem to mind, so he continued to make his requests of Lael, bidding her to bring their guests victuals to fill their bellies. Aidan had come to realize his wife was a skilled diplomat, for she had managed to deal fairly with all his siblings and had won herself a sort of truce with Lael—hardly an easy feat.

"To what do we owe the honor?" Aidan asked Broc, slapping him congenially upon the back.

Broc's face was set in grim lines that seemed at odds with his boyish features and his bonny blond hair. "We come on behalf of The MacKinnon," he said gravely.

Mulling that over, Aidan saw the men inside and stood before the chieftain's table as the tables were being filled to the edge with food and drink. Everyone worked together to bring foodstuffs from the pantry—cheese, bread, whatever fruits remained that had not been preserved for the winter,

salted fish, honey from their store and a new kind of wine Lili
had spiced using late-blooming flowers. As it was not yet time
to sup, they did not assemble the trestle tables, for there was
room for all to sit at the long table. Unlike the halls of others',
here space was limited and they did not employ a permanent
dais. Neither was Aidan inclined to lord it over his kinsmen
so they sat on both sides of one long table, facing one another
as equals. Aidan urged the men to sit once the table was
completely prepared. "What business has the MacKinnon
with us?" he asked Broc, curiosity needling him.

Broc's entourage, all of them eyeing the spread, beat the
giant to their seats but Broc seemed far too troubled to spare
the food a glance. "We received word a week ago of a secret
council David called."

A ripple of foreboding swept down Aidan's spine, though
he covered whatever unease he felt and led the way to their
seats. "Come, give me the news while you sup... I ken you
must be famished after the journey north?"

Acknowledging the truth of that statement with a nod,
Broc reluctantly found his seat at the table and began his tale.
When he was done, Aidan simply sat, staring at the man,
considering everything he had said while Keane poured him
another tankard full and another for their guests.

"So David called his banner men the instant I left
Chreagach Mhor?"

"So it seems," Broc acknowledged, nodding soberly. He
lifted up his cup and brought it to his lips, taking a hefty sip,
and then merely shook his head and cleared his throat. "He
didna invite Iain, or we would have come to you long before
now," he continued, as though perfectly accustomed to the
burn of the *uisge*. "We only discovered the meeting by
chance."

Aidan's reached out for his own tankard. "By chance?"

"Aye," Broc said, but before he continued, he introduced
the men he had ridden with into the vale: his cousin Cameron,
and another three strapping young lads—all MacKinnon
liegemen.

"'Tis glad I am to know ye," Aidan offered. "*Fàilte.*"

Welcome.

"*Mòran taing,*" Cameron replied in the old tongue. *Many thanks.* Aidan thought he might be a few years older than his sister Lael, though not by overmuch.

He gave Keane a nod as he held the *uisge* jug over his own cup, asking for permission. Grinning like an idiot, his face stained with the remnants of bruises, Keane took his seat to Aidan's left, leaving the right-hand seat unoccupied—a subtle nod of respect to Lili, even in her absence. That pleased Aidan immensely.

But the story Broc came to relay was curious, and indeed it seemed to be a matter of happenstance—or divinity, one, depending upon the view—that he had gleaned the information at all. Apparently, David had ensconced himself in the manor house of one called Alma, who had been the nursemaid and healer for the MacEanraig clan, Broc's clan by birth. Broc alone from the MacEanraig chieftain's family had survived a savage raid upon their village, and he had been taken as a boy to be cared for by the old MacKinnon laird. In the meantime, Alma returned to what remained of their village to rebuild their homes. Broc's loyalties to Ian MacKinnon were unshakable, Aidan knew that from the stories he had heard overall. But it seemed a large part of the warrior was heartsick, even all these years later, over the demise of his bloodline. As a child, Broc had buried his entire family and had watched his village burn, reduced to ash. Now this woman whose years should have ended long ago—a bit like Una—and who by the grace of the gods continued to breathe, had returned to him with a tale—one that made Aidan's blood run cold.

"I've nay clue what David means tae do," Broc confessed. "But I know he came here to Dubhtolargg, and I know that whatever he has proposed to you comes with treachery at hand."

Lili came into the hall then, and Aidan blinked at the sight of her, suddenly hesitant to introduce her to his guest. His heart was tripping over Broc's forewarning.

Whatever he has proposed to you comes with treachery at hand.

She may betray you at least once before she finds her true path.

His intuition—the first he'd had upon meeting his wife— might yet prove true, though he couldn't bear it. He called her over nonetheless and introduced her. Aidan smiled at the way his guests all rose to greet her, their eyes widening at the sight of his bonny Scots bride. She had the power to render a man mute, that much was true.

Aidan stood as well.

Broc was the first to speak. "*'S mise le meas—yours respectfully*, my lady, I wish ye both long life and bairns aplenty. My wife is bearin' me another in two months hence and this time, we are hoping for another boy."

Lili nodded and said, "Congratulations to you and—"

"Elizabet," Broc provided and his face nearly split in two at the mention of his wife's name. "She reminds me a wee bit o' you," he confessed.

His cousin Cameron laughed. "He's got himself a daughter— bonny as ye, my lady—and another on the way. Soon he'll be able to start his own clan of womenfolk, one to rival Dubhtolargg's!"

Aidan laughed. No doubt, his indulgence toward his sisters was fodder for much gossip, but few enough witnessed it firsthand. It didn't bother him.

"Aye, well," Broc said, his face turning a bright shade of pink that seemed all the darker for the paleness of his hair. "As to that..." He unsheathed his claymore and Aidan straightened, the hairs on his nape suddenly prickling and standing on end. But the blond giant merely laid his sword carefully upon the table, where the etching on his blade was most easily read.

Cnuic `is uillt `is Ailpeinich.

Hills and streams and MacAilpín.

As the legends went, one did not exist without the other, since the beginning of time.

Aidan peered at his wife. Recognition flickered in the depth of her eyes, and he realized she understood what it was she beheld.

But of course she would, for she knew the old tongue, so

it stood to reason that she had learned her histories as well. It was the sword of the *Righ Art*—the High King and Chief of Chiefs. It was the consecrated blade of Kenneth MacAilpín. Lost amidst the *Síol Ailpín*—the fractured Highland Clans who claimed blood lineage to the original Ailpín line—it had not been seen in more than a century. The sword, along with the stone, belonged to the rightful heir of the throne of Scotia, come to them by way of the Dalriadic kings, along with the stone called *clach-na-cinneamhain*, which as legend would also have it, was then blessed by a Pecht priestess. When the two were rightfully united, the chieftain who sat upon the stone and wielded the sword would rule undivided lands. It should have gone exactly so ... except that, after the blessing, under a banner of truce, Kenneth MacAilpín murdered seven Pecht rivals for his throne. Thereafter the stone was cursed, consigning any man who sits upon it without right to war amongst his own kin. Seeing the way of it, after Kenneth's son Aed was murdered in cold blood, Aidan's clan removed the stone and secreted it where it now remained.

For a long moment, Aidan merely stared at the sword, and though he considered it, he decided not to send Lili out of the hall, for without knowledge of the stone, she could not truly comprehend exactly what it meant to have the sword sitting here before her, gleaming upon his table. And yet ... if she was to become a true member of his clan, he must begin to trust her.

He pulled out his wife's chair and sat in his own, considering the sword and its markings—markings he knew intimately because they matched those of the stone hidden within the ben.

For what seemed an eternity, Lily stood at his side, and then she sat too.

Once his wife was seated, the men Broc had brought along with him sat as well, but they all remained silent, waiting to see what Aidan would say about the ancient sword that had been lain upon his table.

"To whom does it belong?" Aidan asked, feigning ignorance.

Broc hesitated a moment, his eyes meeting Lili's and then returning to Aidan's once more. "To me," he said finally. "The sword is mine."

ᴄ ᴡᴇɴᴄʏ-ꜱɪx

L ili's gaze snapped up to meet the giant's bright blue eyes. His eyes assessed her keenly, watching her reaction and that of Aidan's as well.

For his part, Aidan seemed hardly fazed by the sight of the blade. But Lili knew enough to know that men would kill for the sword Broc had placed upon the table before them.

"How did you come by it?" her husband asked casually, but Lili sensed his tension in the rigid set of his shoulders.

"It belonged to my father," Broc disclosed.

Aidan merely nodded. "Well kept."

A shadow crossed Broc's eyes, dimming the sparkle that had appeared only moments before at the mention of his wife. "I took it from my father's body," he continued. "But I did not realize what it was at the time. I only knew it to be my father's. When Alma came to advise Iain MacKinnon of David's secret meeting, her eyes fell upon the sword in my scabbard and the auld woman wept bitterly at my feet."

Once again, Lili's eyes met that of the man seated at the opposite side of the table. Now his eyes glistened with tears she knew he would never shed in the presence of so many men. His golden hair was long and fell below wide shoulders, much like that of her husband's, except that Broc's coloring was nothing at all like Aidan's. Where Broc appeared much like a golden Gael god, her husband had the dark look of his

Pecht ancestors. And still, though Broc had the appearance of an angel—if ever there were angels—she sensed in him a strength born of his circumstances. Ironic that he had pledged his sword to the MacKinnon, and that sword was the sword of kings. Its presage gave her a little shiver.

Broc continued with a heavy sigh. "Alma begged my forgiveness and told me the tale of the sword. It has been passed down to my blood kin for more than four score years."

Lili recognized the tension in Aidan's voice. "But you call yourself MacEanraig?"

Broc's gaze did not waver from her husband's. "As with you, I call myself naught. Ian MacKinnon named me Ceannfhionn as a child. Almost no one refers to me as MacEanraig anymore, but aye, I suppose to protect my lineage from murdering rivals, the Ailpín name was forsaken somewhere along the way—and perhaps as a reminder that might is not the rightful hand that rules, my clansmen took the maxim, 'Sola Virtus Nobilitat.'"

Virtue alone ennobles.

Aidan sucked in a breath, and Lili thought perhaps the words meant something to him, but she did not know quite enough to understand precisely what.

Word by word the hall grew more silent still. The fire in the circular hearth crackled noisily. One lone cup was set upon the table. It echoed like thunder in the growing silence of the hall.

"There was more," Broc continued solemnly. "She gave me the name of the murdering whoresons who razed my village." His voice was calm as he spoke, but when he looked at Lili she held her breath, somehow understanding that what he was about to say would shatter her view of the world.

"Dougal MacLaren—fighting under the banner of Alasdair mac Mhaoil Chaluim, the King of the North, before his death." His gaze reverted to Aidan.

Stuart and Rogan's sire and her son's grandfather.

"David's brother sanctioned the raid upon your village?"

Broc nodded. "Keppenach is my birthright. Now I wish to take it back."

Kellen is still there.

Lili's heart lurched. She stood, raking her chair backward upon the wooden floor, making a terrible, cacophonous sound. Her stomach roiled. She could not listen anymore. All the men simply looked at her, but to her relief, they said nothing. "Excuse me," she said hurriedly, and fled.

Fingers froze in the midst of serving plates, and even chewing stopped. The hall remained deathly quiet for a long interval after Lili's departure.

Keane peered about warily, sensing the underlying tension, despite that at ten and four the boy had yet to see a battlefield.

"You must know I have wed Padruig Caimbeul's daughter?"

Broc nodded somberly. "I mean her no disrespect, Aidan, but her husband's Da is a faithless cur—like his remaining son. I wadna doubt it if one of the two murdered the auld bastard in his bed. I heard rumors of Stuart's death. To me, it stinks of foul play, not some bluidy ignorant curse!"

Aidan stared at the man, straight into his eyes. "*I* am Lili's husband. Stuart MacLaren is dead and I would prefer never to be reminded that she had another."

He could see himself reflected in Broc's eyes, along with the firelight behind him. "Forgive me, but does she not have a son by the man?"

Aidan crossed his arms, though at the instant, they itched to feel cold steel. "Aye, she does, but once the lad is returned to her, I will raise him as my own."

The mood between the men grew more sober yet as each assessed the other.

Broc was not a craven man. Even outnumbered, he did not refrain from asking what he wished to know. "It could be argued that Keppenach should go to your wife's son. Does the stronghold no' interest ye?"

No matter that it was a much coveted defense position beneath the *Am Monadh Ruadh*, Aidan did not have to consider it. "Nay."

"Then consider joining me … along with the MacKinnon,

and the mac Brodies and the Montgomeries ... to ensure its return?"

"To you?"

"To my sons," Broc countered. "I am Keppenach's rightful heir."

Aidan's eyes returned to the sword, considering Broc's story. Despite everything he had heard, anyone could claim the sword. It was not Aidan's task to influence who might rise to power and sit upon Scotia's throne—not that Broc was implying he would go so far. But it was Aidan's task to keep the stone safe, and that meant staying out of Scotia's wars, petty or otherwise. The rightful man would rise to the throne without Aidan's help... or nay. Until then, the stone must be guarded at all costs.

Broc was still waiting for Aidan's answer, he realized, and he weighed his words carefully. "If I did not burn Padruig Caimbeul in his bed for murdering my sire, what makes you think I would rouse my men to war in order to return your keep?" he asked at last. "Nay. I do not embroil myself in Scotia's politics."

Broc tilted his head. "Not even to secure alliances?"

Aidan tensed. "Is that a threat, Broc?"

Broc was quick to answer. He shook his head at once. "Nay. Not at all, though it would seem tae me that no man should stand alone."

"Our solitude has served us well enough through the years," Aidan countered. "It will serve us many more."

Broc's brow furrowed. "Aye, but dinna ye wish tae fight for what is right?" he persisted. "If the tale Alma tells is true, my sons could stand to rule one day."

Aidan considered Broc a long moment, wondering how much he should reveal. "And what if her tales are not true?" Aidan suggested. "What if that sword was seized from its rightful owner on a battlefield somewhere? What if your father came by it through war, not by blood? Would you see your sons war upon one another simply to wield it?"

No clan in Scotia's history had ever been plagued with more cold-blooded murders by their own kinsmen than the

Ailpín clan. That was something every Highlander knew. Even now, the stone's curse riddled Ailpín blood, for David himself was an eighth son, and every last brother before him had had to die before he could take his place upon the throne.

Broc's face fell, though not because he had not considered the cost of fighting for his patrimony, Aidan sensed. After a long interval, he said stubbornly, "I would see my sons raised at Keppenach."

"Well, then may it be so," Aidan allowed, and he truly hoped the man would someday sleep under Keppenach's roof... just so long as Lili's son would not be caught in the midst of men at war.

"We'll leave it there," Broc relented, and just then Cailin appeared at Aidan's back, brandishing a fresh jug of *uisge*, saving them from further discussion.

Cameron's face lit at the sight of his second youngest sister as she then sat in the chair that had grown cold at Aidan's side. "Anyone gutty enough to swallow a dram o' this?" she asked. "Una sends a verra special batch for our special guests," she says.

"I am!" Cameron replied at once, raising his hand.

* * *

In her mind, Lili saw the clash of swords, the letting of blood and ensuing screams ringing throughout the halls of Keppenach Keep.

White-faced, she hurried down the dock, unable to bear the images that assailed her at the thought of the battle that was sure to come. It did not take a seer to bring such horrors to mind, for she knew the castle well enough to envision the rivulets of blood that would seep into every crevice of those stone floors. Her son might well be among the dead if she did not find a way to remove him from that stronghold, and it seemed the only way she could save him was to betray the man she was coming to love.

What could she do?

She must think!

She could not face Aveline right now. Neither did she wish to face Lael, for fear that Aidan's shrewd sister would see what was in her mind. For that matter, neither could she face Una. Leaving the dock, she ran in the direction of Glenna's hut, but she did not think she could see Glenna either, for that friendship was built upon lies as well—lies all her own. Glenna, like Aidan and his people, had given her nothing but trust, even when they should not have. Forsooth, but she was accursed in truth, for she was bound to curse everyone she came to love—that was becoming clear.

She found a spot along the hillside, cushioned with moss, and sat upon a boulder near a bare rowan tree. Its branches were grey and one lone leaf dangled from a wiry branch, threatening to drop onto a blanket of divested leaves upon the ground. Right now, Lili felt a little like that leaf, alone on the end of a precipice, ready to fall.

She was so confused.

She was in love with the man she had once feared. In truth, Aidan dún Scoti was a man among men, honorable, proud and true. Not one of those who believed themselves better than he were fit to kiss the hem of his breacan. He treated those he loved with far more civility than anyone she had ever known.

And then there was her silly curse—what if it held true? She was grateful not to know one way or another, for she feared Aidan would never have time to come to love her.

But nay, she could not do it.

She could not be the one to put an end to Aidan's life.

She. Would. Not!

And then she recalled the sword, and began to wonder if mayhap she might not have to kill Aidan after all... for what if she were to trade information for Kellen's return?

Would that be enough?

She did not know Broc Ceannfhionn and she owed the man naught. But she did owe her allegiance to her husband... and to her son.

She wiped her tears and slid down to lay upon the mossy ground, thinking, scheming.

TWENTY-SEVEN

The look upon Lili's face as she'd fled the hall hounded Aidan hours later.

He realized she must be worried about her son, but a tiny part of him feared she was aggrieved over the things Broc had said about Stuart MacLaren. That her heart might still belong to a man long dead made his gut ache and his appetite scarce.

Trusting his guests to find their way around once the meal was done, he went in search of his wife and found her lying near the Rowan tree where his mother had been laid to rest. All these years later, there was no sign of her grave, for the mound had washed away with the rains and the moss had clamored atop it, covering it, consigning her body forever beneath the earth, where all men would someday return. The rowan tree had been Aidan's marker. His Da, like most of the warriors gone from this earth were commemorated with piles of stones that dotted the hillside, for they still required a warrior's burial and their bodies were burned upon a pyre. They kept no burial grounds within the vale, and yet, Aidan had not had the stomach to burn the woman who had given him life. He had been but a boy of thirteen... not much younger than Keane was now when she'd died.

It appeared to him that his lovely wife had been weeping; he could tell because her nose was still pink. But as he neared the spot where she lay upon the mossy ground, he smiled, because he could see that she had fallen asleep, and that simple realization returned a sense of wellbeing that had been shaken with Brock Ceannfhionn's tale. If Lili could fall asleep here in broad daylight, in the middle of a field, he was doing his job to keep his kinsmen safe. He sat down beside her and she opened her eyes. Her lashes fluttered gently—so did his heart at the sight of those lovely violet eyes. But her face fell at once into a frown the moment she spied him. "I was worried about Kellen," she confessed.

He placed a single finger to her cheek, tracing the barely visible outline of her dried tears. "Dinna worry, Lili. We will see your boy's return. I meant everything I said. I will raise him as my own."

She swallowed, and unable to restrain himself, Aidan reached to gently kiss his wife upon her beautiful lips.

Her eyes remained open, pleading with him, and he knew that he would do anything in his power to answer her silent prayers. Deep in his heart, he understood that she struggled with something, but she would tell him when she was ready and of her own accord. He sensed her heart and it was pure. No matter that Una claimed she would betray him, he did not believe it. And yet, if that was the way of it, he must accept that as well, for fate had a fickle hand, and it was not Aidan's right to stay it. Each man and woman must choose his own way. Only then could the stone truly come into its rightful hands.

Still, Una's words rang though his head, bedeviling him: *She may betray you at least once before she finds her true path.*

And yet how could Lili betray him when her eyes spoke nothing but truth? Every emotion was right there for him to see.

He lay down beside her, resting upon his elbow and peered about. "'Tis likely the last of our temperate days this year," he said, noting the pile of leaves at the base of the rowan tree.

"Aye, but I love winter," Lili confessed.

She had come to realize that their ancestors loved the seasons fiercely, and so did she. She felt it most keenly in this place... here at Dubhtolargg... this haven away from the rest of the world. The pile of leaves at the foot of the rowan tree stirred with the gentle breeze and she sucked in a breath at the beauty of the place... the beauty of her husband.

She reached out to splay her hand upon his chest, clothed now as the season warranted. But she felt his heartbeat just the same. It thumped against the palm of her hand like a Pagan drum... a drum beat matched by the rhythm of her own heart. She was aware of its thumping every time Aidan was near. He made her body come alive... he made her *feel*... he made her forget all the years she had felt an abomination amongst her own kin.

When her husband looked at her, she wasn't Lili the witch, or Lili the accursed, or Lili the poor widow of a man who dared to love her... she was simply Lili.

And only now, as she looked into Aidan's eyes, did she understand that Stuart had never truly loved her. Stuart had held her as a prize—a lovely trophy to show his men. She could tell the difference in the gazes now... and it filled her with a new fear, for curse or nay, she did not wish to lose this love that fate had unexpectedly gifted her. She wanted to show Aidan how much he was coming to mean to her...

She dared to slide her hand down to his belly and then the crux of his thighs. His chest inflated with surprise. His shaft hardened beneath her palm.

"Lili," he said, and the single word was a warning.

But Lili would not be thwarted. Smiling mischievously, she squeezed gently, her heart racing as she thought of coupling right here beneath the wintertide sky. The very thought of it exhilarated her.

Aidan nearly swallowed his tongue.

Anything he might have said would have come out garbled in that instant while Lili cupped him in her hands. If she slid her hand beneath the folds of his breacan, she would find him as hard as that boulder she sat beside—and nearly as thick.

"Wife," he said low. "You cannot know what you do to me."

She smiled a siren's smile. "Ah, but I do, *Husband*, and I

would have you love me outside those bedroom walls."

"Ye're a bluidy temptress," he swore.

She smiled softly, completely without remorse.

He grinned then, his lips curving roguishly. "Dinna say ye werena warned," he told her, and then leaned to kiss her lips again. She tasted like rain on a summer day, sweet and fresh. For an instant, it crossed his mind that someone might spy them here, but he didn't care. Their guests were all amply provided for, and a new bonfire was being prepared. Tomorrow they would leave the vale, but tonight they would be regaled. In the meantime, they had no need of Aidan while he had a sudden, desperate and irrefutable need for his bonny wife.

He pressed Lili down upon the soft, plump moss, covering her. Of all the places on the hillside, she had chosen the one spot where moss grew as thick as his mattress. She moaned softly beneath him, and Aidan smiled to himself, preparing himself to silence her by making good on his threat.

His hands sailed the ocean of her body, tracing the outline of her curves, reveling in the depths of passion he met in her gaze. She was a goddess. His goddess. His wife. The mother of his children to be—by damn, he would worship her flesh with his heart on the tip of his tongue. With that thought in mind, he slid down, kissing her breasts beneath her gown, leaving it covered to protect her from the chill of the air. He had no need to bare her completely to find the treasure he wanted to share.

His hand sought and found her hem and he lifted the gown to her knees, and then before she could protest, he shifted so that he was settled between her thighs.

Lili gasped in surprise, her eyes widening at the sight of him between her legs, and she sensed at once what he meant to do. She opened her mouth to protest, but he simply smiled and before she could speak, his lips descended suddenly, his tongue seeking entrance to her most secret place.

With another gasp of surprise, Lili lay back again, trembling as he moved to kiss her where no man had ever kissed her before. His tongue swept out, teasing her with abandon, and she spread her legs without any will left at all.

Let him do whatever he may...

"That's it, flower," he whispered, his breath hot against her flesh.

In the next instant, all troubling thoughts fled entirely—like birds taking flight—banished by naught more than her husband's whispers and his tongue.

Twenty-Eight

O nce their guests departed they left behind a pall—a dark presentiment that hovered like an angry cloud Lili couldn't seem to banish. It was a feeling that seemed to be growing stronger and stronger by day. In part, she was certain it was because she was growing more and more desperate to find a way to retrieve her son without bringing harm to her husband or his clan.

All the weeks they'd had without a visitation of sickness came to an abrupt end. Aveline confessed she was with child and spent her days retching in her cottage. Then Fergus' daughter Meara grew ill, stricken with the same mysterious malady Duncan had suffered. It was difficult to believe Lili had spent nearly two months with these people—two months away from her sweet son. It pained her to think that mayhap she would not see him again for so long. If something did not happen soon, the snows would fall and the mountains would become impassable until the snows melted in spring.

Lili took the ring out of her coffer yet again, inspecting it. It was not even pretty. There was little about it to notice, and that was as it was intended, she supposed. She slipped it on her finger and stared at the trinket. Aidan would notice... for she wore no jewelry. She had come with little enough but the clothes upon her back. And yet...

She took the ring off, and put it back into its pouch,

shoving it again to the bottom of her chest. She would not defile her love for Aidan by even contemplating such a thing!

Very quickly, Meara's illness worsened.

Aidan was sleeping when they came to tell Lili, and so she made her way to Meara's home in the middle of the night with Fergus' son. Remembering Una's advice, she followed her instincts, and on the way, stopped by a little stream to gather a bit of water. Fergus' boy slipped away to relieve himself uphill and while he was gone Lili peered up at the moon, silently asking the spirits to bless the liquid in her hand. Adding a pinch of precious salt from the pouch she had tied to her waist, she swirled the cup clockwise … until the salt dissolved. She then held up the cup so that it was illuminated by the moonlight, and said, "By full moon's light, with helping hands, I spread good health throughout the lands." She took that blessed water to Meara's house and set it between two lit candles upon the floor near the hearth, and then she gathered the rest of her medicines from the pouch she had brought.

The lass was gravely ill, and Lili found her sweating profusely, despite that her body was wracked with shivers. Fergus' wife had been one of the first to be taken by this sweating sickness, and he worried now, pacing the floor of his cottage.

Lili did what she could to help the shivering girl. Her brother sat in a chair by the fire, petting their whining dog, his brows knit with worry. Since Meara had fallen ill, their home appeared as though it had been ravaged by brigands. For that reason Lili had set the water down upon the floor, for there was no room anywhere else. Once she had done all that she could and Meara fell into a deep, unsettled sleep, Lili sat by the girl's bedside, watching her sleep.

Her father, for all his bluster, had the look of a terrified Da, and his son only slept once his dog left his feet. Lili was dozing when she heard the animal lapping up the water she had brought from the little stream. By the time she realized, the cup was empty.

Tired and frustrated, she was grateful when Aidan appeared at their door. "Come to bed," he demanded.

"Nay. I shouldna," she argued.

"Have you done all you can?"

"Aye, but—"

"Chief is right, lass," Fergus interrupted. "The waiting is the most difficult part, but ye canna help my daughter any better by making yourself ill as well. Go an' get ye some rest and return in the morn."

The look on Fergus' face was so full of despair that Lili did not want to leave him. These were her people now and she could not bear the thought of losing even one.

Aidan sensed her hesitation, and he went to her and took her gently by the hand. He pulled her away from the sleeping girl, grabbing her arisaid by the door. He gave Fergus a glance, his voice softening. "Call upon us if aught changes."

"Aye," the father said. "Ye know I will."

* * *

"It seems I can no longer sleep without ye in my bed," Aidan told Lili once they'd returned to their darkened room. It sounded much like a complaint, but Lili heard the gentleness in his tone.

The brazier had gone cold, but Lili's thoughts were too pre-occupied with Meara to notice the chill in the air. She smiled at Aidan, grateful for his presence, and even more grateful for his solicitude. "I canna imagine what this illness could be," she worried, as she sat down upon the bed and removed her slippers.

Aidan stoked the fire in the brazier, reviving the flame. "I willna see ye grow ill over this, Lili." She loved the way he said her name now, with such tenderness. Nevertheless, she could not simply leave off—not when a young girl's life hung in the balance.

"What can ye tell me of those who fell ill before?" she persisted.

He turned to face her then, "Fergus' wife was among the first to go."

"She lives verra near Glenna," Lili said, considering the

fact. "Who else?"

"One of my auldest warrior's—a man who fought beside my father."

"Where did he live?"

"In a cottage on the hillside."

Lili thought about that, wondering how near to the other two. She was so pre-occupied that she did not realize until her husband was naked and standing before her.

"What in bluidy hell must a mon do to gain his wife's attention?" he asked standing nude, but not aroused.

Lili laughed, peering up into his face. He was smiling, his teeth gleaming white in the darkness. The fire at his back played with shadows on the wall, casting his form into a sultry firelight dance.

"E'en that weeping maid of yours, the one who doesna seem to realize her place, has a growing belly," Aidan complained, but not with much concern to his voice. "I would have a son by you," he said softly, kneeling to look her squarely in the face.

His hand went to her knee.

Lili's breath caught as the smile faded from his features, replaced with one of concern. "We arena promised tomorrow," he told her. "Meara's illness only makes it clearer to me. If she dies, my brother will weep for what will never be. Come what may, I willna regret a single moment I spend upon this earth. *Buin mo chridhe dhuit,*" he told her gruffly, and Lili's heart squeezed at hearing the words, for she could see them mirrored in his eyes.

You are the love of my heart.

It filled her with joy to hear him say so, but worry quickly followed, for she feared what may come. To say it back somehow seemed to seal his fate, and so she could not find her voice to speak.

She loved him too.

Desperately.

Somehow, the feelings had emerged despite her will to

stamp them away, and now even the possibility that the curse might be true filled her heart with dread.

She couldn't speak, but she could show him... and she pulled him onto the bed, desperate to feel life once again growing in her womb.

TWENTY-NINE

Meara died in the wee hours of the morning.

Fergus did not come to retrieve them, for he and his son had fallen asleep, exhausted by their vigil. By the time the poor man had awakened, his daughter was already gone. With somber hearts, they burned the lass upon a pyre the following day, along with the family dog, who also fell ill within hours of Meara's parting. Fergus believed the animal had perished of heartbreak, but Lili felt a twinge of hope at the discovery, for while she felt terrible over the dog's death, she had an idea burgeoning in her head.

Not wishing to stir a father's grief, or evoke thoughts of regret, she made quiet inquiries into where the family had acquired their water. If she was correct, she thought she knew from where the illness might have come. Their home was far enough from the village well, and so they had gathered it instead from a nearby stream—the same stream where Lili had gotten the water for her blessing. Apparently, Glenna too sometimes used that stream, whenever she could not go herself for water at the well. Sometimes Duncan was too lazy to go all the way. And when Lili inquired further, she discovered that the others who had perished had also used the stream for their supply of water as well. Once the funeral was over, she set out alone to inspect the area, to see if her suspicions could be true.

She discovered that the stream ended in a tiny little pool that settled between Glenna and Fergus' cottages. Fed by a trickling of water from the hillside above, she followed the path uphill, where she discovered the culprit. In a small basin fed by the hill itself, there sat enormous piles of human dung. She remembered that after the guarderobe in her father's donjon had been created, so that offal was discarded down the walls into the motte, thereafter some folks in the village had grown ill, until they realized that the motte was no longer safe to draw water from.

Lili sighed, and sat upon a boulder, remembering Keane's first words to her: *If ye should need tae piss... I can show ye where tae go, lest ye find yourself with an arse full of nettles.*

Keane's heart was broken. The poor lad's eyes were now swollen once more, only this time with grief. With this news, Keane could well blame himself, she knew, so she considered how best to tell everyone what she had discovered. She couldn't keep it to herself; she must tell them so no one else would become ill. Poor Meara! Poor Keane! Poor Fergus!

As she sat contemplating what she would say, her gaze was drawn toward a pile of stones, from whence a thin ribbon of mist seemed to billow from the ground below. She made her way over to it, kicking a few stones from the top.

Suddenly, without warning the ground beneath her gave way, crumbling like old cake beneath her feet and she was cast down into a cold, dank dark hole in the ground.

* * *

Thinking that his wife needed a bit of rest, Aidan searched her medicine chest. It might as well be a medicine chest, for it bore little else, and it surprised him still that she had brought so little with her from Keppenach. As small as the coffers were, they contained almost primarily herbs. Luckily, of her many small pouches, he recalled which bag she had used when she'd given Keane a draught to help him sleep through his most painful nights, so he searched for that one, and found it, but he also encountered another bag that contained a hard lump. Since she had naught but three dresses and a comb—for the most part—he was curious about the contents of the pouch. He lifted it out from between her gowns, and squeezed it.

A ring perhaps? Did she harbor a trinket from Stuart?

Driven by curiosity now, He opened the bag, turning it over so the contents fell into his hand: a single vial of powder and an ugly ring. He turned the ring over in his palm and spied the hole built into one side and blinked, peering down at it, somehow knowing what it was for, despite that he'd never seen anything like it. Inspecting it closer, he lifted it up and shook it. Traces of powder sprinkled into his palm.

Did she mean to poison him?

There could be no other explanation for such a device. And yet she had not used it. What stopped her? She might have seen her task done by now and slipped away with no one the wiser. But she had saved Duncan, and then Keane... ach, was she saving her treachery for him?

He thought of the look of adoration in her eyes when they made love and the very notion turned his gut—and his heart, for he had grown to love his bartered bride.

Accept the things to which fate binds you, his mother had said just before her death. After his father's funeral, he had railed against the will of the world, and despite that she had carried another man's babe in her belly, forced upon her in an act of cruelty, she had caressed her growing belly with such love that Aidan had only been able to love Sorcha once she was born.

Accept the things to which fate binds you, her voice said to him now. Only then could one be certain that the things that came to pass were meant to be, completely free from the will of men. So it was that the stone should come to rest in rightful hands some day.

But at least he knew... so that he could avoid ingesting anything Lili's hands had touched. Thank God Lael was still in charge of the kitchens. Though for the moment, he would not tell his sister, for Lael would skewer Lili in defense of him.

In fact, he was reluctant to tell anyone at all, for Lili had clearly not harmed any of his kin as yet. He could not blame her for the strange malady plaguing them, for it had begun before her arrival. Since she'd come, she had saved lives.

Mayhap she never intended to use the ring …

But he must know where her heart lay.

He *must* know what she intended to do with it.

Placing the ring back in the pouch, he tightened the drawstring, and then shoved the bag back down into her chest, leaving it approximately where he had discovered it.

At least he knew… and from this moment forward, he would be certain to watch his cups… along with every last move his wife made.

* * *

The ground beneath the fissure was hollow. Like a roof thinned with age, it merely collapsed, throwing Lili into the depths of a small cavern. She scraped her arms and legs on the way down, but otherwise she was unharmed, except that there was no way back up, it seemed.

Her arisaid was left hanging from the edge, and she had a glimmer of hope, but when she tugged it, it came free and tumbled down into her face, raining dust and tiny pebbles onto her head. She spat dust from her mouth, and inspected the cave better now.

A cold mist coiled about her feet. Like the inside of a hollowed orb, the sides rounded up and around, so that the walls were flat like a ceiling at the opening of the fissure and the sides were concave and too far away, impossible to climb—except for one tiny spot where the cave wall jutted outward so that if she could reach that shelf, she might be able to use it for support and pull herself up. Except that side of the cavern was damp with water trickling down from the basin above. It left a dark greenish stain on the stone. Nevertheless, Lili tried and found the shelf slippery to the touch. Besides, the scent of the water up close was not unlike a sewer. The thought nearly made her wretch. She wiped her fingers on the cave wall on the other side, not wanting to spoil her dress. And then she wiped them again in the dry dirt at her feet, brushing it then on the hem of her gown. In essence they had been using the basin above for a guarderobe for a very long time, she believed. Some of the water trickled down to the rocks below, and some seemed to have been carried to the tiny pool near Glenna's home.

Peering down at her gown, where she had wiped her hands, she found the hem torn, and frowned. Glenna was quite skilled with a needle she reassured herself; she could fix it. For now she simply needed to find a way out and warn everyone about the basin and the pool.

Dark as it was, there was the faintest light emanating through another crack in the wall, where cold mist poured through, like a warm breath on a cold day. She eyed the crack in the wall warily, and shouted up for help to no avail. She was alone on the hillside today. Everyone was attending poor Meara's funeral.

Feeling the cold rising around her, she retrieved her cloak from the ground, and shook it out, then cast it about her shoulders, cursing herself now for not having told someone where she was off to. Without much choice in the matter, she decided to explore the crack in the wall.

The cave walls, aside from the ceiling from whence she'd fallen, seemed sturdy enough and she could always retrace her steps if there was nowhere to go, but the faint light shining through the wall made her feel there was another exit somewhere else. Twilight was coming and she did not wish to be caught in a hole in the ground in the black of night.

However, the crack in the wall was barely wide enough for her to fit through. She had to work free a few loose stones, but finally she squeezed through. It led to yet another cavern, this one bigger than the last. Light entered here from both the way she had come and another hole that led up... only that one had a rope ladder descending from it. *Odd to find a ladder in a hole in the ground.* Feeling much less panicked now at the sight of the stairs, she lingered to inspect the room a moment, curious now.

In the center of the cave, there was a large oblong block of stone, mayhap a little longer than the length of her arm.

Smooth, as though polished, the top surface had a bit of sheen. In the back of her mind, she thought of the Stone at Scone… where kings were crowned. She had never seen that stone, and yet this one put her in mind of it.

Could it be?

But nay…

She ran her hands along the top of the stone, wondering why a stone like this would be lain as though upon an altar.

As she circled the stone, she found a plaque, but she could barely make it out in the dim light of the cavern. Curiosity made her turn the stone so that it faced the rays of light coming from the crack in the wall from whence she'd come.

Unless the fates be faulty grown
And prophet's voice be vain
Where'er is found this sacred stone
The blood of Alba reigns.

She blinked, staring at the words on the stone plaque—carved long ago, she realized, for the etchings were not fresh. Her fingers traced the ancient markings. There were more on the stone itself. She recognized the markings from the sword of the *Righ Art*—the intricately carved weapon Broc Ceannfhionn had placed upon Aidan's table. And then below the stone, upon the altar, there were three words written in the Latin tongue: *Sola Virtus Nobilitat.*

A prickling erupted upon her flesh—a prickling that would not stop, for the import of the discovery was not lost upon her. She knew of only one stone whereupon kings were crowned… but this was not it… was it? That Stone was at Scone. David too had been crowned upon it. She knew that because Rogan had gone to witness the coronation last year and he had bragged that he too had sat upon that stone, and then joked that it had not made him a king.

Her skin tingled strangely—a sensation that had naught to do with the cold, and she shivered fiercely. As though she had conjured it with the thought, a cold mist spilled down from the hole in the ceiling above, and suddenly Lili was unnerved, wanting nothing more than to be away from this tomb for a stone.

Climbing the ladder quickly, she realized that she had discovered something Aidan did not wish her to see, and she felt clammy and sweaty despite the cool air.

But then little might have prepared her for what she emerged into, for if the cavern below seemed forgotten over the ages, this one was well lived in. Misty and dank though it was, it was lit by a fat candle braced upon the far wall. In the center of the room sat a small table, along with a smaller crystal about the size of Lili's head. Mortar and pestle sat to one side and the remnants of powder peppered the surface, along with notches from the pounding of a pestle. Lili recognized the marks for she had her own worktable at Keppenach where she ground her herbs.

Inspecting the rest of the room, she found very old manuscripts upon a shelf on one wall and an old matted wolf skin rug lying upon the ground. A chair sat beneath the torch, strewn with an old blanket that was woven in the clan's colors. Spiders wove their webs up high, but for the moment the room was devoid of human life, though clearly not for long.

This then, was Una's home—dark and deep within the earth.

Drawn to what appeared to be a scrying stone, Lili reached out to touch it. She only knew what it was because she had been told of them, though she had never actually seen one. The instant her finger touched it, white light flashed through her head, startling her. She withdrew her hand at once, and backed away from the table, peering around for an exit.

She did not belong here, and she suddenly had the most incredible urge to be gone, before someone could discover her snooping.

Once again, she found a ladder leading through the ceiling—this one made of wood—and not daring to linger a moment longer... somehow feeling as though she were desecrating a holy place... she hurried toward it and pulled herself up, thanking the heavens above that she had not harmed herself in the fall and that she could hie away as quickly as possible.

That cavern led her to another one yet, but this one was filled with foodstuffs—winter stores, no doubt. How advantageous, for in the dead of winter, the room would be cold enough to freeze water, she was nearly certain. But Lili didn't linger to see what goods were stored here.

Like a maze of caverns, she made her way through each, until the light grew brighter in the last cave. From there, she hurried out into the waning daylight, and onto the worn path that led down the mount. Never in her life had she ever been so unnerved, and yet as she raced down the hill, she felt a burgeoning hope, for she realized that she had discovered the means to save her son and her husband as well.

* * *

Una was among the last to leave the funeral.

For long hours now, the smoke would continue to curl into the gray sky, darkening the immediate horizon. The stench of burnt flesh was one she would never grow accustomed to, no matter how many years she spent upon the earth. And yet, she knew ... Meara's soul was not lost after all. She had simply returned to whence they had all come, to where one day they would all go.

The stone in her staff winked despite that the sun was gone, and she waved it over the pyre, and spoke words:

The peace of the lochs be with you, child.
The peace of the earth be with you.
The peace of the stars be with you.
Now and evermore.

And then she sighed and closed her eyes, giving Meara farewell love, and trying not to grieve over a young woman who would never know the cries of her own babe, or the spirit of life growing in her womb, or even the love of a good man. Keane's life was destined for another turn... one that may not much please his brother.

But that was neither here nor there.

Lifting her gaze, she spied a figure racing down the hillside and her fist tightened about her staff, for she recognized the gait and the long flowing auburn hair. Lili was coming down the mount from the direction of Una's home, hurrying down as quickly as her feet could carry her.

A fierce prickling assailed her, flowing into every limb. Sadness threatened, but she sucked in a breath of smoke-tinged air and closed her eyes... now it would begin.

The fate of the clan—of the stone itself—was in the lass' hands.

 THRTY

When Lili returned to the *crannóg*, the sun was barely an orange glow rising above the shrouded peaks. Aidan was standing in the middle of the dock, peering out over the water when she found him. She stopped beside him to glance out as well, nibbling nervously at the inside of her lip. Despite that she'd intended to wait until they were completely alone, she was too anxious to broach the subject. "I was thinking, my love..."

He turned to look at her, offering her a half-hearted smile. "My love?"

Lili's heart flipped over the way he'd said the words—the way he was looking at her. For an instant, she didn't realize he was echoing her own words.

"'Tis the first time ye have ever called me such a thing," he said, enlightening her.

Lili blinked. Forsooth, it was true... she might in fact need something from him now, but she did love him. Those words had come out her mouth of their own accord. It wasn't simply a means to soften him, for she would never ply a man with sweet talk just to gain her way... she didn't even know how. She turned away, feeling awkward suddenly that she would require something of him. She stared at the sliver of orange that spilled across the surface of the water toward the *crannóg*... a watery flame inching toward them as the sun set behind the distant peaks.

A gaggle of geese flew by, their wings beating in harmony, their V-shaped flight silhouetted in the water. For the longest instant, Lili couldn't tear her gaze away. She watched as the image of the birds skated across the loch to the distant shore.

"Do ye mean it, Lili?"

Lili was quick to answer, though she couldn't look at him for fear that he would see the secrets she needed so desperately to keep. "Aye," she said and sensed his lingering gaze... then he turned away and she felt like she could breathe again.

This was the only way, she convinced herself.

She had already spoken to Aveline. Aveline knew what she must do. There was no other means to disembroil them from this mess. She had the means now to retrieve her son and mayhap even to prevent Aidan's death... at least by her hands.

For long moments, Lili stood staring at the gleaming water. From somewhere, the sound of a lone reed lifted upon the air, a melancholy note that moved her heart. The mournful sound shifted her thoughts for the moment. "How is Keane?"

"Well enough," Aidan said, without looking at her.

Lili sensed his withdrawal, and when at last he turned to acknowledge her again, she spied only a lingering sorrow in his eyes. She assumed Meara's death troubled him— particularly since only Lili realized as yet that the illness was not so mysterious after all. Nobody else need die. And remembering her discovery, she thought at once to put him at ease, though couldn't remember how she'd left the area— would he know she had stumbled into the caverns?

While he was watching, she refrained from looking to see how badly her arms and legs were scraped. She had all but forgotten her injuries in the excitement of the moment. Now, suddenly, like a stab of guilt, her elbow stung, and the dirty stains on her dress seemed like evidence of her sins.

His voice was gentle. "What is it ye were thinking, *mo chride?*"

Lili cleared her throat, unable to keep the news from her husband. "I believe I know what malady plagues your kinfolk."

His brows collided.

Lili pulled her arisaid higher about her shoulders to hide her trembling. "I'll show ye," she promised. "But first … I must beg something o' ye."

"There is no need to beg for aught, Lili. Ever. All I have is yours, and these are your kinfolk now as well as mine."

Lili's heart fluttered in her breast. It seemed to her that he meant every word, and it only made her all the more determined to see this done. She gathered her courage then, and asked him to return Aveline to Keppenach to bear Rogan's babe where she belonged. There were no assurances Rogan would do the right thing by Aveline or the child, but Aveline did not wish to remain at Dubhtolargg any longer. The girl was miserable, weeping every day, heartsick, for she believed Rogan loved her. Lili knew better, but it was not her place to dash the girl's hopes, and mayhap Rogan might come to love Aveline if he saw his babe.

"Ye wish me to send the lass back to Rogan? Why the change of heart?"

"Because I canna live without my son," Lili answered, her heart in her eyes, and her words full of emotion. In this there was only truth, but she also wished to save the man she loved. And yet that she could not tell him. If there truly was a curse, she would find a way to prevent the course Una had predicted so long ago. The old woman *must* know a way! Until then, this seemed the right thing to do to save him from a fate decreed by lesser men.

"Soon, the snows will come and the mountains will become impassable," she contended. "I would have my son with me through the Yuletide."

He simply stared at her, and Lili tensed, fearing his answer.

He *must* agree to this! Sending Aveline back was the only way she knew to get a message to Rogan. She planned to trade her son for information she knew beyond a doubt would be far more valuable to David of Scotia than the death of Aidan dún Scoti. But she would not give them a bloody thing unless Kellen was returned to her.

"Rogan promised he would send my son once I was settled," she lied. "He only wished to be certain—" Her mind raced for a plausible excuse.

"That we were not savages who might corrupt his nephew?" Aidan provided, his green eyes glittering.

Lili nodded, hating herself for the lie. Inasmuch as it was true that Rogan believed them barbarians—and she had as well—it was not true.

"Please," she beseeched. "Please…"

His green eyes bore into her own, reaching too deeply into her soul. And yet to her dismay, and to her relief, he agreed without argument, saying only that it was not his desire to keep a woman prisoner within his vale.

Lili exhaled in relief, hardly aware that she had pent up her breath until it rushed from her lungs, leaving a puff of mist lying in the air between them.

It was that simple. He would send Aveline home escorted by three of his best men, and Aveline would take a message to Rogan from Lili. If Rogan dared to release Kellen, the men would escort her son home, but she knew it would not be so easy.

Once they were agreed, Lili took Aidan by the hand and led him up the hillside to show him the basin she had discovered. As she feared he would, he spied the fissure as well and Lili was forced to give him half-truths.

"I nearly fell," she explained, and showed him where she'd scraped her knee. "I stumbled backward and fell upon my rump." She showed him the scrapes on the palms of her hands, and his look darkened, his jaw clenching. "I was so excited I ran down the hill to tell you what I'd found."

"You might have killed yourself," he scolded, but that was all he said, and Lili shrugged, and explained about the water that both Glenna and Fergus had gotten from the pool downhill. She showed him exactly where it was then.

Lili believed that the offal had contaminated the pond, for it was small enough and the water was not clear—something she had not been able to tell so late at night the evening she had gone to tend poor Meara.

From there forth, Aidan's attention shifted to filling in the fissure that had appeared so suddenly, and making certain the water from the basin didn't flow anywhere near the village well.

Thankfully, there were no more questions, but Lili thought she sensed in him a change of mood—a brooding darkness that only deepened as he labored with his men up on the hill. He came to bed late that night, and every night thereafter, and abandoned their bed every morning before sunrise. For more than a week, he barely touched her, but Lili busied herself, helping Aveline prepare for her journey home, reassuring herself that this was the only way.

* * *

There was a moment when Aidan had begun to believe in something more—something magic, if one must use that word. But Lili's miraculous healing was naught more than hard work on her behalf. Una's tricks were merely that—an old woman's trickery. The curse was fantasy, an old woman's rage put to verse. Men were prone to believe in faerie tales so it was no surprise to Aidan that the bloody curse had become a song for wandering minstrels to carry door to door. Stuart's death was probably no more than a simple accident—just a clumsy dolt who didn't know better not to stare up into the sky after sending an arrow into the air. Ach, but he loved the woman madly and here he stood, barely alive but hardly dead, shoveling dirt into a god-forsaken hole in the ground! Their purpose here in this vale seemed a mockery at the moment. All these years they'd held the stone in keeping for a worthy king to arise, and now, because he had gone and wed an outlander bride, their efforts would all come to naught.

Every spade of dirt he tossed into the fissure grew heavier and heavier, until his mood turned as foul as the stains on his clothes.

His men all worked in silence, fearful of his mood—and

bloody good for the lot of them! He'd like to smack every last one upon the noggin with his spade, including Keane, who was still recovering, for putting the lives of their kinsmen at risk—all for a crude game of "who could shit the bigger log of bloody rotten shit!"

Peering down into the fissure, Aidan marveled that it seemed never to fill, and his curiosity needled him. He *must* know what Lili may have seen. He couldn't see the stone from where he stood, and she *claimed* she hadn't been down there, but he suspected she had, and there was only one way to appease his curiosity. The only reason he hadn't gone down as yet was simply because he was a coward. He *wanted* to believe his wife. But he was a fool if he did not!

Hurling his shovel to the ground with the force of his anger and commanding his men to cease their work while he explored, he jumped down into the crevice, finding the hole in the wall and cursing beneath his breath as he slipped through to the other side, straight into the cavern that housed their precious stone. From there, he climbed straight up to Una's grotto, finding her standing alone, staring blankly at her *keek stane*. When she looked at him, she didn't appear surprised to see him.

"I suspect Lili has seen the stone."

Her head bobbled rather calmly. "I suspect she has."

To Aidan's liking, she didn't react well enough, and he told her, "She has asked me to return Aveline to Keppenach." By the sins of sluag, he'd yet to tell a bloody soul, and the fact was needling him to the bone!

The old woman merely blinked. "This I know."

Aidan's shoulders tensed, his anger rising. "By the gods, Una! What if she has told Aveline of the stone? What if Aveline should lead them here?" he asked, demanding answers, and then he wondered when Lili might have told Una about her request—and more, why the hell hadn't Una come to inquire about it?

The old woman merely peered up at him then, leaning on her staff for support. The mist was gone today. It was likely that the caverns had aired out with a second entrance to the caves. But without the curling mist about their feet, the grotto appeared little more than a filthy, dank cave, devoid of any mystery.

And yet Una's good eye did not lose its sparkle, even if the stone in her staff was gray and dull. "It is our charge to guard the stone, until such time as the rightful heir finds his way to the throne—not to choose who will be the one to find it."

Aidan willed himself to calm down. He found her rickety old chair and sank into it, feeling weary to his bones. If Lili were to tell anyone at all—anyone!—David would march upon the vale—and that was if his rivals didn't beat him to it. By all that was sacred, if they should fight to protect the stone, they would invite bloodshed to their door. Aidan would not allow it! They were simply not strong enough to defend one small vale against the whole of Scotia. He would sooner tie a ribbon around the oversized rock and hand it over to the first to ask.

Una hobbled over to the chair and stood before him, reminding him of her presence. By the light of the fresh candle burning overhead, she looked tired and old, and her voice was gravely and weaker now than it seemed to be yesterday. "Our history is not our destiny, Aidan. I was coming to believe we were approaching the end of our days, though it appears to me now 'tis merely the beginning."

Aidan gave her an incredulous look, his heart squeezing painfully. "How the bluidy hell can ye say such a thing, Una? The end has never seemed more near. We might as well send Cailin and Sorcha to England to wed, and match Keane to a bluidy Scotswoman. Our Pecht lineage will be no more!"

Una stood before him another moment, shaking her head with disappointment and then she turned away, hobbling back to her worktable. "I suppose it could be true … if ye have no faith in the lass."

"Why the hell should I?" Aidan roared back. He stood, tossing out his hands as a plea for Una to listen to reason.

"Ach! It seems to me that men will trust their ears far less than their eyes, but they trust their hearts e'en less!" And with that, she huffed and tossed her staff upon the table, abusing

the ashwood stick as he had never seen her do before. It
rattled noisily over the table and came to a halt beside the
grey, dull *keek stane*.

Aidan frowned. His gut began to ache. He stood there
looking at Una, disheartened and heartsick over the way he
had spoken to her. By god, she might not truly be the Mother
of Winter, but in so many ways, she was the mother of them
all. "Forgive me," he allowed, swallowing a whole new lump
of grief that appeared. And then he left her, returning to the
hillside.

Without another word from anyone, Aidan and his men
filled in the entire cave beneath the fissure, moving mountains
of dirt into the hillside, until nothing remained to evidence
the caverns below.

ᏟᎻᎡᏟᎽ-ᎾNᎬ

As Aveline's mood lightened and her smiles increased with thoughts of returning to Keppenach, Aidan's mood grew darker yet.

Lili thought mayhap he suspected something but he said not a word. Troubled over his mood, she double-checked her coffers to be certain the ring and vial were still secreted inside. Certainly if her husband had discovered the horrible device by now, he would have questioned her about it. But, nay, there it remained, right where she had left it, and so she could not account for the change in his demeanor.

In truth, though she had considered many times hiding the offending pouch somewhere out in the fields, it had become quite apparent that the one place it would be safest was right here where she kept it. Aidan's people spent little enough time indoors, and she could not guarantee someone might not find it out there—no matter how well she hid it. But no one ventured into this room without permission aside from her and Aidan, and unlike Stuart and Rogan, her husband did not seem to feel the need to govern every aspect of her life. He had never once questioned her about her belongings from the moment he had dumped her coffers in his room. And despite his bluster upon her arrival, he had embraced her wholly as his wife, giving her nothing but respect and affection. Not one thing had she asked of him that he had ever denied her, and in fact, she did not have to ask for much. He cared for her in a manner that no man had ever done before him—no man.

With her husband's help, she scribed a formal request to Rogan—or rather, Aidan wrote the missive himself. Her husband was an accomplished scribe, more so even than Stuart or Rogan. What irony, she thought, that the man they'd hailed as a savage was a great deal more educated than most men she knew. In spite of his seclusion by choice, Aidan knew far more about the designations and positions of the men who ruled this land than she did. His choice to abstain from politics did not mandate that he remain ignorant of their machinations.

Lending the weight of his position to her request, so that Rogan could not deny her, he wrote:

> *To Rogan, high chief of clan MacLaren, laird of Keppenach and lesser keeps,*
>
> *In the matter of Aveline of Teviotdale, since the lady is thick with child and too heartsick to remain at Dubhtolargg, I return her forthwith to Keppenach, with apologies to David, though it is the lady's wish that her child be born under the protection of his father, the laird of Keppenach. In the matter of Kellen MacLaren, son of Stuart MacLaren, grandson of Dougal MacLaren, I would see him returned to his mother Lileas, the now and future lady of Dubhtolargg …*
>
> *The now and future lady of Dubhtolargg.*

Lili's heart swelled over the proclamation, for by it, he declared to one and all that she was his wife in truth and that he would never, ever rebuke her.

However, she noted how carefully he worded his next words so as not to provide an endorsement to David as his king.

> *… It is acknowledged that because a full year of hand fasting has not yet elapsed, proper dispensation must be received by David mac Mail Choluim, Prince of the Cumbrians, Earl of Northhampton and Huntingdon, King of the Scots, but not of the Pechts, As I am certain*

he will be pleased to find this union suits me well, please convey to me at once when the child may be retrieved, at which point I shall send a fully equipped garrison with all due haste in order to amend the current situation and see the boy safely to his mother before the first snows fall.

Subscribed and sealed on this sixth day of October by me, Aidan, High Chief of the dún Scoti, laird of Dubhtolargg, forebear of Kenneth MacAilpín, the Righ Art, the High King and Chief of Chiefs.

Alas, but the true message—the one Lili dared not scribe on paper—that one, Aveline must deliver herself in secret. Rogan was to bring Kellen to the stone cairn near the Faerie Glen—the ancient ruins that sat before the pathway leading down into the vale. He was to bring her son on the first day of the Blood moon in October. Somehow, Lili would find a way to slip away in order to exchange the information she had discovered. She must also endeavor to put her guilt aside for she was convinced there was no other way.

Aidan sealed the message and handed it over to one of his men on the day he dispatched the troupe to escort Aveline to Keppenach. Another messenger was sent with a similar letter for David. And thereafter, Lili resigned herself to wait. There would be no way to know whether Rogan would accept her bargain or nay, but in any case, he could not entirely ignore her husband's letter. He must send a message back, and in that message she would listen carefully for his answer. And then, no matter how he replied, she would hie herself to that Faerie Glen on the first night of the Blood moon.

However, to Lili's dismay, once Aveline was gone, Aidan kept even more to himself, drawing his men into the fields to spar, as though preparing himself for war. Long hours the men spent practicing while Lili busied herself with designs for a garden come spring, preparing her seeds with a bit of Una's guidance as there were some she did not know, and the soil up here was far different from the soil to be found below the ben. Despite the fact that the vale sat upon a carpet of green, the layer of good loam was lean, and below it was a table of stone. For some of her plants that needed deeper roots, it might behoove her to raise a bed or two.

Upon her request, her husband had ordered a worktable to be constructed and placed near the window in their chamber so that she might work while enjoying a view of the loch.

But as the first snows fell upon the vale, still with no word from Rogan, Lili began to worry. Fat flakes danced about the sky, like white butterflies. Lili watched them, thinking about the mountain path by which they had come only a few short months before ... wondering how the ground fared below the rise of the first ben.

So much had happened since that day... she was not the same girl she had been, and it came as little surprise that she no longer considered Keppenach her home. These, in truth, were her people now...

Guilt-ridden for having lied to Aidan, and worried for her son, she took her frustrations out upon mortar and pestle.

Una stood watching while she prepared a measure of white willow bark... and another of valerian. The concoction of white willow bark was the same mixture she had used for Duncan and Keane both, to help them with pain and to reduce their fever. The valerian... well, she hoped Una would not recognize the root. Betimes, Lili took a small dose during her woman's curse, but a far more potent mixture could be used to put grown men to sleep. The only drawback was that it had a very bitter taste, but she was not too concerned about that. Their *uisge* was so stout that she could easily hide the taste of the root, and the alcohol would greatly amplify the *drogue's* effects.

She and Una had developed a strange fellowship. The old woman was hardly affectionate, and yet Lili sensed the great love she bore her clan. It was for love of them that Una had cursed Lili in the first place, she realized.

Una watched her ground the dried valerian root, saying little, and Lili dared to ask her then about the curse, hoping to distract her from the concoction she was making. Anyway, what good would all her work be if Aidan was still fated to die?

As though her leg troubled her, the old woman shifted her

weight upon her staff and said, "All that we are, child—all that we become—arises from the depths of our hearts. Be the two of ye as one and even death willna part ye."

Lili considered the old woman's answer, but was still not appeased. She did not want merely to be connected to Aidan in spirit. She wanted him present body and soul, flesh and blood. The possibility of losing him now was heart-rending!

While images of Aidan's demise darkened Lili's thoughts, the old woman continued. "'Tis impossible to unshed blood, or call back words spoken in anger. And yet I once heard it said that forgiveness is the remission of sins," she concluded. "If there is hope, it must be found there."

Lili frowned and peered down at the pestle in her hand. Forgiveness? For what she was about to do? Was the old woman predicting bloodshed over her schemes? Or was she saying perhaps that Lili ought to forgive them for the misery she had suffered over the damnable curse? In truth she had already found forgiveness in her heart, for if the old woman had never cursed her, she would have never found her way to Aidan and she loved him with all her heart.

Frustrated by the answer she received, she ground away at the valerian root, reducing it to dust. It seemed everything Una did or said was shrouded in some form of mystery, and yet the woman never truly confessed to any sort of magic at all. For all anyone knew, she might be simply an eccentric old crone, although Lili sensed something otherworldly about her. Nor could she forget the blinding sensations that had assaulted her when she had touched the woman's scrying stone—that flash of light that had filled her head at the moment of connection. As yet, Lili had not admitted to being in her grotto, but she sensed Una knew.

The old woman's green gaze was canny—eye-color much like Aidan's and his siblings'—but they were reserved today as she watched Lili set the crushed valerian root aside.

More and more, Una had been coming about—betimes helping, betimes simply watching. And betimes Lili thought she might simply be keeping an eye on her. Sometimes Sorcha also came to watch and help, and during those times Una sometimes told them stories of the early days of Dubhtolargg.

She told Lili about a chieftain—a man who had followed his sire up the mount, full of doubt. His father died, Una said, and the new chieftain buried him up on the ridge—beneath the same cairn she had spied coming into the vale—and then he nearly went back down the mountain, plagued by doubt and grief. Apparently, he had been visited by a faerie, with whom he later fell in love, and it was their offspring who dwelled here now. It was a fanciful story—one Sorcha seemed to love. After hearing it, she ran out of the room, searching for someone to whom she could recount the tale.

Once she was gone, Una turned to her and said, "'Tis true what they say… sisters are merely different flowers from the same garden."

"I would love to have had one," Lili replied absently. It had long been her secret wish—far less lamented now that she felt, at last, a kinship with Aidan's people. For so long she'd had no one at all.

"Ach, the eyes are blind!" Una railed unexpectedly. "*See* with your heart, child!" And then shaking her head as though with disgust, she hobbled away with her staff, leaving Lili to look after her as she went muttering out the door.

But then suddenly, as Lili stared out into the darkened hall… and she heard Sorcha's voice telling Keane the tale somewhere nearby, the tenor of her laughter so familiar… And in that instant, Lili grasped the true depths of her father's sins, and she blinked, understanding.

Sorcha, the little girl who had embraced her long before any of Aidan's kinsmen had—was her sister by blood. And once Lili knew it, she knew it deep down in her soul, like a perfect truth uncovered by the light. The realization left her dazed. It would explain how and why she had felt so connected to this place from the instant she had ridden into the glen.

She was bound here already by blood.

* * *

With the approach of twilight, the echo of steel on steel ceased to ring through the hills.

Aidan craved solitude, needing to feel the sting of cold upon his flesh. Stripping fully, he stood beside Caoineag's Pool.

An icy mist rose from the water. Soon the shoreline would be congested with ice. Like frost in an old man's beard, the grass would turn crystalline. But even then, Aidan would find a moment to immerse himself in the icy waters of the loch, for it gave him a sense of euphoria to emerge and feel his blood flow into his limbs like warm *uisge*. In those instants, he felt more alive than at any other time, save the moments he spent in his wife's arms.

The *Am Monadh Ruadh* could be a bitter foe, unless a mon were at one with the land. Aidan's daily plunge into the loch kept him acclimated to the cold. Tonight, as the sun set over the *crannóg* in the distance, he felt a sense of calm that came, not simply from a good-day's practice with the blades, but a peace that settled over him with simply knowing that Lili awaited him at home.

In the waning daylight, he spied the first flurries of winter and he sucked in a breath and plunged headlong into the icy loch, trusting his instincts. If war came to the vale, he would be ready—so would his men. But faith, like the bone-chilling cold, rushed through him as he immersed himself in the waters of the loch.

Thrty-two

It was a king's prerogative to change his mind.

A letter arrived from David. His green eyes glinting, Aidan brought the missive to Lili, handing it to her while she stood at her desk, a half smile turning his lips. With trembling hands that were stiff from the cold, Lili quickly unfurled the parchment, her heart surging into her throat. She held her breath as she read. Apparently mistaking Aidan's carefully worded letter for a form of alliance, David wrote:

To Aidan, High Chief of the dún Scoti, laird of Dubhtolargg, forebear of Kenneth MacAilpín, I give thee greeting.

As it pleases me greatly ye are so agreeable to this alliance, I see no reason not to grant your lady's wish. Please give your lovely bride my regards, and convey to her my deepest regrets over the manner and implementation of her circumstances. Long life to ye and yours.

Subscribed and sealed on this twentieth day of October by me, David mac Maíl Choluim, Prince of the Cumbrians, Earl of Northhampton and Huntingdon, the Righ Art, the High King of the Scots and Chief of Chiefs, forebear of Kenneth MacAilpín.

Lili's hands shook with relief as she handed the parchment back to Aidan. David's message was clear to her, even if Aidan could not read between the lines. The king had had a change of heart, and regretted his part in Rogan's scheme.

Long life to you and yours…

It was a blessing upon their marriage from Scotia's reigning King.

But Rogan would not so easily conform, she realized. And yet once her son was safely in their hands, Rogan would not dare undermine his liege. With but a single day remaining before the Blood moon, she knew David's letter would have missed Rogan at Keppenach, for he would surely be on his way north—if indeed he intended to bargain with her. And she knew in her heart of hearts that he would. All she had to do now was convince Rogan to make the trade—to relinquish her son into her hands—and that she vowed to accomplish however she must.

For the first time in so long, she felt hopeful. She glanced up at her husband, loving his face—loving everything about him. If either of them must leave this earth too soon, she would not go without showing Aidan what was in her heart.

Be the two of you as one, Una had said.

That was precisely what Lili intended to do, for now she understood what the old woman had meant.

With a twinkle in her eyes, she walked to the door of their bedroom and closed it, then turned and smiled at her husband. That was all it took—a smile on her behalf, and she watched his breacan stir below his belt. And seeing that she spied the evidence of his arousal, he laughed huskily and she flung herself into his arms, seizing him by his face and kissing him wantonly, wanting him to feel everything that was in her heart. Answering with unreserved passion, he kissed her back, all the frustrations of the past weeks evident in the ardor of his kiss. She dared not let him go as she drew him into the bed, intending to love him as a true wife should. This time, their coupling was not gentle. Lili wanted him to understand that not even death would part them because, aye, he was her one true love.

* * *

Inhaling a rush of stinging air into her lungs, Una watched

as Lili stole away from the *crannóg*, up the hill toward the crumbling ruins at the edge of the Faerie Glen.

The twilight of the year was knocking upon their door—the time between times, when the days descended into darkness and the nights grew cold and long. A blanket of fresh snow lay untrodden below the ridge, tinted copper beneath the full Blood moon—but this would not be simply any Blood moon. Tonight, the red sphere in the northern sky would eclipse itself, and the division between this world and the next would be at its thinnest. It was a time for rebirth, a time for growth, a time for atonement... and aye, a time of rest for the Mother of Winter...

But tonight, before the full eclipse, there would be no rest.

Her face painted the pale color of snow, Una ignored the exhaustion that threatened to steal into her old bones, and stood watching the night unfold. Fog swirled at her feet. The staff in her hand, with the stone in its claw, winked under the red moon, like the slow, waking blink of a weary mother whose child wailed in need.

For a moment, she watched the girl's dark form creep up the hillside... alone, her bright red cloak fluttering behind her in the wind. And then, with a satisfied smile, she blew upon the milky stone in her staff...

Her breath warm against the night, she blew until the mist coalesced about her lips. After a moment, she puffed it away, and continued to blow softly... until the cold night fog slipped like a protective blanket over the entire hillside.

Down below, for an instant, before she was obscured from view by the lowering mist, Lili froze, her arisaid swinging about as she peered in Una's direction... as though sensing she was being watched. Unbidden, the girl's gaze lifted to the tabled rock, and it was then Una knew for certain as she turned and hurried up the hillside... some day... aye, Lili would be The One.

Prickles traveled the length of the old woman's spine, despite that her old bones could no longer feel the cold, and she felt gratified to the depths of her soul. Relief wound its way through the tangled coils of her mind, freeing her from worry.

Nay, they had not spoken since yestereve... since before the king's missive had arrived, but she sensed in her heart that Lili would do what was right. This would not be the end ... for even with the wind whispering through the crags, she did not hear Caoineag's weeping.

Not tonight.

* * *

The storm seemed to have descended without warning.

With each step along the ridge, Rogan's boots sank deeper into the frozen ground. If that weren't enough, a carpet of mist swept over the landscape, tangling about his feet, obscuring them from view. The whiteout did not alarm him—he was a Highlander to his bones. But the color of the moon gave him pause, for despite his men's complaints about the ominous place they had made camp, and despite his assurances that the fields behind them held no more magic than his little toe, it gave him a strange sense of malaise. It would all be over soon, he assured himself, as he paced the camp, ignoring the quiet shivers and the worried looks of his men.

Lest they attract attention coming up the mount—and set Aidan's entire clan of barbarians upon them—he had brought only six armed warriors... it was too late to worry over their numbers.

His choices had been plain: Ignore Lili's summons and keep his arse behind Keppenach's walls, but he was not a coward; come armed to the teeth with his army, though he realized Aidan's men would outnumber his still and, more, they knew this terrain better than he did; or finally, steal up the mount with a handful of trusted men and keep the child near. He knew beyond a shadow of doubt that Lili would never endanger her son.

Even now, one of his men held a knife at the boy's back, and Lili must know he would not hesitate to command the deed done. He had little love for the brat.

If there was one thing Rogan knew about Lili it was that she was incapable of lying. Aveline had further convinced him of that with her tearful promises: Lili had discovered something significant here at Dubhtolargg. What it was Rogan did not know because Lili had apparently refused to speak of her discovery to Aveline. But there was something... And just to make certain Aveline's tongue was not forked, he had driven the blade of his dirk into each of her fingernails— until she had screamed with pain, beseeching him to stop.

Never again would the bitch defy him.

He would never have allowed her to be a vessel for his children. The very thought sickened him. She was no good to him there at Keppenach anymore, and when and if they discovered her body, they would mistake her bloodied nails for a desperate attempt to free herself from the wooden prison he had confined her to.

But they wouldn't find her.

With his half-dozen men he had stolen up the mountain pass, careful to keep to the shadows in the crags. Once here, he had refused to light a fire, despite the cold, for they would not tarry here overlong. He had ushered the child into the remainder of an ancient cairn, just to shut his complaints over the biting wind. Peering out from the ruins, the boy sat, looking blue, shivering beneath the light of the full moon shining down through the cairn's open roof. Cast with the red of the moon, he had a devil's face that was unnerving his men. Would that he could kill the boy and simply be done.

"D-d' ye th-think she'll come?" worried one of his men, stuttering over his half-frozen tongue.

In answer, Rogan swung about to peer down the mountain path, turning his back to his men. "Of course she'll come," he said, more to himself. "She sought this meeting, did she not?"

But the night was black, revealing not a single torchlight below. The vale appeared from the ridge much like a black hole, except for the moon's reflection upon the distant loch.

"W-what if 'tis a trap?" fretted another.

Rogan did not care that the child could overhear. "Then

we slit the boy's throat," he said his voice devoid of emotion. He was not so much fazed by the cold, because vengeance gave him sustenance. Their weakness annoyed him, and he cursed them for all fools, wondering why he could not find good men to garrison his keep.

Where the hell was she?

Lili would not leave her son out here to suffer the cold overlong... that he knew. And when she came, he only intended to linger long enough to glean whatever information she thought to barter, and then he would take both her and her brat child back to Keppenach, where they belonged, and he would use the information she gave him to curry favor with the king—and her child to keep her in line.

He watched the mountain path closely with his back to the Faerie Glen, knowing instinctively that these superstitious folk would never come that way—and since Rogan did not believe in ghoulies, neither would faeries or brownies. He'd hidden their horses just beyond the cairn. And finally he was rewarded. Down below, a flurry of red caught his eye, and he grinned.

The rest of his men spied Lili's cloak, whipping blood-red in the wind, but her face was not yet visible. "Ach! W-what if it b-be a *doonie*?"

Their gullible minds no doubt imagined all manner of *brollachans* in the swirling snow. Twas little wonder they saw shape-shifting brownies instead of a bonnie familiar face. Rogan cast them a quelling glance, and smiled and said in a tongue he knew they did not understand, *"Toll-tòin." Arse hole.* "We'll be on our way afore long."

* * *

Wind and snow whipped Lili's face, obscuring the way uphill, but she had walked this way a thousand times in her mind. Knowing her son must be just beyond the rise made her skin prickle with excitement and fear. If aught went awry, Kellen could be the one to pay the price.

To her surprise, Rogan had not responded to Aidan's

letter at all, but she knew him well enough to know that he would be here despite that fact, for he would wish to possess the one thing Lili claimed David would covet even more than Aidan's death.

Aye, but she had already decided she would never give it to him.

In her hand, she carried a gift of *uisge*—the stoutest batch she could find in their stores—enough for Rogan and all the men he may have brought to drink themselves into a stupor, especially considering that it was *drogued*.

The cold froze her nose and snow peppered her lashes, but she brushed the flakes away and kept marching, knowing that there was no turning back now. Whatever was to come, her path was set.

Despite the mist and blinding snow, she found Rogan's camp easily enough. The men's silver armor winked under the moonlight. Aidan would think their armor an abomination, she knew, but she was glad for it tonight. And because she was looking for him, she spied her son, shivering inside the cairn. Seeing her, Kellen stood at once, looking first to Rogan and then to Lili. Lili wanted only to hold him in that instant and for a dazed moment, she could think of nothing else. His sweet face appeared just the same as it had the day she had left him, though his eyes were haunted and full of fear.

"Lili!" Rogan said in greeting, and offered her a tentative hug. Lili forced herself to allow it, and even hugged him back, but not with much feeling, lest he suspect. "Please... first I must see my son," she insisted, and made her way toward the cairn.

Rogan held her back by the crook of her arm and she forced a smile. "What is this?" he asked, lifting her hand and along with it the jug of *uisge*.

She gave him a wan smile. "I brought a bit o' warmth," she said. "And ye may have it only once I have seen my son." She met his gaze with a practiced look that revealed naught.

With his free hand, he took the jug, laughing low, but he would not let her go.

"Please, Rogan! I *must* see my son. I've missed him so!"

He released his hold suddenly and she tugged her arm away and ran to Kellen. He hurled his little body into her arms, crying out, "Mama!"

Lili choked back a sob. He had not called her by that name since he was but three. "Kellen, Kellen, my sweet little boy!" She set him down and looked him squarely in the face, examining him, pulling his cloak up about his neck. "Are ye well?" she asked, noting he was a bit gaunt.

He nodded jerkily, and realizing that Rogan was right behind her, listening, she added quickly, "Tomorrow we will go home, you and I."

"To Keppenach?" he asked, his dark eyes full of confusion.

"Aye," she swore. "To Keppenach. And then mayhap to see your grandminny, for I know she would love to meet her only grandchild."

A grin broke across her son's face. "Ach, mama! It worked!" His eyes sparkled as he unfurled his hand between them, revealing the little talisman he had found that day out in her garden. The tiny stone was black as coal against the paleness of his hand. Snow fell between them, tangling in his lashes, alighting upon red cheeks that puffed suddenly with a grin.

He shivered from the cold and Lili's heart nearly broke. She nodded, choking back another sob, and closed his hand so he could hold it secured, knowing that the hardest of her lies were yet to come.

Behind her, Rogan sniffed the cork, watching them closely. The man who had been guarding Kellen within the Cairn stepped out, a gleaming knife in his hand. His smile had missing teeth.

"You were ever a horrid liar," Rogan said. "Di' ye think to bribe me with a gift of *uisge*, Lili?"

Lili stood, clutching her son before him, pulling her arisaid about his shoulders to keep him warm. "Nay, but I bring good tidings," she swore, hitching her chin with false bravado and watching nervously as Rogan examined the jug. "Once you hear it, you may in truth wish to drink a toast," she suggested.

His eyes glittered through the darkness. "So I am told."

Lili silently counted the men he had brought with him, far fewer than she might have guessed—six if all were present and accounted for. Their horses must be hidden somewhere else.

As she watched, Rogan made his way to one of his men and offered the man the jug. "Ye look cauld," he said to the man. "Take a wee dram."

The man looked first to Lili, his look full of suspicion, and then to the jug, accepting it though reluctantly. He hesitated and Rogan commanded him, "Drink!"

Shuddering, the poor man nodded and gave Lili another wary glance.

Lili prayed the *drogue* was not so strong it would bring him to his knees at once. It would not kill him, but if he fell into the snow and no one warmed his bones, he would surely die from the cold.

The man pulled the jug away from Rogan. He bit the cork out with his teeth and spat it out, then took a long chug, and brought the jug away and wiped his mouth. For a long moment, Lili ceased to breathe. She held her son close, her heart beating frantically as Rogan's man stood looking at her, cradling the *uisge* jug before him.

When it seemed he was unaffected, Rogan turned to her at last, his eyes glittering dangerously. "So then, what is it ye believe to be so momentous that David may wish to spare your dún Scoti's life?"

Again Lili lifted her chin, eyeing the man with the jug. As long as there was still a chance Rogan might drink from it, and that she might slip away with her son without bloodshed, she intended to continue playing her role. "First, I would beg safe passage to my father's home. No matter what he says he feels for me, the instant Aidan realizes I have betrayed him, he will kill me, and I have no place else to go."

Rogan seemed to like the sound of that, for he smiled, and Lili shivered, more afraid than cold. She felt her son's shivers beneath her cloak and knew he could not remain out here so long without a fire. Rogan's camp was dark and cold. It was clear to her that he did not intend to stay long, and her minutes were numbered.

"Tell ye what I'd do, Lili," Rogan offered after a moment, bartering with her. "If I like what ye have to say, I will indeed send ye home to your Da... that is, if Padruig will have ye. And if nay... then ye may still have a place as the lady of Keppenach. Does that suit ye?"

Lili blinked. She commanded herself to breathe. But the possibility of being trapped under Rogan's roof for even a single day made her stomach clench. Unwittingly, she pressed her fingers into her son's shoulders, clutching him hard. He didn't protest, for he too was watching Rogan. Rogan was like an adder loose in a room, dangerous and ready to strike with a deadly bite.

"Aye," Lili agreed. But in her peripheral, she saw the man who had drunk the *uisge* waver on his feet, and she stifled a gasp.

Rogan laughed, not yet noticing the man whose shoulders teetered. "So then... what is it ye may know that could change the fate o' the world?"

Lili inhaled a deep breath, and began to speak, but the man who had drunk the potion dropped the jug suddenly. Soundlessly, it sank into the snow, melting ice as it drained liquid fire at his feet. Without a word, the man followed the jug, crumbling to his knees.

Rogan's gaze cut to his fallen man.

Lili held her son close, ready to fight unto her last breath.

Aidan realized Lili could not see him through the billowing drifts.

He and his men waited in the forbidden fields, knowing the Scots would not expect them to violate the Faerie Glen. Most men believed that to do so invited the wrath of the gods.

Painted white to camouflage horse and rider against the weather, seven riders sat upon pale horses, white mares born to this terrain and trained to ride over these craggy bluffs. The Scots and English might prefer geldings, but Aidan's warriors preferred spirited mares, with bloodlines as pure and old as theirs, mares who did not look at each other with bloodlust in their eyes during battle. Sleek and sturdy, they were a warrior's greatest ally, alongside the kinsman fighting at his back.

He and Lael shared a glance. The handles of his sister's knives were covered with skins to keep the cold from icing them to her fingers and so their shine would not betray them under the moonlight, but tonight it wouldn't have mattered, for the red shadow that had embraced the moon was not bright enough to pierce the billowing snow and mist. They didn't speak, but he knew she would play her part. His sister was as capable a warrior as any of his men.

In the distance, he saw the dark outline of a man topple to his knees and then plant himself face down into the snow. Fifteen more warriors were climbing the bluff below to block their retreat. He must know they were in place before he gave the signal, but they were out of time. Rage burned within his breast as he gave his warriors the sign to attack...

Lili's heart jumped at the sight of the pale riders emerging from the mist.

They came out of the darkness, looking like white demons on ghostly steeds, with blue war paint smeared across their white-painted faces.

She threw open her cloak and screamed. "Run, Kellen! Run!" She pushed her son in the direction he should go. But for an instant, he faltered, reluctant to leave, and Lili's eyes pleaded with him to go.

Growling like an angered beast, Rogan fell upon her then, and only then did Kellen run.

Lili saw the eyes of the rider who rode after her son, green and sparkling with vengeance. Her black hair concealed by silver-wolf furs, she met Lili's gaze only an instant before she rode toward Kellen and scooped him up into her arms without halting in her stride.

Kellen screamed, but Lili could not reassure him, for Rogan dragged her to her feet and set his blade to her throat as her husband's horse came to a halt before them, showering them with snow from beneath his horse's hooves.

Immense pride brought tears to her eyes and she did not feel the slice of Rogan's blade against her skin, nor the words Aidan spoke to him, for her ears were pounding with the beat of her own heart and her eyes were clouded with tears. She met Aidan's gaze, telling him with her eyes not to cow before this demon among men. If she must die tonight, it was a fate she accepted, for she knew now that her son would be safe. Tears brimmed in her eyes, frozen for an instant...

The moon slid completely behind its shadow, and it was as though God blinked. Even the sound of her heartbeat quieted in that instant. If this would be the end, she would not allow the words to remain unsaid. Her heart constricted painfully. "*Tha gaol agam ort,*" she whispered.

The words hung between them, neither here nor there, frozen like the mist in the air.

Shrieking in outrage, Rogan saw his men—all four who had remained—abandon him. No doubt they believed the dún Scoti to be demons arisen from the Faerie Glen.

Lying bitch—she had betrayed him!

One of his men lay face down in the snow—poisoned by the whore in his arms. He had trusted her word enough to lessen his numbers by one—had thought her so virtuous that she could not have lied to save her life. But there he was, face down in the snow, and Rogan refused to take responsibility for the man's downfall, no matter that he had been the one to hand him the jug. Another man was cut down before he could lift his sword from his scabbard.

Hearing Lili's words were the final blow to his injured pride, and he smacked her hard against the temple with the hilt of his claymore as Aidan dún Scoti descended from the saddle into the snow.

By God, if he would die tonight, he would die like a Scotsman, not a coward!

Lili's body crumpled to his feet, and the last thing he spied was her blood, red as rose petals, trickling into the snow.

With a war cry, dún Scoti swung his blade.

Red was all Aidan saw—the Blood moon and the red of his wife's blood fueled a rage unlike any he'd ever known.

Abandoning their laird, Rogan's warriors escaped down the mountain path. Unfortunately for them, none would live to carry tales tonight. Rogan sealed his own fate the instant he discarded Lili at his feet.

With a bellow full of fury, Aidan swung his heavy claymore. The blade caught the man's upraised sword with a metallic crash that lit sparks in the air between them. With the sheer force of his blow, Rogan's blade went flying backwards out of his hands. It plunged into the snowdrift at his back. Between them, Lili's body lay crumpled across a bed of frozen white and Aidan drove Rogan back, away from his wife.

He stumbled backward, righting himself as Aidan pulled the axe out of his belt, and once he was far enough away from Lili, he tossed the weapon at Rogan's feet. "Let it never be said I would slay an unarmed mon, but ye dinna mistake me, Rogan MacLaren, for I will kill ye tonight!"

The breath from Rogan's nostrils puffed into the air like a maddened stallion. His black eyes looked like those of a cornered beast's. Aidan inched closer, ready to strike the instant he lifted the axe, but his quarry merely eyed the weapon.

Somewhere down the mountain path, the clanging of swords could be heard, but Aidan was only interested in the death of one man. Those poor bastards below had simply made the mistake of swearing fealty to the wrong man.

Rogan backed away as Aidan stalked him, never averting his gaze as he groped in search of his fallen sword. "*Faigh bàs!*" he spat.

Aidan grinned. "Aye, but if I go to hell, I will see ye there!"

Almost as though the heavens offered agreement, the moon slid behind its shadow in that instant, but Aidan saw clearly enough to follow Rogan's movements. He knew this land like a lover's body. Closing in upon his prey, he bent to retrieve the axe from the ground, but he did not sheathe it. It had been a mistake for Rogan to forgo the weapon, for Aidan was far better with his axe than he was with his sword.

At last Rogan found his weapon of choice, the sword he knew still bore the remnants of Lily's blood. Now he snarled with renewed confidence, and lifted the claymore, lunging after Aidan.

Aidan flung his axe. Unerringly through the darkened night, it found its mark in the center of Rogan's chest, imbedding itself so deeply that he could hear the man's ribs crack above the din of the wind. A look of stunned surprise crossed Rogan's features as he fell backward into the drift, dropping his sword and grasping for the blade buried in his chest. The axe did not move, but death would not find him so quickly as he might hope for the blade had missed his heart.

Aidan hesitated only long enough to clear his mind of battle-rage, wind and snow whipping his face. And hearing the shouts of his men returning up the mountain path, he retrieved the jug of *uisge* Lili had brought with her. Plucking it out of already frozen hands, he walked over to Rogan and tossed it down beside him. "Enjoy it while ye can," he spat, offering the man a greater mercy than he deserved. "It'll be the last ye e'er taste."

He propped his boot against the man's belly and withdrew the axe from his chest, cracking more ribs with the effort and leaving the bastard to whatever fate his men would allow. If he managed to crawl away before they chanced to find him, he would die prostrate in the snow while wolves tore the meat from his flesh, leaving nothing but bones. Without another word, he spun about, removing his cloak to cover his wife and scoop her up from the snow, praying he was not too late...

Epilogue

The pain was almost unbearable.

Lili placed a hand to her belly, worrying. For as long as anyone could recall, Una had been the only one to deliver babes here in the vale. She had never before gone away during the winter months, but Aidan swore she would return long before the Beltane celebration to give the spring blessings before setting out once again on her yearly sojourn through the Highlands.

However, the snows had long since receded, and still she had not come home. When Lili considered the old woman's occasional remarks—that she was "growing old," and "now that Lili was about to care for their kinsmen, she could rest at ease"—she worried mayhap this time would be the one time Una may not return.

Even now the bonfire was being constructed as they prepared for the Beltane celebration, and she and Lael together were counting the sheep they would slaughter for the feast. The rest of the livestock they had set aside for Una's blessing. With but a single night remaining before the festival, all hearth fires had already been extinguished. They would be re-lit with an ember from the bonfire after it too was blessed by Una.

Sorcha, Duncan and Kellen were in the fields now with the rest of the children, picking mayflowers they would place upon every living creature in the vale. Spring was here at last and the rowan trees were in full bloom, their white buds at the ends of their branches looking like the memory of snow.

On a day like today, Lili did not worry so much about Kellen, and she took much joy in the simple fact that for the first time in his life her son was free to be a child. The babe in her belly was another matter entirely... first he would need make it into this world, and for that she needed Una.

Lael's brow furrowed, noting the hand that had gone to Lili's swollen belly. "Are ye well?" she worried.

"I am fine," Lili reassured.

Since the night of Rogan's fall, and from the instant Aidan's eldest sister had placed her arms around Lili's son, her manner and mood had changed toward Lili. Aside from Glenna, she was Lili's dearest friend now. Betimes she found herself wishing Aveline had remained, for she had heard from a messenger that the poor girl had gone missing and had yet to be found. Of course, Lili feared the worst, and now that she had discovered such joy amidst these people, she couldn't help but wonder if Aveline might have encountered the same. What a pity.

"Ye dinna look so well to me," Lael scolded. "Does she Glenna?"

Glenna knew Lili was struggling to keep the babe from being born, and she understood why, and said, "Lili, dear, leave the counting to us and go and rest a bit. Una will return soon."

Ach, but Lili was running out of time!

Another pain shot through her belly and the babe squirmed, giving her one warning after another.

She peered up near the ridge, where Aidan stood supervising the men as they hauled down cabers. Some they would leave for the games, but most of the new logs were to be used to repair winter damage on the *crannóg's* piles, walls and floors. Some traditions were destined to continue. Others would be no more. Thankfully, they had not buried another man, woman or child—not since the day Lili had discovered the cause of their maladies. Not even on that fateful night... up on the ridge had they lost a single life.

Of Rogan's troupe, that was another matter. That night,

they had burned Rogan's body up on the ridge, along with his men. Only one had survived, but because Lili had not told any of them anything about the stone, no one knew what she had promised to reveal to Rogan. And no one would ever know as far as she was concerned. For all David knew, there had simply been a skirmish over the return of her son.

Two days hence, MacKinnon men had ventured into the vale, asking once more if Aidan would lend his sword to their cause. Broc had petitioned David for the return of Keppenach, but David had refused, claiming that the fate of the fortress was undecided now that Lili had wed. Although it could be argued that her son was still its rightful heir, it was not worth going to war with the MacKinnon's over. Still, she sensed a battle coming soon over the fate of her son's patrimony, and Lili worried Aidan would feel compelled to help defend the fortress from those who might seek to encroach upon the *Am Monadh Ruadh*. She only hoped he would not be forced to decide before the babe arrived—the way her belly was cramping, she feared any moment now!

As for Sorcha, she still did not know that she and Lili were sisters by blood. Aidan had asked Lili not to reveal it as it was her husband's wish that his youngest sister not know the circumstances of her birth. Lili wasn't so certain she agreed, but it was his sister first, after all, and what mattered most was that Lili could give the girl the love of her heart no matter what she knew of their blood.

"Lili?" Glenna prodded.

The work was nearly done for the day anyway. Lili was just about to agree to go lie down, lest she tax herself and bring upon her labor too soon, and then her gaze lifted toward the tabled stone and her heart leaped against her ribs. She cried in relief and buckled to her knees that very moment. "Oh!" she exclaimed, and clutched her belly.

The babe was coming.

Now.

And just in time, because Una started down the hillside in their direction, with her white hair blowing in the breeze like billowing clouds, and her staff winking under the noonday sun.

"Oh, my!" she cried again, this time over a new pain that shot through her pelvis. Whether her excitement had brought on her labor, or Una had simply given the babe permission to be born would never be known, but Lili felt a sudden wave of pain that felt as though someone had dropped Una's *keek stane* straight over her pelvis. "Oh!" she cried again, nearly fainting as she felt the child's head beginning to crown.

Girl or boy? In either case, the babe was as impatient as his father!

Glenna screamed and caught Lili as she stumbled and Lael went screaming up the hillside, calling for her brother.

They barely had time to carry Lili into the *crannóg*.

Their daughter was born on the eve of Beltane. Her hair, black as raven's wings, was so long that Cailin tried to braid it. Surrounded by the ones she loved, Lili knew beyond a doubt that she was not cursed at all… nay, for she was blessed.

With tears in his eyes, her husband ushered everyone out of their chamber and came to Lili's side, falling to one knee.

"*Sùilean geala,*" he whispered to their daughter—*Bright Eyes*—for her eyes were a rare color for an infant—more green than blue, and unnaturally bright—like Aidan's mother's and his father's. It was the birthmark of the guardians, Una claimed, although it was not telling in of itself, for there was much else that must be true in order for a true guardian to arise. Lili's eyes were violet and yet Una claimed she would someday inherit Una's staff. Still, it was clear that their child was a daughter of Aidan's noble blood.

And Aidan suddenly understood, and he swallowed the lump that appeared in his throat as he realized what Una had been trying to tell him on that night so long ago… the night she had bade him to look to the stars to sustain his faith.

Aidan stared down into the eyes of his nameless child, and knew he would never again doubt his wife… or his faith. Before that night upon the ridge, Lili had confessed everything to him, trusting him to protect her and her son— his son now. And now they had two precious children… and the one squirming before him was the star Una wanted him to see with his heart.

"I'd like to name her Ria," he told his wife, his throat almost too thick to speak. "*Riannag*, after my mother. It means star."

Tears swam in Lili's eyes as Aidan reached out to trace the fine raised scar that encircled her neck, the scar Rogan had given her before his death. That was all that remained to remind him how close he'd come to losing everything.

"Nothing would please me more," she said.

"Ach..." His voice was thick with emotion. "I will never give you a stone castle to buttress the sky," he whispered. "Nor will I rule nations. I am but a mon, a guardian of the stone—can ye love a simple mon without aspirations to greatness, Lili?"

"With all my heart," she swore, and he believed her, for her heart was there in her eyes. "But I disagree, my love. My daughter's father is the greatest among men!"

His own eyes swam with tears as he smoothed the sweat soaked hair from his wife's brow and whispered back, "I love you, Lili," he said.

"*Tha gaol agam ort-fhèin*," she replied. *I love you too.*

Their child gurgled between them and in the shadow of the hall, Una lingered. But when Lili met her gaze, she smiled and hobbled away.

AFTERWORD

First I'd like to note that I took liberties with the geography a bit. The valley I chose for the setting of this story was inspired by the setting of Loch Einich, and is in the general vicinity, but I purposely wanted to keep the location a bit of a mystery. Also to be noted is that the first accounts of whisky distilling didn't come until much later, though I must believe the practice came long before the writing about it. Likewise kilts, plaids and tartans, as well as the Picts themselves. By most accounts the Picts were gone by the Ninth Century.

As for *An Lia Fàil,* otherwise known as the Stone of Destiny, or the Stone of Scone, and by some as *clach-na-cinneamhain,* there are many legends surrounding it. Throughout history it's been stolen, hidden, absconded with, placed under thrones, and still to this day no one can tell you with absolute certainty where/which is the real stone.

One account tells us the true stone was hidden somewhere in the mountains near Scone, secreted away by monks in 1296, sometime before the Hammer of the Scots, a.k.a. King Edward of England could take it and use it to subdue the Highlanders. Pointing to that theory, there's a Nineteenth Century story about two boys who had been exploring a landslide on Dunsinane Hill, near the site of an ancient hill fort, known as Macbeth's Castle. There the boys found a fissure and a hidden cave, where they also discovered a mysteriously carved black stone. Later, going by the boys' accounts, the cave was relocated and there they discovered not just the stone in question, but two plaque-like tablets. Amidst much excitement, the stone was sent to London for examination and was never seen again. But, of course, knowing this really engaged this writer's mind.

What if—that magical question—the Stone of Destiny were in fact hidden, but not in 1296, when the chroniclers would have us believe? What if it were hidden *much* earlier... say, at a time when Scotland's history was in its infancy? And what if the guardians of the true stone had been disappointed by the warring of Alba's noble tribes. What if after Kenneth MacAilpín's treason, where he murdered seven rivals for the Pictish throne, that real stone were cursed by the last of the Picts? And what if then, after Kenneth's son Aed was murdered by coup, what if the guardians of the stone feared their sacred relic had fallen into the wrong hands? What if they stole that stone–the real stone–and hid it away in a cave and what if it remains hidden to this very day deep in the hills of Scotland? This would be the story of the Guardians of the Stone.

The truth is that the Picts pretty much disappeared from Scotland's history, with no one the wiser about where they went or why, but I'd like to re-imagine them this way, as a people who clung to their heritage until the very end... and who lent us their traditions through their tenacity to survive.

This one's for all those who, like me, even now don't want to let these people fade completely from the annals of history.

Slàinte mhòr agad!

Tanya Anne Crosby

AVAILABLE NOW

The true stone of Destiny remains hidden, but now comes a new battle to determine who will hold the sword of kings.

Defying her laird and brother, Lael of the dun Scoti clan takes up her sword to fight beside the MacKinnons to return Keppenach to its rightful heir—to Broc Ceannfhionn. She'll risk everything to keep the stronghold out of the hands of King Henry's Butcher... even her life.

They call him The Butcher, but not even Henry's henchman would hang a woman. Riding into the gates on winged fury, Jaime Steorling cuts the raven-haired beauty down from the gallows only to find himself a willing prisoner of her heart. In the end, only a bond of love between bitter enemies can bring healing to broken nations.

ABOUT THE AUTHOR

Tanya Anne Crosby's novels have graced numerous bestseller lists including the New York Times and USA Today. Best known for stories charged with emotion and humor, and filled with flawed characters, her novels have garnered reader praise and glowing critical reviews. She lives with her husband, two dogs and two moody cats in northern Michigan.

FOR MORE INFORMATION:
Visit www.tanyaannecrosby.com
Join Tanya on Facebook at facebook.com/tanyaannecrosby
Follow Tanya on Twitter @tanyaannecrosby

CPSIA information can be obtained
at www.ICGtesting.com
Printed in the USA
LVOW12s1510010616

490793LV00004B/162/P